THE SHAPESHIFTER'S CAULDRON

a metaphysical comedy
by Lisa Bonnice

also by Lisa Bonnice

Shape Shifting – the Body/Mind/Spirit Weight Solution

The Shape Shifter's Daily Diary

Fear of Our Father
(co-authored with Stacey M. Kananen)

A Faery on My Shoulder

The Faery Falls

Castle Gate
(Book 1 in *The Maxwell Curse Trilogy*)

in the works ...

Books 2 & 3 of
The Maxwell Curse Trilogy:

A Curse by Fire
&
Kind Miss

THE SHAPESHIFTER'S CAULDRON

a metaphysical comedy

by Lisa Bonnice

THE SHAPESHIFTER'S CAULDRON

This is a work of fiction … mostly.

Sensitivity note: This book contains a character in the form of a trans woman. She is based on a combination of real-life experience, conversations and interviews with friends and experts, and tremendous love for this character. Her experience is her own and not intended to imply any commonality. No disrespect to the trans community is intended.

Dedicated to Jeff, who goes along with me

in my travels into the unknown ...

or am I going along in his?

THE SHAPESHIFTER'S CAULDRON

Table of Contents

SYNOPSES OF BOOKS ONE AND TWO

Warning: Here be Spoilers!

The faeries, of course, would prefer that you read those books first because they're whopping good tales, and so you won't spend any time while reading *The Shapeshifter's Cauldron* wondering what on earth these characters are talking about when they refer to an incident from the past. If you insist on plowing forward, here is the bare minimum you must know about Lola and Twink's previous adventures for this one to make sense.

Book 1—*A Faery on My Shoulder*

Lola Garnett used to live an ordinary life in the nostalgically charming little town of Chagrin Falls, Ohio. While it was a *lovely* life, it was a *boring* life. Lola one day fell asleep wishing for a more *interesting* life. Boy, did she get what she wished for!

As Lola napped, her neighbor Melinda Underwood was cooking up a revenge spell aimed at her straying man. While Lola dreamed of fluffy clouds and wistful wishes, Melinda created a tear in the fabric of time and space through which to pull down extra power. Lola's dream-self drifted into the portal and ※**POOF**※ her life was no longer boring. She woke from her nap with psychic abilities beyond her comprehension and control.

As Lola's life spun out, she beseeched the heavens for guidance. The powers-that-be took pity and sent a faery named Aethelwyne Eglantina who was ordered, due to her own bad behavior, to use this assignment as a lesson in understanding humans.

The faery resented assisting a novice like Lola, who clearly needed a kick in the arse. After all, Lola insisted on calling her the humiliating name "Twink" solely because she couldn't properly wrap her human tongue around such an elegant utterance to pronounce it correctly.

As Lola and Twink developed a cautious comradery, hijinks ensued.

Melinda behaved badly, drawing a reluctant Lola into her schemes. Long story short, Lola and Twink foiled Melinda's evil plot.

Book 2—*The Faery Falls*

Fast forward about nine months. Lola has accepted that her psychic abilities are permanent, so she has started taking classes to develop and control them. In a class on shamanic journeying, she runs into the owner of a local antique shop in which she discovered an irresistible topaz pendant, which she now owns. That shop owner is a trans woman, Madeline Laurent (or Maddie, as she prefers) with whom Lola clicks immediately. They become fast friends.

Enter Seth.

Seth was, at one time, the unfortunate boyfriend of the equally unfortunate Melinda Underwood and through a series of magical misadventures, poor Seth ended up trapped on the other side of the veil, unable to come home.

With the reluctant assistance of Twink and a growing cast of faeries, our heroine set out to do the impossible: retrieve a human man from another realm using little more than intuition, improvisation, and a questionable understanding of magick.

Along the way, Lola and Maddie engage in some "girl detective" action and formulate a plan so audacious it really ought not to work. And yet…

Through a chaotic blend of human determination, faery magick, and a last-minute burst, of "Oh dear God, I hope this works," Lola pulls Seth back through a portal beneath Chagrin Falls—nearly drowning in the process, because apparently risking her life is becoming something of a theme.

Against all odds, Seth makes it home, solid, human, and extremely hungry.

In the aftermath, Seth finds a place in the human world, Maddie's romantic life takes a dramatic turn, and Lola is left to reckon with a reality that is no longer even pretending to be ordinary.

The rest you can gather as you read *The Shapeshifter's Cauldron*. Whatever you do not understand within the upcoming story was probably covered in Books 1 and 2…

… which the faeries would prefer you read first because they're whopping good tales and you won't spend any time while reading *The Shapeshifter's Cauldron* wondering what on earth these characters are talking about!

ONE

I had just come home from work at Karma Korner when the phone rang. It was my best friend Maddie. Normally I'm always glad to hear her voice, but I'd done five readings that day. Not that five was too many—that number was pretty average—it was two particular clients that sapped me.

Three of them were very nice people, easy to connect with. We shared down-to-earth conversations, a few good laughs, and I felt good about helping them achieve an "Aha!" moment, revealing insights that had been hidden by their own blind spots. They each left the store feeling better about their situations, which always leaves me feeling good about what I do for a living.

But one was the kind of customer I struggle not to lose patience with. Raven knows this. She even winked at me when she sent the woman to my table, as if to say, "Better you than me!"

This woman was one of those know-it-all poseurs, positively dripping with crystals and draped in silky chakra colors, who don't even want a reading. They want an opportunity to show off how much they already know.

She plopped down across from me, pointed at my deck of oracle cards, and demanded, "Why don't you use Tarot? All the best readers use Tarot."

I nodded. "Yes, many of them do. Personally, I love this deck. It speaks to me ... "

The woman opened her mouth to interrupt, but I finished my thought. "... and honestly, I don't really need the cards. I mostly use them when too much information is pouring through and I want to narrow my focus."

"Hmph," she said. "Well, I always use Tarot. It's what *my* guides prefer."

I bit my tongue to keep from asking what I really wanted to know: *Why are you even here?* Instead, I asked, with a smile, "What can I do for you?"

As if she had been practicing her line for a school play and this was her big moment, she declared, "My guides have been showing me about an upcoming timeline shift. What are you getting on that?"

'*Oh, geez,*' I thought. '*Which timeline shift? There are so many to choose from. Pull one out of a hat.*'

I hoped she wasn't as psychic as she was putting on. Otherwise, she'd 'hear' my inner monologue, and she was not bringing out the best in me. I had to check myself and throw up a quick thoughtwall before continuing.

Instead of speaking my mind, I said, "Well, there are an infinite number of timelines to choose from. Every action we take creates a new one. Are we talking about your personal timeline, or the big picture … the future of humanity?"

"Oh. Well." She was flummoxed. "My guides didn't say."

"Okay," I said. "Which would you rather focus on?"

"Can we do both? Like, how does my personal timeline fit in with the big picture? You know, why am I here?"

"Sure, we can do that." I handed her the cards. "Think about that question as you shuffle the deck."

She fumbled them a bit, then handed them back. They pulsed with the perfect response, ripe with her answer. I couldn't wait to see what they had to say.

I only flipped three. It's the way I always began. If I needed more, I'd pull them one at a time.

Right away, she gasped and clutched her chest with both hands. "I know what that means! This is perfect!"

"Excellent! Do you want to tell me what you see, or should I do the reading you're paying for?"

"No, go ahead," she said with a fluttery wave over the cards.

"Alright. It looks to me like you're in the wrong profession." I wasn't even reading the cards at this point. The images were downloading faster than I could process them. I saw her working directly with patients in a medical center, brusquely pushing them through the system.

"Yes! I see that, too … the wrong profession."

"You're working in the medical field …"

"Yes! Yes! I'm a healer," she mewed. "I love working with patients."

No, she didn't. And no, she wasn't. Her place was behind the scenes. She had no people skills. But how to say this?

"Actually," I began, "I see you being more helpful to those patients if you worked to improve the broken system. You know enough about how it works … or doesn't work … and you have the type of personality and know-how to fix it."

"Ugh!" she gasped right at me, horror filling her indignant eyes. "No! That's not at all what I want to do. See these?" She held up jazz hands. "These are healing tools."

"That may well be," I said. "I'm just telling you what I see. You've got a very powerful healing ability, but it will be much more effective—and you'll reach more lives—if you change things from the inside."

"Well, that's not what I see, at all," she said, pointing at the cards.

She then proceeded to interpret them herself, telling exactly the story she wanted to hear … that she was a star who simply radiated healing light. Those fortunate enough to come under her miracle hands would have their illnesses lifted forever.

I knew I'd never convince her otherwise. I saw what I saw, and I felt what I felt. There was nothing loving or healing about her vibe. She irritated me just being in her field. Her entire beingness was discordant with personal healing.

But put her in a boardroom with stubborn insurance reps or doctors-turned-businessmen, and she would be a force to be reckoned with. She could do so much good for humanity.

She didn't want to hear it, and I wasn't going to force it. If she wanted to cross my palm with silver just to demonstrate her own psychic prowess, she could go right ahead. I'd gladly sit and listen as she answered her own questions … incorrectly.

It wasn't her, though, that put me through the ringer. It was the fifth client that put me on edge.

An attractive woman in her mid-twenties sat at my table, her low-cut top exposing more than I would have been comfortable revealing. She started right off with a question I dread: "I need to know if my fiancé is cheating on me. What can you tell me?"

I shuffled and flipped a few cards, not really needing them. I could already see the answer, and she wasn't going to like it.

He wasn't cheating on her; he was cheating on his wife.

She was the other woman.

The backstory played out on my clairvoyant screen, the internal movie house in my head: a charming scene of this man, her "fiancé," proposing to his high school sweetheart on bended knee.

Then I saw a sweet little wedding, so much love between the happy couple. Without any lurid details, I saw their adorable honeymoon night, their embarrassed fumbling as two virgins discovered one another.

Fast forward, and two babies later, the happy couple settled into a routine with her raising the kids and keeping the house, and him being steadily promoted through the ranks to top mechanic at a local car dealership's repair shop. His trusting wife was okay with him leaving his wedding ring at home after a co-worker's finger was torn off when his ring got caught during a repair gone wrong.

This same shop is where my client and her man met, when she dropped off her car for repairs. He'd never had any intentions of straying from his marriage, but this woman was exciting and sexy … the whole thing felt just a little bit dangerous. Yes, he loved his little wife, but their sex life had become dull and borderline nonexistent.

He bit the apple and now he was in deep. He soon found himself engaged to my client, through her persistent machinations. She had a way about her. He couldn't say no and she wanted to nail it down.

I took a deep breath before responding to her question, buying myself some time. There was no way to tell her what I saw without upsetting her, and I knew—I could practically smell it on her—that we wouldn't like her when she's angry.

Besides, what if I was wrong? I probably wasn't. It doesn't happen often. That's not ego. That's experience.

Even so, no one is 100% accurate and inaccurate information can destroy lives. So, unless I metaphorically see a solid 'YES' in flaming letters, I sidestep the question and ask the client's guides for suggestions to help them be happier—not more miserable or … perhaps … vengeful.

If I do see a flaming YES, I still don't come right out and say their partner is cheating. Instead, I'll say something like, "Start doing things that make you happy again and if you drift away from that relationship, that's what you really needed to know."

I know it's frustrating for a sitter to hear a non-answer like that, but bitches be crazy sometimes and I'm not going to be responsible for a newspaper headline.

And, yes, I saw that as one of her possible futures: a newspaper headline. I had to step carefully.

I said, "I don't see that he's cheating on you." True. Mostly.

She heaved a huge sigh of relief.

"But," I went on, also relieved to be hearing from her guides what to say next, "I'm hearing that he's not the man for you. The two of you are like ships passing in the night."

"How do you …" she interrupted, but I continued.

The information was flowing now. I described what I saw as it came.

"This man is just a temporary stopgap while the man you're supposed to be with finishes school. Right now, your future husband is concentrating on his studies and is not in the market for a companion."

"Oh!" she said, her eyebrows raised and her posture straightening. "When will that be?"

"I don't see that it will be soon," I said, "maybe a year or so …" I paused, waiting for more information. I heard very clearly that I should continue to word this carefully. That possible future of a headline story had not quite been cleared away.

This is when I consulted the cards for clarity, getting out of my own way. Grateful for their guidance, I pointed at one of them and spilled the new information that was now pouring into my mind, "This card is suggesting that you take a break from men for a while and work on yourself. Otherwise, when Mr. Right is finished with his degree and looking for you, you might not match his vibe. He's kind and gentle and you … well … you have a bit of a temper that you could work on toning down."

Tears gathered in her eyes, and she dabbed at them with a tissue. "I would love that," she said. "I need some me time. But … how do I break up with my fiancé? He'll be so upset."

Visions of headlines vaporized as she asked, and I replied, "I think he'll be okay. You just think about you."

The rest of the reading was less fraught, thank goodness, but I was rattled for the rest of the day. I was really on the spot there. One wrong word, and a crime scene may have been in that couple's future—and I may have been dragged into it if she told the police that a psychic gave her upsetting information.

Readings for other people don't work the same if I ask that same question in my own life. If I was able to easily see any flaming letters between me and Chuck, we wouldn't have drifted as far off track as we have.

I vowed years ago to stay with Chuck in sickness and in health, but wedding vows don't address what happens if he turns into a butthead. Sometimes I look at him and wonder what I ever saw in him. That scares me. It scares me even more when I see him looking at me the same way.

I don't think he's cheating … my psychic skills are way too tuned for that to slip past me, especially in light of Melinda's efforts to break us up. Even dear Seth, if I'm honest, tried to drive a sexual wedge between us (although he was under Melinda's spell at the time, so I'm still pinning the blame on her).

So, yeah, I'm not worried that Chuck is dipping his wick elsewhere, it's that … sometimes I just don't *like* him and I'm not sure he likes me, either. I don't want a divorce, but neither do I want to be married. I don't know what happened. I can't pinpoint a direct cause, so it's hard to know how to fix it.

Raven says we're all blind to our own wounds because they're so interwoven with who we are. We cannot see the forest for the trees. I'm lost in the forest with someone I would rather wasn't there.

Here's a perfect example…

Maddie called that evening to ask me to go with her on a ten-day trip to England, and she wanted to go the next week to attend an estate sale at an actual English estate, like Downton Abbey. She was practically salivating to get her mitts on some truly old antiques to sell in her store. Her man Paul couldn't go because of his work schedule, and she didn't want to go alone. She offered to pay my way … all expenses.

"You know I can afford it," she reminded me. "The cost is just a drop in the bucket, nothing considering how much fun we'll have. We'll rent a car in London and drive across the gorgeous English countryside, wind in our hair, sheep in the road, and rub elbows with charming, posh gentlemen. You can't say no to an offer like this!"

Indeed, I could not, but do you think Chuck agreed? If so, you'd be wrong.

"What are Amanda and I going to do while you're gone for two weeks?" he pouted, plopping into his dining room chair while I finished setting the table for dinner.

I rolled my eyes as I turned back toward the kitchen and inwardly kicked myself. Maybe I should have made a special meal to butter him up, as I once might have done. It didn't even occur to me this time. I used to care about getting his go-ahead for big things and he apparently still does. The older I get, the less he gets to tell me what to do, so I wasn't asking permission. I was telling him what was going to happen.

I took a deep breath and swallowed my aggravation. "Well, first, it's ten days, not two weeks," I replied. "Both you and Amanda are capable of fending for yourselves for ten days."

"Yeah, but who's going to do your chores?" he asked. "I don't know how to do laundry or grocery shop, not to mention cooking dinners for two weeks. Neither does Amanda."

"Maybe it's time you both learn. Besides, it's *ten days*," I reminded him, through slightly gritted teeth.

"Fine!" he said, throwing his hands in the air. "Ten days! That's still a long time!"

"Are you saying you cannot survive without me for a mere week and a half?" I stomped over to the kitchen junk drawer, pulled out a stack of carry-out menus, and slapped them down on the table in front of him. "Take out and frozen dinners are your friends."

Shifting the argument, he replied, "And going with Maddie … you two get into things … you know, all that psychic mumbo jumbo with the faeries and whatnot. I don't need to be worrying about what you're up to on the other side of the world."

"It's not Maddie that stirs the pot," I reminded him. "It's that damned Melinda. Every time I've gotten into trouble, it's because of her. And she's not a part of our lives anymore. No one has seen or heard from her since the summer of the fire at Raven's shop. Even Seth hasn't heard from her. He's happily ensconced in running Maddie's antique store, and neither Raven nor I have had any psychic inklings that she's even thinking about us."

It was true. Ever since Seth recovered from Melinda's psychic attack, and I began doing readings at Karma Korner, Melinda has been completely out of our thoughts. Maybe it's because of the protective field I've learned to build.

Hold on. Twink just tapped me on the shoulder and said, "Credit where credit is due …"

So, yeah, it's also because of Twink and Precious Pea, and Myx and Maj … and Jennett and Olfen … and whoever else I'm forgetting from the land of the Fae.

Not yet out of steam, Chuck came back with another question, "Why does it have to be such a long trip? Surely an estate sale doesn't last …" he caught himself before repeating the 'two weeks' trope "… ten days."

"Maddie says we need to allow for travel," I explained. "She said two of those days will be taken up by the long flights alone, and we should allow a day to recover from jet lag. Then we have to drive across southern England to the estate, and …"

This is where I hesitated, because I knew this would be a sticking point, "… on the way back, she wants to spend a couple days in some town called Glastonbury."

I tried to be casual about Glastonbury. I didn't want him to pee in my Wheaties.

Even so, Chuck immediately pounced on that tidbit of information. "So, this isn't just a business trip in search of antiques. You two will be lollygagging as well."

I rolled my eyes and didn't bother to take the bait.

"Look," I said instead, "Maddie is paying for the whole thing and if she wants to spend a couple days as a tourist while she's in another country, can you blame her? It's not like it's going to cost *you* anything."

"That's another thing," he argued, "I don't like you taking charity from her, and I certainly don't want Paul knowing that his … woman … is paying for mine. He's one of my most important clients and I don't want him to think I can't support my family or send my wife on an expensive trip. And it is expensive, isn't it?"

"Well, yeah," I said. "That's why Maddie offered to pay. She knew I couldn't cough up that much on such short notice. She doesn't want to go alone and doesn't want excuses like money to keep me from going with. She makes it sound like I'll be doing her a favor. You have to remember that Maddie is independently wealthy. *She* will be paying for it, not Paul."

"It sounds like you've already decided to go," he harumphed, folding his arms over his chest.

"Yeah," I said, returning to the kitchen to get the rest of the serving dishes, "it sounds like it, doesn't it?" I turned toward the stairs and hollered, "Amanda! Come and eat."

Once I heard her feet shuffling overhead, I finished laying dinner on the table and sat across from Chuck. He didn't like it when I psychically tapped in, so I usually respected his wishes. This time, though, I allowed myself the briefest scan, just enough to pick up on a flicker of fear … *what will happen to us if …*

As he scooped food onto his plate and dug in, stuffing his face, I allowed myself to get lost in thought. '*Does my happiness bug him?*'

In flaming letters, the answer appeared.

And, yes, it scared me.

TWO

"I think I'm going to regret letting you talk me into flying in the main cabin," Maddie said as we squeezed into our seats.

"I think you're right," I grumbled. My butt barely fit between the arm rests. "When did airline seats get this tight? What happens when someone even slightly larger tries to fit into these contraptions?"

"They get fat shamed," she said, tsking as she fastened her seat belt.

Twisting my hips in the confined space, trying to get comfortable, I said, "I foolishly assumed international flights would have more comfortable seating. If I had known we'd have to sit like this on an eight-hour flight, I might have let you pay for first or business class, but the thousands you saved mattered more to me during the planning process."

"Live and learn," Maddie sighed, craning her neck to peer into the business class section up ahead of us. "Looks like a full flight. No upgrades today … maybe I'll arrange better seats on the way back … whether you approve or not." She grinned at me, knowing that this was exactly what she would do.

I stifled an urge to continue grumbling about the airline's blatant cash grab and decided instead to focus on the extra legroom we had in our bulkhead seats … for which, yes, Maddie had to pay extra.

"Now listen, Lola," Maddie said, leaning toward me so no one would overhear, "I get that you're having a hard time with Chuck and Amanda guilt-tripping you and whatever else is going on, but we're here, on the plane, and we have a fabulous ten days ahead of us. You're going to have to lighten the eff up or I'll … well, I don't know what I'll do, but it'll be drastic."

"You're right," I said, trying to smile. "Thank you … for trying to cheer me up and for giving me a reason to be cheery. I promise, I'll leave all that behind starting … now." I punctuated that 'now' by snapping my fingers.

The flight attendant approached and pointed at my carry-on, a backpack with my purse tucked inside. "Ma'am, I'm going to have to stow that in the overhead. Personal items must be placed under the seat in front of you, and …" she gestured at the empty space where a seat should have been.

"Oh," I said, flustered. "But everything I need is in there."

She smiled but didn't budge. "It's FAA regulations."

"Give me a minute," I replied. I dug through my bag and pulled out my phone and charger, my book and a bag of trail mix, tucking them into the narrow space between my hip and the armrest. I handed her the bag and she thanked me, before hoisting it up into an overhead bin a couple of rows behind us.

She then turned to Maddie, who was already retrieving what she needed before relinquishing her bag, and we both settled in for a long, uncomfortable flight.

Once we were in the air, Maddie pulled out a notebook brimming with loose sheets of paper. "Let's go over the itinerary. This is the first chance we've had to do this uninterrupted." She showed me a printout of our schedule for the next ten days.

"When we land at Heathrow, it will be evening. The clocks will be five hours later than in Ohio, so we'll grab a hotel room near the airport and try to sleep off the time difference. I've made reservations …" she flipped through the notebook and pulled out a sheet confirming two rooms.

"I would have been fine sharing …" I began, but she interrupted.

"Honey, we *both* need my own space," she teased, laying her immaculately manicured hand on my arm. "Besides, wouldn't Chuckles be upset if we shared a hotel room, considering …" She glanced conspiratorially downward.

I asked, "Considering what?" Then I remembered. "Oh, yeah. I didn't even think about that. To me, you're just … Maddie … and I don't care if 'Chuckles' doesn't like us sharing a room. I'm focused on cutting costs and there is nothing sexual about our friendship, even if you are technically male. After all, you're my best *girl*friend."

"You're sweet," she said, "but let me worry about the costs. I'm not good at sharing hotel rooms. I take over the entire bathroom with my gear and, besides, Paul tells me I snore. So … there's that."

I laughed and agreed, "Okay, maybe you're right."

"Good," she said. "That's settled. Next," she shuffled the papers again, "we pick up the rental car at Heathrow tomorrow morning …"

"Why do you have this all printed out?" I interrupted. "Surely there's an app to keep track of all this."

"Of course there is," she said, "but this ain't my first rodeo. I always print everything just in case, and sometimes it's easier to keep track of so much information when you don't have to scroll on a tiny screen. Besides, we're in airplane mode, so I can't access the internet and I'm not paying the airline's sky-high … no pun intended … fee for wi-fi. I may be able to afford it, but I was raised in a very frugal family. Old habits die hard."

"Aha!" I pounced, "See? You do care about cutting costs!"

She rolled her eyes. "I may be fabulously wealthy now," she said, "but remember when we first met? How poor I was? I've learned to pick and choose my splurges, and I don't mind paying big bucks for a comfier seat on a long-haul flight or an extra room so we can both enjoy some alone time. Those can be written off as business expenses. I don't *need* wi-fi. I downloaded plenty of music and movies at home, and I can live without doomscrolling for a few hours."

A flight attendant with a service cart handed us both a bag of pretzels and asked if we'd like anything to drink. We both ordered a beverage—me a glass of orange juice and Maddie a cola on ice—then continued our conversation.

I asked, "Weren't we supposed to spend the first day getting over jet lag? Why are we picking up the car right away?"

"Oh, right," she said. "I realized that jet lag shouldn't be too bad on the way there. As I said, it'll be evening in London when we arrive, so we'll have an entire night to sleep. Plus, I plan to snooze away some of the eight hours ahead of us … if I can get comfortable in this torturous monstrosity," she grinned, wiggling dramatically in her narrow seat.

"Besides," Maddie continued, "I thought we could make a quick stop tomorrow to break up the long trek to the estate sale. It's just a ninety-minute drive from London to a cute little village called Avebury, and we'll spend the night there before heading to Devon. That way we're not pushing ourselves into a long drive with possibly too little sleep."

"I've heard of Avebury," I said, sipping my juice and eating a tiny pretzel. "Raven suggested a visit there when I told her we were going to England. I think she said it's a bigger stone circle than Stonehenge. Is that on the way? Can we see Stonehenge?"

"I don't know," Maddie replied, "I'll have to check once we have internet again." She shuffled through her itinerary papers and continued, "The next day we'll drive to Devon, and the following day is all business for me. You can take the car and go sightseeing if you don't want to hang out with me drooling over antiques."

"We'll see," I said. "I'm not real keen on driving on the wrong side of the road."

She took a big slurp of her beverage. "I hear you, sister. It does take some getting used to. I'm going to depend on you as my navigator."

Ignoring my grimace, she went on. "After all the tax-deductible business is done, we are free to be tourists and we're off to Glastonbury. I've rented a charming little two-bedroom farmhouse cottage at the foot of the Tor, with a spectacular view of the hill and the tower at the top. Maybe your faeries will meet us there!"

"I think you can bet on it," I said, surprised that none of them were hovering overhead, eavesdropping. Then I remembered how much the faeries hated riding in the car, which moved so fast it boggled their minds. I supposed that being inside a plane, going ten times as fast, would be more than they could deal with.

When I told them about our upcoming travels, Twink and her younger sister, Precious Pea, were so excited they both throbbed and sparkled in anticipation. I even teased Twink about it, much to her chagrin.

"You know, Twink," I said, "I'm used to Pea blinking when she gets excited but I've never seen you lose control like that."

"I haven't lost control," she sniffed, pulling herself back together. "How dare you?"

Meanwhile, Pea flickered and squealed, "Glastonbury! Eeeee! Are you going to climb the Tor?"

Twink didn't squeal. Twink never squealed. But she certainly pulsed with more clouds of glittery faery dust than I've ever seen. Aethelwyne Eglantina—or, as I called her, "Twink"—tried to present herself as terribly grown up and above it all despite her young age, the faery equivalent of someone in their early twenties. If I had to guess, Pea was closer to Amanda's age, in her late teens, so Twink reacting like an adolescent was kind of cute.

As for the Tor, I couldn't answer that. This was Maddie's plan and I didn't know much about Glastonbury, just that there was a huge festival every summer and I'd seen YouTube videos of bands performing.

But I hadn't realized, until the faeries filled me in and I Googled it later, that the Tor is a hill crowned with the ruins of a stone tower, sitting at the intersection of two ley lines, and widely considered to be the heart of Avalon.

I had to look up ley lines, too. I still don't fully understand what they are, but from what I've gathered, they're like Earth's acupuncture meridians, lines of energy connecting sacred sites.

Glastonbury is at the intersection of two of the most powerful—the St. Michael line and the Mary line—so the energy there is supposed to be especially strong. Because of this, Glastonbury attracts spiritually minded people. They climb the Tor and get some kind of buzz out of being at the top of the hill.

Raven even commented, "How exciting! I can't wait to hear your take on the energies because you'll be there during the equinox and an eclipse. Of course, you'll have to tune in without picking up on all the other pilgrims who climb the hill with you. With your ability to focus getting better every day, I don't doubt you'll have a lot to report."

"Yes," I said, "but one reason I'm looking forward to the trip at all is to get away from all this."

While I loved Raven's shop and her customers and my reading clients, I needed a break from people. The idea of fighting crowds in a sacred spot wasn't at all appealing.

Despite my overall grouchiness (which Maddie had just pointed out) my anticipation began to build after Twink later dropped a tantalizing hint. "Never mind the ley lines or Avalon," she said, dismissively waving off her strobing younger sister. "What about the king of the Fae who lives beneath the hill? Isn't he a bit more important?"

"It's all important, Thel," Pea huffed back at her. using Twink's preferred nickname … a shortened version of her full moniker, Aethelwyne. "You celebrate what you want, I'll celebrate what I want."

"I don't think I've ever met a male faery, have I?" I asked them. "All the faeries I've interacted with seem to be female. I wonder what the king will be like … if he presents himself as available to meet, that is."

"Yeh've only stepped a toe into our world," Twink reminded me, "and those were controlled visits."

I'd love to travel to Jennett's Foss someday, but it's not on the itinerary for this trip. That's where I met Twink's Aunt Jennett, a queen of the Fae, though only in the spirit realm during a shamanic journey. In real life—if that's even the right way to describe it—Jennett is based further north in Yorkshire while Glastonbury is in the southwest, in Somerset.

As I continued gathering wool—wedged there in my seat, recalling my conversation with the faery sisters, and considering what 'real life' even meant when it came to the Fae—Maddie said, "Well, doll, I'm going to try to get a little nap in. Wake me when they bring the meal cart around." She tucked her notebook next to her hip and reclined her seat.

"Will do," I replied. I wasn't tired and wouldn't be able to sleep yet, so I reclined my seat as well and pulled out my book. I tried to read, but my mind kept swirling with thoughts of ley lines and faeries I might meet along the way … perhaps in the physical world and not just the spiritual dreamtime.

I couldn't focus though. My mind drifted back to Chuck and the way we left things when Maddie picked me up for the airport. We were barely speaking. I hoped that a little time apart would help us miss each other. I'd like to come back to a warm welcome, instead of the resentful grump I'd left behind.

'*Oh well,*' I thought. '*I'll call him once we land … let him know I'm thinking about him and promise to text every day.*'

I decided to join Maddie in a little shut eye, even if I couldn't sleep. It was going to be a long, uncomfortable flight and none of my friend's light-hearted threats about my mood would change that.

ThRee

I didn't give it much thought before arriving, expecting England to be just like America except with different accents. But so many of the buildings were centuries old and the locals didn't even seem to notice them. Meanwhile, in the airport shuttle on the way to the hotel, I sat with my jaw agape marveling at houses built hundreds of years ago … with people still living in them!

In contrast, our hotel was ultra-modern. I couldn't figure out how to check in at the self-serve kiosk and had to go to the only manned station at the front desk. The young clerk there made a valiant effort not to stare at me as if I had two heads when I asked where their little shop was. "You know," I explained, "if I wanted a can of pop, a bottle of water or a snack … if I forgot my toothbrush at home …"

She was kind enough to not say, "Okay, Boomer," as she absently pointed out the tap-to-pay self-serve checkout machine across the lobby where snacks and toiletries sat waiting for purchase on the honor system. She then moved on to the next in the line of guests checking in from all over the world, speaking many different languages.

We checked out the next morning dressed for chilly weather in jeans, sweaters and tennies, with hoodies tied around our waists and our hair pulled back in ponytails. The main contrast between us was that Maddie's casual duds were expensive and stylish and mine clearly came from the outlet mall. Her ponytail was held back in a sparkly clip while mine was gathered in a rubber band. She looked so cute she even got a wink from the shuttle driver when he dropped us off at the rental agency.

As we gathered our luggage to go inside and pick up our car, I said, "You always look more feminine and put together than I do. I clearly don't care as much as you."

"I don't think it's so much about caring," she said, hoisting her heavy bag over a wrinkle in the welcome rug. "Maybe it's more about enjoying the process. I love sparkly, girly things. Always have. You're just … more practical."

I chuckled. "Thank you for dancing around my feelings. I, unlike you, always experienced girliness as cause for derision and dismissal."

"Honey," she said, breezing through the automatic door, "you don't have to be female to attract that kind of nonsense. Now let's get our car and hit the road for our girls' adventure!"

Thank God Maddie took the wheel of the rental car because I would have totaled it within minutes of pulling out of the lot at Heathrow. Driving on the wrong side of the road is more than a minor detail. It's also a matter of turning into the wrong lane whether you're going right or left, and understanding their different road signs. You have to pay sharp, close attention—no wool gathering. It's a whole new way of being, especially in one of the biggest, busiest cities in the world.

Even with guidance from the built-in dashboard GPS (which they call SatNav), we went around in circles just trying to get onto the freeway (which they call the motorway) because of the wagon wheel shaped roundabouts (which I call "OMFG!").

I was almost in tears when I pointed out to Maddie, "Ya know, back home a roundabout is a decorative traffic circle with a tree in the middle and a 35 MPH speed limit. And they're tucked away in posh neighborhoods, not on the main roads every half mile instead of traffic lights."

She merely smiled and sped forward, paying my dismay no mind.

I went on. "And since they're on side streets, there's no need to learn how to maneuver. You just … go … because there's no one else there!"

Maddie grinned in agreement. "Not here, boy! Here, if you don't know the rules … You. Will. Die."

"Or," I continued the banter, "you'll drive around in circles until you figure out what the nice SatNav lady means by 'Take the fifth exit at the roundabout.'"

To me, an "exit" is on a highway—*only one* exit. Not this wagon wheel nonsense where every spoke is an exit. And you bloody well better be in the correct lane entering and exiting or you'll piss off a truck (lorry) driver who'll scream obscenities and hold up two fingers at you. In the U.S., it's a peace sign. In England, not so much. Here, flipping the bird is double the fun.

During my initial panic—which I spent shrieking, "LOOK OUT!!!"— Maddie reacquainted herself with the rules of the British roads. It was only after we made it to the motorway that she finally educated me how to be a good navigator. This was her third trip to England, and she had apparently forgotten what it was like to be a newbie.

It would have been nice if she had done that *before* we drove off in our Mercedes convertible with only 900 miles on it. I said that, too, leaning forward as if proximity to the SatNav screen would help me digest what we just experienced.

I moaned, "It would have been nice if you'd told me what you want me to navigate, *before* we drove off in this death trap!"

"Hey, we're alive and well, right?" she asked, zipping down the M4 in the far right, fast lane. "We survived our first crisis … and it wasn't as bad as you're making it out to be. This ain't my first rodeo. I just forgot how to get out of a roundabout."

I moaned again and sank back into my seat on what should be the driver's side but is the passenger side, here.

Once we dropped into the flow of motorway traffic, I was able to unclench my butt and relax into the luxe leather seat. There were definite advantages to having a friend who didn't mind spending a few coins for her own comfort. I was especially appreciative that she didn't insist on putting the top down. The temperature was in the 50s (whatever they call that in Celsius) and, even though the sun was out for now, it was too chilly to be doing 70 in a convertible.

I pulled out my phone to see if Chuck had responded to my chat message. I'd sent it the night before, explaining that I hadn't realized my cell service didn't include international calls, so I had to buy a local SIM card from the hotel's self-serve shop.

That was quite a learning curve. I mean, do you even know where your SIM card is located? Or how to remove and replace it? And what about your phone's settings? Would you know how to tweak them? Me either. But at least now I had plenty of data and a British phone number, albeit no way to call or text internationally.

The things we don't think about, eh?

No response yet. Not a huge surprise, as Chuck isn't one for private messaging on social media apps. He prefers texting and it probably hasn't even occurred to him to check if I've contacted him another way. He was probably wondering why I hadn't called or texted.

At least, I hoped he was wondering.

It dawned on me. "Hey," I said to Maddie, "do you have international service on your phone? Do you mind if I text Chuck and tell him to check his DMs?"

"Sure, go ahead," she said.

I typed out a brief text and hit send. He and I would be limited to Messenger and email. Inconvenient, yes ... but a relief, if I'm being honest. It might be nice to have a little distance from my real life.

Once that was taken care of, I joined Maddie in singing along to '80s music on the radio, tuned to a station called BBC2, and watching the scenery whizzing by. Surprisingly, it didn't look much different from Ohio. Lots of green, lots of trees, just a hint of the foliage beginning to change color. The first day of fall was only days away, too early for full autumn splendor.

"It's so weird hearing the radio DJs speaking with that accent, when it looks so much like home. And where are all the castles?" I asked. "I thought there would be castles."

"There are," she said, "but they aren't on the motorway. You have to get off onto the smaller, less traveled roads ... and if you think driving here is scary, I don't even want to tell you what it's like on a single-track road."

"I don't want to know," I said.

Time passed quickly, and before long the SatNav lady chimed in with her posh British accent, "At Wickham Interchange, take the first exit onto A338."

As we exited the motorway onto a ramp on the wrong side of the road, the SatNav displayed a massive oval-shaped roundabout with multiple exits. I was deeply grateful that the blue directional arrow showed us taking the first one. Maddie expertly maneuvered into the appropriate lane and waited her turn to enter the roundabout, then made that left turn.

"Boom," she said. "There we go. It's a lot easier when you're not dealing with London airport traffic."

"Indeed," I agreed.

We still had about 30 miles to go, but it went fast. There were plenty of roundabouts on the way to Avebury, but because the speed limit was low and traffic was light, it became good practice instead of a near-death experience. Before long, I was navigating like a pro, directing Maddie into the correct lanes and off onto the proper exits.

I was getting used to … well, I don't know if I'll ever get used to … the old, old, old buildings. The homes, the churches and the municipal buildings were in sharp contrast to the shiny new supermarkets and gas stations (which they call petrol).

Each town we passed through seemed to have the same church: a smallish stone structure, with tall, pointed windows, arched wooden doors and a sturdy, square tower. The churchyards were dotted with weather-beaten headstones, some leaning, others toppled over with age and covered with green lichen.

Even so, I wasn't prepared for my first view of Avebury.

We were tooling along on a two-lane B-road, green fields stretching out on either side, when suddenly the landscape changed. Those fields were now dotted with massive stone megaliths, ten or fifteen feet high, some just as wide, others tall and slender. In a fenced field on the left, they were lined up in a row, but on the right they didn't seem to follow any placement pattern … just huge stones plopped in the middle of another fenced-in field.

My jaw dropped, as did Maddie's.

"Wowwww …" I said, "… they're right there. I thought we'd have to hike to see them. Or … pay to get in."

"No, didn't I mention?" Maddie said. "Part of the village, just up there, is in the middle of the stone circle."

Sure enough, directly ahead was a tidy, quaint pub—hundreds of years old, of course—with white exterior walls, a brown thatched roof, and a patio filled with wooden picnic tables. Maddie pulled into the tiny parking lot.

"Our B&B is up the road another half mile and it's not check-in time yet, so let's grab some lunch and wander."

I climbed out of the car and took it all in. We were in the center of the stone circle, with two more fenced fields behind us, one on either side of the main road. The village was divided into quadrants at a central crossroads, where a busy two-lane road curved through town.

It was like a theme park or a movie set, and I had to remind myself—this was *real*. People *live here!* I had never felt like such a fish-out-of-water American.

An undercurrent—a throbbing, pulsing energy—called, and I ached to tap in, but it could wait. First, something to eat. I was starving.

We entered the pub where an electronic tablet was mounted on the wall in front of us, asking for our car's license number. Parking spots in this tiny village were at a premium and, if you were going to take up a spot here at the pub, you'd better be a customer. Maddie dug the rental agreement from her bag for the tag number and typed it in, allowing us permission to leave the car there for the rest of the day.

The bar to the right was a blend of old and new. The building itself was hundreds of years old, but the bar was decked out with modern taps and glitzy lighting.

Maddie said to the pretty young barkeep, "We'd like to have some lunch. Do we seat ourselves?"

"You certainly may, anywhere is fine," she said in her English lilt.

"Americans, are yeh? Tourists?" asked a scruffy, bearded man leaning against the bar, his accent thickened by a drink or two, "Be sure to sit at the well table, if no one's already there. It's haunted!"

Encouraged by our puzzled expressions, he continued, "Hundreds of years ago, this was a farmhouse. The owner came home from the wars to find his wife with another man. He killed them both and threw them down the well, and she haunts the place to this day." He guffawed, "There's some sightseeing for yeh!"

The bartender smiled and shook her head. "Pay him no mind. Florrie won't bother you."

"Aye," he bellowed, "Florrie won't bother yeh. Neither of yeh have a beard. She hates a man with a beard!"

"Thanks for the warning," Maddie said, winking conspiratorially. "Good thing I shaved this morning!"

We all laughed, but I was the only one who knew she wasn't kidding.

We wandered into the dining area, also a mix of old and new furnishings, and spotted the well table—a round brick structure with a glass top allowing a view down into the well—but a trio of people were already seated there.

The table by a bay window overlooking the stones across the street was open, so we sat there. "This is actually a better view," I said. "I don't know if I'd want to sit at the haunted table anyway, staring down into an ancient crime scene. I'm not in the mood to pick up on murdered ghosts."

"I was wondering about that," Maddie said. "How are your psychic senses doing on the trip so far?"

"Not too bad," I said, picking up the menu. "I think we've been too on-the-go for much to get through. I'm more concerned that I haven't heard from Chuck."

I pulled out my phone and checked again. Still no reply to my message from the night before. "Have you received a response from the text I sent?"

Maddie looked at her phone. "Nothing from Chuck, but plenty of other things I need to respond to. Give me a sec while you look at the menu."

She got busy, bipping her keyboard, while I perused the options.

As I sat deciding whether to order the fishcakes with poached egg or an ordinary salad, I heard a buzzing near my ear. I didn't even need to look. If Twink or Precious Pea were going to show up anywhere, a haunted pub in the middle of an ancient stone circle would be the place.

Maddie set her phone down. "You know, maybe you haven't heard from Chuck yet because it's still early back in Ohio. He might not be up and around yet. Or," she added, "you said that your cell account didn't have international service. Maybe his doesn't either so he can't text me back."

"Of course," I said, relieved. "I'm sure everything is fine."

We ordered lunch and took our time, to the faeries' dismay. Twink and Pea were both there. They weren't showing themselves, but I heard them talking to one another:

"What's taking her so long?"

"I don't know, do I?"

"It's like she doesn't even know where she is!"

Finally, I said aloud, "Would you two knock it off? I'm trying to eat."

Maddie chuckled. "Oh, are our friends with us? I guess I'm back to not being able to see them."

"They're here," I said, "but I don't see them either. They want me to hurry up and get out there amongst the stones."

"Aye," Twink's disembodied voice said, "but yeh need to make a stop first, in yon shop. Over there, across the road."

I looked out the bay window. Across the curving, narrow road stood another old brick building that I hadn't noticed before. A bus had been unloading passengers in front of it, blocking my view.

Now that traffic had cleared, I could see into the windows. Crystals hung and sparkled in the light, along with the usual assortment of mystical doodads. This was a shop like Raven's, back home.

"Oooo!" I said to Maddie, "Twink wants me to go to the crystal shop across the road!"

She laughed. "You don't have to twist my arm!"

With that, we ate a little more quickly and settled the bill. Although Maddie had offered to cover all my expenses, I insisted on paying for my own food. I could afford it and, besides, when someone else is footing the bill it's hard to order what you actually want if it's on the pricier side.

I was also paying for my own souvenirs, so I hoped Twink hadn't set her mind on my buying something expensive across the street. She had no concept of money or the value humans place on things, so any objections to high prices would be met with a tiny pair of rolled eyes.

It was colder outside than when we arrived, and we were met with drizzling rain. "Get used to your hair looking crazy here," Maddie warned. She retrieved a waterproof silk scarf from her purse and tied it over her tidy coif. "This time of year, it's always misting or raining … or as the locals say, 'pissing down'."

My scarf was in the car, so I put my purse up over my head as an umbrella and we darted across the road, dodging local drivers who knew the narrow bends well enough to zip through them.

I'd been to a lot of metaphysical shops back home. I knew the look. Candles, crystals, incense, books ... each place decorated and shaped by the personality of its owner.

None of those experiences prepared me for this.

Stepping over the threshold, my initial impression was that this was a cute little shop—clean and tidy, smallish rooms, decked out with the usual candles, incense, crystals and such, two women chatting amiably near the cash register in their lilting British accents.

But once I was fully inside I felt a sort of ... psychic suction ... pulling my consciousness inward to a dimension beyond 3D.

While the shops back home reflect the creative visions of their owners, this one carried the imprint of the land and the stone circle surrounding us. This shop's vibe wasn't just curated; it emanated from the ground beneath our feet.

Everything—the people, the products, the crystals—glowed with an almost blinding light. I had to blink my eyes a few times to adjust. Although my vision settled, everything still sparkled with shimmering edges. Each object had its own rainbow halo, as if I was seeing through hologram glasses.

And ... right there in the middle of the shop's main room stood Twink and Precious Pea, full-sized. Twink was slightly taller than Pea, but both were about the height of a nine-year-old girl. They beamed and glowed, sparkling and shimmering so brilliantly that I could almost not make out the colors of their clothes ... Twink in her usual peacock hues and Pea in her standard pink.

Both grinning, each grabbed one of my hands—Twink on the left, Pea on the right—and pulled me toward one of the other rooms, exclaiming, "Come on! Back here!"

The looks on the faces of the women at the till, and Maddie as well, told me that they didn't see the faeries. Just me, arms outstretched, seemingly falling forward.

I pulled my hands back to my sides and tried to walk normally, which was difficult because the sisters didn't care how I looked to the others. They just wanted me to hurry, still tugging at my hands.

They led me to a smaller room, filled with bins and shelves of crystals. The light in this room was even brighter than the front of the shop.

"Over here," said Pea, pointing to a set of glass shelves.

On one shelf were numerous crystal spheres, carved out of different stones … dark obsidian, speckled jasper, rose quartz, amethyst, and the most sparkly of all, quartz.

"Pick one of these," she urged, indicating the quartz crystal balls.

Choosing wouldn't be difficult. They were all beautiful, but one stood out. A quartz sphere, about the size of a golf ball, glittered more brightly than the rest.

I picked it up and gazed into it, its internal fractures creating an illusion of depth that drew my eyes inward with the promise of 'more to see here'. As I turned it in my hand, rainbow flashes flickered in the light.

"Excellent choice," said Twink, "but more importantly, come over here. See this one?"

On the opposite wall Twink directed me to a display of dark, greenish-gray stones, each with a shimmering aurora from within that flashed and changed with the angle of the light. I had seen labradorite before. Raven sells it at her shop. I had noted its beauty but never felt drawn to bring one home.

That changed now. One of the stones—maybe two inches wide and shaped like a flying saucer with the most magnificent blue flash—practically shrieked, "Me! Me! Take me!"

Decision made.

I looked at the prices of both stones, the tiny white stickers with the costs written in British pounds. After juggling some conversation rate math in my head, I concluded that buying both was outside of my budget for the day. I'd have to choose between the two.

"I can't afford both …" I began, but Twink interrupted me.

"Nonsense," she said. "Do yeh think we brought yeh in here just to buy trinkets? Cut yehr costs elsewhere."

With buyers' remorse already rearing its head, the vortexy pull returned: the shop … the stones … the land on which I stood. I had to buy them. I was led to these two crystals by my trusted companions.

Maddie wandered into the room then, her lack of reaction informing me that she still didn't see the faeries, so I said, "Look at these gorgeous stones. Twink and Pea want me to buy them."

She beamed. "Well, then I guess you better buy them! Are they here now? Hello, ladies!"

They both replied in kind, but she didn't hear.

"Yes, they're here, and they say hello," I said. "I better get out of here before I spend any more."

"Good thinking," she said. "Besides, I want to get out there amongst the *big* stones."

We made our way toward the cash register and that's where I spotted a display of essential oils. One bottle in particular caught my eye, the same way the two stones had. The oil was only a few pounds, so I added a bottle of Clary Sage to my collection and paid the nice lady.

Why Clary Sage? I did not know, but Twink had made her point: I wasn't here just to buy trinkets. There must be some purpose for these items that had not yet been made clear.

I tucked my purchases into my purse while Maddie showed me the box of oracle cards she'd bought. "Aren't they gorgeous? They have the Avebury stones on them."

"They are beautiful," I agreed. "Maybe we can do a reading with them later."

The rain had stopped while we were inside, but now it was misty and chilly, the cold seeping into my bones. The radiance from inside the shop carried over only slightly outdoors.

We approached the entrance of the closest fenced-in field, the southeastern quadrant of the stone circle. Behind us was the pub where we just ate. Only a handful of tourists were about, probably due to the weather.

Ahead of us, a young couple entered the field through a latched gate. The woman was dressed like a hippie from the Sixties, long hair, bell bottom jeans, and a shaggy fake fur coat. The man was clothed in long and flowing garb along with a battered top hat bedecked with a feather. Neither was cosplaying. Both glowed a little more brightly than any of the other people scattered about the field.

We followed along, giving them space. The land pulsated with aliveness and there was no rush. This was a sacred place, and allowing them room to move about, not hurrying behind them, was appropriate.

The wooden-framed gate was latched from the inside, with a metal pole jutting upward as a handle. I jiggled the pole back and forth to open the gate, but no joy. The young man turned around and saw me struggling, so he strode back to the gate and easily unlatched it.

I blushed with embarrassment and said, "Thank you."

He nodded politely and returned to his woman's side, and Maddie whispered, "You've just been given entrance to the stones by a wizard!"

I knew she was joking … at least, *she* thought she was joking, but there was more truth to her jest than she knew. I silently agreed that it was more than a coincidence that the 'wizard' had let me into the field … this was synchronicity.

We walked through the field, our shoes getting wet from the grass, stopping at each large stone to lay hands on them. I wasn't picking up anything beyond the throbbing hum that I had noticed upon our arrival. No lofty, spiritual messages as I had expected.

However, a small group of glowing beech trees up ahead caught my attention.

I wandered away from Maddie, who stood with her back against one of the monoliths.

The trees were on a slight hill. The closer I got, the stronger their presence became, calling me forward. I climbed up the short incline and approached the trees, recalling what I'd learned over the years: *Ask a tree for permission before entering its space.*

I didn't count how many trees were there altogether, because only the three at the top of the hill replied, *Yes, come in.* Their thick roots covered the ground beneath them, curving about like a pile of serpents.

Stepping carefully so I didn't twist an ankle, especially as my vision was again challenged by overwhelming light, I moved in among the roots until I was centered between those three. Their trunks were so massive I wouldn't be able to touch fingers if I reached around them. I closed my eyes and listened … it was the thing to do.

The power building within the trees was like an airplane engine revving up. It was as if green made sound and was growing in intensity.

After enjoying the bliss of the moment for a few beats, I finally wondered why I was called into this pillar of green light. Then I recalled the labradorite I'd just purchased and tucked into my purse. I thought to reach in and retrieve it, but instead psychically 'heard': *No need. It's with you here.*

So, I didn't need to hold the stone. Its presence there with me in this space was enough.

Then, I heard something else … with my actual ears … a deep male voice saying, "The King awaits."

I opened my eyes and spun around, looking for any nearby men … perhaps the wizard … but no one was there. Not even the faeries. I was alone among the trees. Maddie still stood out there in the field of monoliths, her palms resting upon a different stone than before.

As I stepped out of the tangle of roots and began my descent down the hill, the lighting and the thrumming vibe returned to what most would call 'normal.' Everything from here on would be ordinary, like for anyone else who gathered here hoping for something otherworldly to happen.

Except something otherworldly already had.

FOUR

I finally heard from Chuck. He received the text I sent from Maddie's phone and had to reinstall Messenger to reply because he didn't have international service for his cell either. I had no idea he had uninstalled Messenger but he said that he never used it … we always texted one another.

Anyway, all is well. He was relieved to hear from me, and I was relieved that he was relieved. I read his message as Maddie and I sat in the dining room of the B&B, experiencing my first Full English Breakfast. Good lord, that's a lot of food!

"Try that," Maddie said, pointing at the round slice of sausage on my plate, which was an unnerving shade of charcoal gray.

"Give me a sec," I said, pushing the baked beans into a contained pile so the sauce wouldn't seep into any of the other foods. I hate when my food touches, and this crowded plate was a true challenge. "What is it?"

"It's black pudding," she grinned.

"That doesn't look like pudding. Why is it black?" I asked. "And what's with the grilled tomatoes and mushrooms? So much of this isn't breakfast food." I cut into the mystery sausage with my fork and took a bite.

"I don't know why it's called pudding," she said. "It's just another one of those words that means something different here." She watched my face for a reaction as I sampled the enigmatic not-dessert.

"It's good," I said, taking another bite.

She grinned broadly and said, "You don't want to know why it's black. Just enjoy a new experience."

I stopped chewing and swallowed quickly. "Why is it black?"

"Google it," she said, digging into her own breakfast.

The B&B's Wi-Fi was sketchy so I couldn't get a signal. Overall, my British SIM card offered good service, but out here in the sticks it was unreliable. Meanwhile, the sausage was delicious so I finished it off, trying not to think too much about it.

Maddie pulled her Day-Timer out of her purse and flipped to her itinerary. "We can take the motorway straight to Devon, or we can take the smaller A-roads and drive past Stonehenge … you can see it from the road. The Stonehenge route is a little longer, but more scenic. Which do you prefer?"

I thought for a moment. The motorway was quicker and we wouldn't have to deal with roundabouts. But it would be fun to see Stonehenge, even if it was just a drive-by.

"If we have the extra time, let's take the long way," I said.

"We have nothing but time. Today is a travel day," she said, tucking her planner back into her bag.

We finished our breakfast and signed the guest book on our way out, saying farewell to our genial hosts. With our bags loaded in the trunk (which they call the 'boot'), we headed off on our next adventure, waving goodbye to the Avebury stones on our way out of town.

"I've been thinking about that guy you called a 'wizard' … the one who let us into the field yesterday," I said, as we drove past the raised grouping of beech trees I'd been drawn to. "I don't think he was a phony. I suspect he really lives a magical life. He and his woman did stand out as rather …" I thought for a moment before saying, for lack of a better word, "… sparkly."

"I think so, too," said Maddie. "Did you notice that there weren't any of those poseur types here? I expected the place to be crawling with new-age pretenders, but that wasn't the case. Everyone was very genuine."

Maddie knew how much people like that bug me. Almost as much as her man Paul used to when he became the neighborhood Tennis Jerk at the court across the street from my house. I've complained to her about both often enough.

"I was surprised by that as well. No one was trying to be more enlightened than the rocks," I said, as we zipped through a roundabout with no effort. I was silent for a moment, tuning in to the Avebury vibe while we were still nearby, then said, "I think the stones would say, 'We've been here longer than you can imagine and we'll be here long after you're gone … it would take more than a few silly humans to overwhelm our presence.'"

Maddie guffawed. "That makes sense."

"What has me wondering," I said, "are the words I heard beneath those beech trees. 'The King awaits.' Twink and Pea mentioned a king of the Fae that lives in Glastonbury, but is that who the voice meant? Is King Charles going to be visiting anyplace on our path?"

She frowned with thought. "Not that I know of. I really doubt it. And even if he was, there is literally no chance that we would run into him."

"Not even if the faeries intervened?" I asked, one dubious eyebrow raised.

"Well," she chuckled, "now that you put it that way … who knows?"

Maddie drove on, both of us silent and lost in our own thoughts. We passed another one of those little churches with the square stone tower along the way and I made a mental note that I'd like to see the insides of one. Do they all look the same inside as they do from the outside?

I was Googling King Charles' public itinerary for the week to see whether our planned travels crossed paths when Maddie drove right past the official entrance to Stonehenge. She turned left instead of right at the next intersection onto the A303, causing the SatNav to say, "Recalculating …"

In just a couple miles, there it was … Stonehenge … right there in a field off the left side of the road, rather like the Avebury stones but further away, tiny in the distance but still easily visible from the car. It was so unlike the U.S., where landmarks are often hidden behind a paywall.

"Wow." I stared out the window. "That's it. That's the famous Stonehenge. Looks like we can't get there from here, though."

"No," Maddie said, "we passed the entrance a couple miles back, where you have to pay to get close. Since we're not stopping, this is a place where you can see it from the road."

She waited until there were no cars coming in either direction and pulled a U-turn on the two-lane highway. Heading back in the opposite direction, now going west toward Devon, she asked, "Are you picking up any vibes here, like you did in Avebury? I mean, I know we're not up close and personal, but …"

"I'm not," I admitted, "but, like you said, we're not up close and my feet aren't on the land. Besides," I said, "from what I've been reading online, Stonehenge isn't on the same ley line as Avebury … not sure what that might mean. Different vibe?"

"Oh! I forgot to show you …" she said, reaching for her purse in the back seat, swerving into the other lane.

"Jesus!" I shrieked. "Let me get it! You just concentrate on not killing us, okay?"

She laughed and said, "You're such a worry wart! There aren't any cars for miles. Go ahead and grab my purse. There's a book in there about ley lines that I bought in Avebury yesterday … I forgot to show you, being so busy with giant stones and faeries and wizards and whatnot."

"Well, that's very different," I said, mollified. I took off my seatbelt and turned around to dig through Maddie's gigantic designer purse. I finally found the paperback, so I sat back down and buckled up.

The book was called *Ley Lines and Fae Lines*, and its glossy cover included photos of sacred spaces like Stonehenge, Avebury and Glastonbury, along with several others that I didn't recognize. Superimposed over them was a map of the British Isles, crisscrossed with gridlines.

I was flipping through the pages when, out of the blue, a wave of terror took my breath away. Something horrible was going to happen, something unexpected and unknowable, so there was no way to brace or prepare.

My breath seized up and the only sound I could utter was, "Hnnnnnnnh…" as I grabbed at my chest and tried not to shit myself. The intensity faded over a minute or so, leaving me shaken, scared, and wondering what the hell that was.

Maddie couldn't help noticing. She asked, her voice filled with concern, "You okay, doll? Want me to pull over? I can put the top down to get you some fresh air … it's a gorgeous day for a ride in a convertible."

"No," I said, shaking my head to clear it, "I think I'm okay. Thanks. I don't know what that was, but we've been immersed in some intense energy shifts these past few days. I think I need to step back from the woo woo stuff."

"You sure? Want something to eat?" she asked. "Maybe it's your blood sugar. I have some protein bars in my purse."

I blew her an air kiss and replied, "No, I'll be fine. Thank you. Besides I'm still full from breakfast. Which reminds me, I wanted to look that up …"

I pulled out my phone and Googled *Black Pudding*.

Once I saw the list of ingredients, my jaw dropped. "Oh my God! I can't believe you let me eat blood sausage!"

Maddie whooped with laughter and finally said, still gasping and giggling, "It was delicious, though, wasn't it? Sometimes it's best not to know. Good thing we're not heading to Scotland. I'd have to make sure you tried some haggis."

"You don't suppose that caused whatever just happened to me, do you?" I doubted it as I was saying it, but stranger things have happened. "I mean, blood sausage? Isn't that a little macabre?"

"How is it any worse than eating meat?" she asked.

"I don't know." I didn't have a good answer, beyond the gross out factor.

I did have to wonder, though. My old panic attacks had a pattern: chest pains, hyperventilation, scary thoughts and gut cramps. This was exactly the same only completely different—sharper … scarier—and my hands were still shaking, my heart still pounding.

With no anxiety meds handy, I continued to ground myself and center in my heart with deep breathing exercises. I set the book down on my lap and reminded myself how to breathe … in … and out … in … and out …

After a few minutes, all was well again.

The book was still in my lap and, since I was feeling better, I went ahead and flipped through the pages. Almost immediately, it happened again, only harder this time.

"Oh my God!" I cried, flinging the book into the back seat. "Enough!"

"Enough?" Maddie asked, her brows furrowed.

"I give up," I said, hands raised in surrender. "No more!"

"Good idea," she said. "Let's crank up the tunes and just enjoy the ride. It's a sunny day, and we're surrounded by beautiful English countryside."

That's exactly what we did for the next couple hours until we came to a town in the county of Devon called Tavistock, where Maddie zipped into the parking lot of the first grocery store she spotted. "Let's stock up on snacks and stuff, maybe a frozen meal or two. We're staying in a place with a kitchen. I don't know if we'll even find any restaurants out there in the boondocks."

I picked up some cheese, crackers, and grapes, and a premade prawn sandwich as part of a meal deal, with a bag of cheddar and onion potato chips (they call them crisps … chips here are French fries) and a drink. From the freezer section, we both chose a couple nights worth of meals.

Back in the car on the way to our final destination along a narrow two-lane road, I spotted a directional sign for something called *Brent Tor* up ahead. I pointed it out, "Hey, there's a tor here, too. Is that like the one we'll see in Glastonbury?"

"I don't know," Maddie replied. "Look it up. That must be it, up ahead," she said, indicating further up the right side of the road.

I looked where she was pointing and there—clearly in view just off the side of the road like Avebury and Stonehenge—was another one of those churches with the square tower, but this one was atop a very large hill.

Once again, I was instantly overcome by intense, helpless dread … the kind where there's a monster under the bed and you're so frozen with terror that you can't even move to pull your feet back under the covers. I choked on my breath, unable to speak.

With both hands clasped to my chest, I forced myself back to calm with more heart-centered deep breaths as Maddie cried, in a near panic herself, "Lola! Are you okay? Should I pull over?"

I waved for her to keep driving and did some more deep breathing. After a couple minutes, I found my voice again and sobbed, "This isn't normal."

"Oh, honey," Maddie said, her tone motherly, "let's turn around and head back into town. I'm sure they have an emergency room."

"No, it's passed," I panted. "We're almost there. It'll do me good to get out of the car and put my feet in the grass."

Soon we came upon the remote pair of darling stone cottages where we were staying for the next two nights. By then I was feeling less wobbly, but not entirely well, so I took off my shoes and socks before getting out of the car and stepped into the grassy yard in front of one of the cottages.

Meanwhile, Maddie popped open the trunk so we could retrieve our luggage and grocery bags. She then consulted her phone and said, "I have the door codes here. You choose which cottage you prefer. They're essentially the same, just decorated differently."

"I'll take this one." I pointed at the cottage in whose yard I was standing.

"Perfect," she said. She punched the code into the lock pad, opened the door and entered. She called out to me from inside, "There's a gas fireplace! Would you like me to start it for you?"

I grabbed my grocery bags from the trunk, enjoying the cold grass on my bare feet on the way, and joined her inside the little stone cottage. It was decorated with a mixture of old beams and modern country charm.

"Oh, how pretty!" I gushed. "You sure know how to pick 'em!"

She grinned and said, "I do, don't I? So? Fire? Yes or no."

"Yes, please," I said. She got busy lighting the gas fire while I explored the tiny kitchen, unpacking my groceries into the mini-fridge.

There, on the counter, were individual packages of shortbread cookies and an assortment of teas, coffee and instant hot cocoa, along with sugar and creamer packets. "It's a good thing we bought food," I commented, "because I didn't see anywhere to eat between here and town. We wouldn't survive long on hospitality snacks."

"As I suspected," Maddie replied, finishing her fire-lighting task. "Alright, doll, if you're okay, I'm going to get settled in my own cottage. I wouldn't mind a little nap. Want to meet up again in few hours?"

"That sounds perfect," I said. "I need some time to gather my thoughts."

"Okay, honey. You let me know if you need me." She blew me a kiss and said, as she closed the door behind her, "Your key code and all the information you need about the cottage, including the Wi-Fi password, is there on the kitchen table. See you in a bit."

After she left, I checked out the rest of the dwelling … the quaint little bedroom with its girly décor and double bed, and the tiny bathroom with its claw-foot tub and pedestal sink. I used the toilet and finally plopped myself down on the bed, lying back into the fluffy pillows.

"Twink? Pea?" I asked, hoping they were present.

Twink popped in, miniature-sized as she usually appeared, floating above me on the bed. "Aye?" she asked.

"Oh, thank goodness you're here," I sighed. "What was that all about, that horrendous fear? It happened both times I picked up the book about ley lines and then when I saw the Tor down the road. Is there a connection?"

"How would I know that?" she replied, as if that was the end of the discussion.

"Well, I need help figuring this out," I huffed, "especially if I'm going to be climbing the Glastonbury Tor. I won't be able to function, much less climb a hill, if I can't even catch my breath."

"Maybe it *is* the ley lines," she said. "Yeh're more sensitive than most. This place is … strong. P'rhaps yeh're feeling more of it than yeh're used to, being so close and all. Don't forget to eat something and drink plenty of water. That'll help ground yeh."

"Good idea," I said.

With that, she popped out of sight in a puff of glittering dust, leaving me alone with my thoughts—thoughts which soon faded as I drifted off to sleep, joining Maddie in a much-needed nap.

FIVE

I was sound asleep until I heard a voice just as I had in Avebury. This time it said: "We are one."

The words startled me awake and I bolted upright in bed to dart my eyes around the room, only to see no one there. I can't say whether it was the same voice that said, "The King awaits." I was sleeping and don't recall the tone or timbre … only that it was real, not a whisper of intuition.

Waiting for my heart to stop pounding, I gazed out the bedroom window where I saw the twilight sky. That explained why my stomach was rumbling. The Full English Breakfast had lasted most of the day, but now it was time for a meal … one without creepy ingredients.

I messaged Maddie before heading to the kitchen: *You up? If so, bring your dinner. We'll cook here.*

She messaged back almost immediately: *Be there in a few.*

I turned on the oven to preheat and puttered around the kitchen, familiarizing myself with its layout. The owners had decked it out with everything a guest could possibly need. I'd have to leave a good review.

Just as the oven dinged to tell me it was hot, Maddie opened the front door and stepped inside, shivering and carrying a grocery bag, with her purse slung over her shoulder.

"Brrr," she shuddered. "It's cold out there. A perfect night to sit in front of a fire." She hung her purse on the wingback chair and unloaded her groceries on the kitchen table … a ready-made salad, a frozen slice of lasagna, a bottle of red wine and a corkscrew. "Grab some glasses, doll, and I'll crack open the vino."

"Perfect." I retrieved two wine glasses from the cupboard.

She poured while I read the instructions on the frozen meals. Fortunately, both her lasagna and my spaghetti and meatballs required a similar temperature and a surprisingly fast cooking time. I popped them in and set the timer. Finally, I put together a plate of cheese and crackers and placed it on the coffee table.

Maddie handed me a glass of wine and we settled into the cushy furniture in front of the fireplace, she in the leather wingback chair and I curled up on the upholstered sofa. We sat in silence for a long while—relaxing, eating cheese, and sipping the excellent wine—before she reached into her purse and retrieved the paperback about ley lines.

"Look," she said, leaning forward, "I know the book gave you the willies earlier and I'm not trying to make it happen again by bringing it with me, but it seemed important. I've never seen you react like that, especially to something so … well … not scary."

I grimaced a bit and she continued, "Anyway, I've been reading it, since you don't seem to be able, and it's pretty interesting."

"Oh yeah?" I asked. "Give me the highlights and we'll see if I need to drown my fears in wine." I took a clownishly large gulp and set my glass down on the table.

She offered a pity laugh and then began. "Well, first, the concept of ley lines is fairly new. The man who coined the phrase wrote his book only about a hundred years ago and he didn't think they were mystical at all."

"No kidding?"

"Yeah. I was surprised, too. I could have sworn this was one of those … things," she said, waving her hands, failing to find the word. She gave up and went on. "He just found it interesting that ancient Britain was crisscrossed with straight travel routes, dotted with landmarks like standing stones, hilltops, churches and the like, in deliberate alignment."

"Huh," I said, nodding. "So not woo woo after all."

"Well, not back then," she said, "not until the Sixties when people started singing about the moon in the seventh house … you know, the Age of Aquarius and all that."

"Oh, that sort of changes things," I frowned. "Is this modern-day mumbo jumbo?"

She started to reply but I cut her off.

"I hope that doesn't sound judgmental, especially from someone who makes their living as a psychic. But you know that I'm careful to keep a foot in both worlds. It's too easy to go down rabbit holes when a theory sounds interesting and mysterious."

"I understand," she said, raising her hand to interrupt. "I don't get the sense that it's mumbo jumbo. Some may be, but that's part of the game, isn't it? Discernment."

"Sure. Go on."

"Thank you," Maddie replied and paused for a sip of wine. "Anyway, the first guy—Alfred Watkins—came up with the idea and named them 'ley' lines after an Old English phrase meaning 'open land.' It had nothing to do with energy or magic."

She kicked off her shoes and curled up her legs beneath her, getting comfy. "He never said anything about a St. Michael line … which we're still on, by the way. Avebury, Glastonbury and Brent Tor—the one we saw on the way here—are all on that line … but we'll get to that. In Watkins' view, sacred sites on ley lines were just built on high ground with long sightlines, or near unusual landscape features. Nothing supernatural about it."

"Interesting," I nodded, hoping Maddie couldn't hear my stomach growling. The cottage was filling with the aromatic scent of baked pasta and I was sincerely hungry.

Maddie continued, "One day he had an 'Aha!' moment, which he called a 'flood of ancient sight.' Suddenly, the straight sightlines just … made sense. He eventually titled his book *The Old Straight Track*. But, again, he wasn't seeing this as mystical, just interesting."

"What changed over time?" I asked. "Who decided on their current meaning?"

"Not sure, exactly," she shrugged. "The mysticism started in the Sixties, when modern writers began connecting ley lines with sacred geometry and Atlantis."

That piqued my interest, so I tuned in. Yes, I could see it, the grid upon which our reality is hung. And, yes, the ley lines were lit up with meaning.

To know more I'd have to focus, but I was in the middle of a conversation and didn't want to be rude. It was enough to see this was more than conspiracy—that ley lines may indeed be linked with lost, advanced wisdom from ages past.

Good thing I didn't let myself drift too far, because Maddie was in mid-sentence and I'd missed the first part. "… in the Eighties, ley lines were linked with Archangels and Saints. They represent masculine and feminine currents, and some locations along the lines are considered Earth's chakras. In fact, Glastonbury is often named as the heart chakra."

She paused, letting it all sink in. By now, the room had grown warm from both the fire and the oven's heat, and the wine bottle was noticeably lighter.

I nodded, then asked, "Did you see anything in the book that might explain what happened to me? I've never felt such instant and unexplained terror like I did just holding that book or seeing Brent Tor."

"No," she said. "That's why I skimmed it, to see if there's something you needed to know. But there's nothing scary at all. No warnings or cautions … nothing. Are you okay now?"

"Weirdly, yes," I said. "Except I heard another voice, like I did in Avebury. I was conked out when a voice woke me up, saying, '*We are one.*'"

Maddie furrowed her brow. "What do you think it means?"

I said with a shrug, "It's a phrase I hear a lot in metaphysical circles. You've heard it, I'm sure."

She nodded.

"You know," I continued, "they say all of humanity is like facets of one big diamond or single drops making up the entire ocean. We're all mini holograms of the greater Is … microcosmic expressions of something larger. I'm running out of metaphors."

"Yes," she said, nodding more vehemently, "I get it. I wasn't asking what 'We are one' means. I meant, what does it mean for you? Here and now."

"I don't know, but in any case," I said, "I don't think the standard definition is what this voice meant."

"Have you asked your faeries?"

"No, I haven't had a chance." I finished my wine and got up for a refill. "I messaged you as soon as I woke up." I gave Maddie's glass a top up and opened the oven door for a peek. The food was progressing nicely. "Give me a sec to tune in …" I said, still in the kitchen. "Twink? Are you there?"

This time Precious Pea popped in, instead. "What a charming abode!" she said, fluttering about the kitchen and then zooming over Maddie's head. Maddie didn't react.

"Pea is here," I told her. "Can you hear her?"

"No, doggone it," Maddie sighed. "Why can't I see them now, when I was once able?"

"It's all about wavelengths and whatnot," Pea explained. "It's not that she *can't* see and hear me, it's that I'm off-resonance. There are a lot of folk, living and dead, here with us now, but the human wavelength is different. They may not see us either. All of time and space is one giant … thing … and everything is happening here and now. We travel through the layers by changing the tune we hum."

I repeated an abbreviated version of Pea's lesson in metaphysics to Maddie, saying, "She says you *can* see and hear her, you just need to be tuned to the same station."

"Oh, whatever," Maddie scoffed. "I hear that same hoohah in every class I take in psychic development. Tell me how, not why!"

"Right?" I laughed. "Meantime, Pea said something else that caught my attention." I turned toward Pea, fluttering over the fireplace mantel, and asked, "You said that all of time and space is one big thing. Is that what the voice meant by 'We are one?'"

"Yes and no," Pea said. "'Yes' because of course that's true, but 'no' because we're looking at a microcosm here."

I repeated her words to Maddie, then said, "Pea sounds like she's gone to college since our last adventure. Have you been studying Einstein or something?"

The wee faery laughed and said, "Yeh may also have noticed that I'm no longer blinking as I used to. I've leveled up, so to speak."

My jaw dropped and I said, "No, I had not noticed! Are congratulations in order? I don't even know what that means."

She grinned—hard to see from several feet away—but the glow of faery dust around her sparkled with smiley vibes. "I don't know if congratulations are suitable, but I'm no longer considered a child, so … no more embarrassing adolescent displays."

My mind reeled with questions, but I didn't want to get dragged off topic by the mysteries of faery puberty and rapid maturation … especially now that she was responding like a learned adult instead of a teenager.

Instead, I said, "Tell me more about the microcosm you mentioned."

"I can't tell yeh much more than yeh already know," she said. "Just that you and yehr friend are on a path toward some big experiences. There are no coincidences surrounding the places yeh're visiting. They're all connected."

As she spoke, it all snapped into place like Watkins' "flood of ancient sight." *We are one* brought Avebury, Brent Tor, Glastonbury and the St. Michael line into alignment,

Then my own flood of sight rose—a mind-expanding vision from far above this island nation: a straight line cutting across England from the far southwestern tip, as if drawn with a ruler. The line was dotted with an unusual number of sacred places dedicated to Archangel Michael, the slayer of dragons, guardian of thresholds on high places between this world and the next, a gatekeeper of the veil.

"Oh, that makes so much sense!" I cried, then asked Pea, "But what about the other thing I heard, back in Avebury, '*The King awaits.*'"

"I think yeh can figure that one out, if yeh try." She vanished in a flash of glittering pink dust.

"Damn it." I returned to the couch. "I hate when they just disappear like that in the middle of a conversation. It's like they get a kick out of messing with my head."

"Join the club." Maddie raised an eyebrow. "How do you think it feels to be a third wheel and watch you talking to thin air?"

"Good point," I said. "You asked earlier for the how, not the why … let me show you how I did it when Twink first started showing up."

"Oh, goodie!" Maddie sat up straight, her warmed feet now on the floor, and clapped her hands.

"Do you happen to have a crystal in your bag?" I asked. "Otherwise, go outside and grab a small stone or piece of gravel from the garden. Doesn't matter, it just needs to be an anchor object."

"I do have a crystal. I bought it in Avebury," she said, rummaging through her purse until she found a small paper bag, from which she retrieved a heart-shaped stone carved from rose quartz.

"That's perfect!" I cried. "It's even pink, like Precious Pea always wears."

Maddie winked. "I'd be lying if I said I didn't think about that at the time."

"Okay," I said, grinning, "hold it in whichever hand feels most comfortable, then bring it over your heart." I watched as Maddie followed my instructions, then said, "Now close your eyes and lightly feel into the room. See if you can sense a difference between now and when she was just here."

I didn't say it aloud—I didn't want to lead Maddie's thoughts—but when Pea was present I felt the light-hearted sauciness of a sparkly young woman and a hint of floral tones … not quite lilac, but close. Now that she was gone, it was just a cozy and rustic room—warm and homey, but lacking Pea's twinkle.

"Are you noticing anything?" I asked.

"Not really," Maddie frowned, her eyes still closed.

"Can you smell anything?"

"Smells like blue lotus, but that could be lilacs from the garden. They smell similar," she said, opening her eyes and sighing.

"Maddie," I said, getting up and opening the front door, "look outside. There are no lilacs. Besides, they don't bloom in the fall."

"Well," she said, looking out the door with me, "some do, under unusual conditions, but I take your point. I don't even smell them anymore."

"That was Pea," I said, just as the oven timer buzzed. I hurried into the kitchen to turn it off and remove our meals. "Besides, you wouldn't smell outdoor lilacs in here with the door shut, especially with the aroma of yummy frozen dinners filling the air."

"By the way," I said, busying myself with meal prep, "Thank you for helping me work through this. I feel much better."

Instead of responding, Maddie gasped. I spun around to see why.

"I saw her!" Maddie cried, pointing upward. "At least I think that's what it was. It was just the briefest flash, like an orb you might see in a photo. A sparkling little pink bubble."

I remembered, grinning, "She told me when we first met, 'You can call me Blink, you can call me Pink, you can call me Precious Bubble Pea.' You must have seen her, even if it was just for a split second. Keep working on it. Just remember that scent."

"Oh darn," Maddie said, joining me in the kitchen to set the table. "I have blue lotus essential oil at home. I wish I had brought it with me. It'd be useful right now."

"I bet you can pick up a bottle in Glastonbury," I said, placing our dinner trays and ready-made salads on the kitchen table. Maddie refilled our wine glasses with the last of the bottle. We sat down and dug in, and I continued, "You don't really need the oil. It might make it easier, but I'm sure you can conjure up the scent in your memory."

"You're right," she said. "I'll give that a try. In the meantime, I'm going to appreciate the delicious scent of this lasagna."

She blew on a hot forkful of noodles and cheese, then said, "British food gets a bad rap. The stereotype is that it's bland and flavorless, but that is so wrong."

Maddie took a bite and rolled her eyes back, moaning dramatically. "So. Effing. Good."

I blew on a forkful of pasta, took a tentative bite, and immediately agreed. So. Effing. Good.

SIX

The next morning, I was on my first cup of tea at the kitchen table—still dressed in a rumpled T-shirt and pajama pants—when Maddie rapped on the door. I hollered, "Come on in," then heard her beeping the code into the lock.

She entered, dressed for a day of antique treasure hunting in a slimming pencil skirt and matching jacket, a flowered silk blouse and stylish yet reasonably heeled shoes. Her makeup was impeccable. Her lipstick even matched her blouse.

"Gurrrl, you look gorgeous," I laughed, running my hands through my wild, unbrushed bed-head hair. "Good thing I'm staying here today. I'm still in my jimjams."

"Thanks, doll," she said, pursing her lips and voguing, hamming it up. "If you've got it, flaunt it."

"What time do you figure you'll be back?" I asked, sipping my hot brew.

"Not sure," she said. "That's why I wanted to double check. Are you sure you don't want to drop me off and keep the car for the day? You're insured on the rental policy as a driver, so we're covered."

"Nah," I replied. "I'm not comfortable with that whole wrong-side-of-the-road thing. I have plenty of food, so I think I'll just hang out here for the day, maybe take a stroll. We're not far from Brent Tor. I may take a chance and walk over to see if I can suss out the weird panic."

She parted the curtains to peer out the front window. "It's a bit of a hike. Can't see it from here, with those trees blocking the view. Are you really going to walk all the way there?"

"We'll see. Not if it's too far, but I'll decide later," I said. "Worry not, I'll be able to fill the day one way or another. Might as well go ahead and open the drapes, since you're standing there."

Maddie pulled open the curtains and let the daylight in. "Looks like it's going to be a beautiful day, a bit warm for this late in the season," she said. "Lucky us! Alright, sweetie, message me if you need anything. I'll be about fifteen minutes away."

She turned to leave but then stopped. "Oh! I almost forgot! We talked so much about ley lines last night that we didn't even get to the other topic in the book." She reached into her bag to retrieve the paperback and placed it on the coffee table, face down. "No pressure, I'm even hiding the front cover, so you don't get creeped out by the photos of the tors. Just leaving it here in case you get curious. Don't forget, though, the title is *Ley Lines and Fae Lines*." She said this with emphasis on the last two words. "There's a bunch more in that book that needs to be examined."

She blew a kiss and left, closing the door behind her.

That topic did indeed need examining. I had forgotten that Maddie's book was about more than the not-so-mystical "old straight tracks" crisscrossing England, and the possible links between St. Michael and the line we were on. I was so focused on figuring out why the sight of ancient holy places could send me spiraling into a gibbering mess.

I fought the urge to tune into what was going on with the sudden attacks—that would take me down a rabbit hole—an interesting one, but not necessarily a safe one. That route felt like I'd be inviting a vampire into my chamber.

Before picking up the book I closed my eyes, laid my hand atop my heart and focused my attention there, visualizing my body surrounded by a shimmering bubble of Divine Love. "I am protected," I chanted, "I am protected, I am protected."

Once I felt my body begin to tingle and my heart lighten, I took a few more deep breaths and smiled. All was well. I opened my eyes and took a sip of tea. I didn't bother with the book yet. I now felt an intuitive nudge to take a shower instead.

The bathroom, while small, included a full-sized clawfoot tub with a large, modern, shiny shower head—sure to deliver a luxurious experience. The window above the far side of the tub offered a private view of a field of blooming heather. If only the morning temperature was a bit warmer, I could have opened that window to bring in some fresh air, completing the nature vibe.

I turned on the water and pulled up on the shower toggle. The ray of sunshine streaming through the glass turned each drop of falling water into a glittering prism of light. *This* was why I felt the nudge to shower now, while the sun was at this angle. It wasn't about bathing as much as using perfectly timed laws of nature to create a cascade of mini-rainbows, expanding the radiant vibe I was building.

I quickly undressed and stepped into the tub, closing the white shower curtain, allowing the lightshow to wash over me. I stood there inhaling the steam and absorbing the light-bath until the sun's angle finally shifted enough for the refractions to end. Just in time, too, as I was beginning to run out of hot water.

With no need to wash my hair, having done that yesterday, I unwrapped the bar of scented guest soap and washed quickly, catching a familiar whiff. What was it? I wracked my memory. I recognized it … flowery, but with a bite to it. Was that bite citrus or pine? I had smelled it before but couldn't name it.

I turned off the water just as it turned cold and enveloped myself in one of the fluffy, oversized towels supplied by the generous host. The soap wrapper was on the floor, so I picked it up to throw it away but noticed first the label: *Blissful Soaps – Clary Sage*.

That was the scent I recognized! I had just purchased a bottle of clary sage oil in Avebury.

I hurried to get dressed—jeans and my favorite sweatshirt with the logo of the band Queen—and sat down with my phone to Google the oil's properties. My jaw dropped when I read: eases anxiety and overwhelm, encourages intuition and clarity, useful when logic gets in the way.

This was exactly what I needed.

Initially I had planned to loll about all morning, maybe do some meditating and journaling, perhaps watch some TV to see what British shows were like, and then go for a casual stroll after a bite of lunch, but that all changed. I was raring to go.

I looked through the kitchen drawers to see if the hosts had supplied any kitchen bags and, sure enough, there was a box of zipper sandwich bags. I took a sheet of paper towel and deposited several drops of my oil onto it, then popped it into the bag before zipping it shut.

Then, I dumped my backpack out onto the bed and refilled it with my "meal deal" prawn sandwich and crisps, a bottle of water, my journal and pen, my phone, the sandwich bag with the oiled paper towel and, finally, Maddie's book.

Just as I was walking out the door, I heard one of the faeries … not sure which one, as the voice was distant … saying, "Don't forget your new crystal."

Right. Of course. I went back to the bedroom to find both stones I bought in Avebury among the pile of stuff I'd just poured out onto the bed. Unsure of which crystal I was supposed to bring, I grabbed both and headed out the door.

It was just a short stroll down the tree-lined drive to the road, about a quarter of a mile. And there it was, Brent Tor, just across the road beyond a hedge and a small field. I thought, '*Maddie was wrong. It's not far away. It's right there.*'

My heart leapt in my chest, but the discomfort passed quickly so I knew this was not a reaction to just seeing the church atop the Tor. It felt more like something didn't want me to get any closer.

I stood for several minutes—feet planted firmly, hip distance apart—taking deep breaths and retrieving the clary sage zip-bag for a few inhalations.

Unsure how to get to the entrance to the property, I took an intuitive guess and turned right out of the cottage driveway. Cars were few and far between, so I didn't have to worry much about remembering which was the 'wrong' side of the road to safely walk on.

It was about another half a mile to what appeared to be the entrance, where I found a sign that said, "*13th Century Church of St. Michael de Rupe.*" The sign also said, "*Visitors Welcome*" but a heavy wooden gate blocked the road uphill. It further said, "*Sunday Service 6PM Easter to September*." Here it was, almost the fall Equinox, late September, so the sign must have meant up until September.

I didn't mind not being able to get closer. Just standing there, I was inundated with visions of me climbing that hill alone and tumbling down the steep side, breaking a leg and lying there, birds pecking at my eyes, hoping someone would find me before next Easter.

My logical mind told me, "Silly Lola, you have your phone to call for help," but a scared little voice then lit up my threat-detection system with the doubt, "You probably won't get a signal out here!"

Just to be sure, I pulled out my phone to check. It wasn't a strong signal, but I had a couple bars. I took a few photos of the church up on the hilltop which included, go figure, one of those square towers. The scene was exceptionally photogenic and I briefly regretted that I couldn't get closer to see it better, but I was more relieved than regretful.

Not ready yet to go back to the cottage—after all, I had the whole day ahead of me—I wandered down the road a bit until I found a pretty little grassy spot off to the side with a sturdy wooden bench, facing the Tor. That was one of the things I had noticed about England … plenty of little benches in off-beat places.

Plopping myself down, I gazed up the hill at the stone church and let my mind wander. I was safe here, across the road … or … was I? Another wave of fear washed over me as it occurred to me that I didn't know where I was or who lived around there. Hadn't I just passed a grouping of trees? What if a man was hiding in there, lying in wait to rape and murder me?

'*Whoa*,' I thought. '*That came out of nowhere. What's that all about?*'

I jumped up from my seat and crossed the road to put some distance between me and the trees, praying for a car to come along so I would no longer be alone. I could flag them down if I had to. I hurried up the road to the driveway of my temporary home just as the telltale signs of an oncoming panic attack—shortness of breath, urgent and painful stomach cramps— began to kick in. Again. Just as I was feeling safe.

Finally in the yard, I breathed a huge sigh of relief. Even so, I hurriedly unlocked the door and went inside to get my bearings and use the toilet, which had become a pressing issue.

As I sat in the bathroom, waiting for the pain in my gut to fade, I checked my phone for messages and found one from Chuck. It was a selfie of him at our kitchen table in front of an uncooked TV dinner tray. He was holding the frozen slab of gravy and meatloaf up to his mouth as if to take a bite, with text superimposed on the image saying, *Miss you!* <3

I laughed out loud and even typed *LOL* in response.

Touching base with home helped fade the stomach cramps and I was soon able to head back to the kitchen to reply with my own photo. I fetched the sandwich from my backpack, knowing he'd be amused by the Brits' use of prawn instead of tuna. I took a selfie with it held up to my grinning face, adding text that said, *Mmm mmm ... prawn ... them's good eatin'* :-*

Smiling and calm again, I opened the sandwich package even though it was a little early for lunch. Wandering over to the kitchen window, I took a bite and gazed outside, enjoying the surprising goodness of new and different food.

I hadn't paid attention yesterday to the view of the back yard, so I only now saw that there was a well-tended garden out there with a manmade pond and waterfall, a hammock and, of course, a little bench.

Grabbing my backpack, I took it—along with my yummy sandwich—outside through the back door. Stepping into the garden was like entering a little slice of heaven. Just over to one side was the field of heather that I saw out of the bathroom window, and around the other side of the house was an apple tree filled with chirping birds. I eased into the hammock and finished half of the sandwich, watching the waterfall trickling into the pond.

I felt a nudge then to retrieve the quartz sphere from my bag, so I dug it out and held it up toward the sun to watch its rays filter through the stone's inclusions, flashing with rainbows when it was held at just the right angle. It reminded me of the shower of sparkling diamond water drops that morning—the scent of clary sage soap lingering in my memory—and immediately brought me back to that exquisite state of mind.

Inhaling deeply, I made a conscious effort to anchor into that bliss with the crystal in my hand. I closed my fist around it and shut my eyes, holding it to my heart. A few more deep breaths and I sensed an energetic 'click.' The stone was now programmed. Whenever I needed to pull myself quickly out of a spiraling panic, I could hold it like this … or even just hold my closed fist to my heart as if the crystal were there, if it wasn't handy.

My heart welled with joy. Such a wonderful tool and I was so grateful to have learned to do this! What a life-changer.

I set the small crystal ball next to me on the hammock and picked up the UFO-shaped labradorite, the one with the breathtaking sky-blue flash. I couldn't wait to see how it would glitter in the sun.

Similar to the quartz sphere, the flash was almost blindingly beautiful, but there was that stab of fear again, right on cue. This time, though, it came with a chorus of voices—definitely not in my head—words streaming so fast and full blast that I couldn't understand them.

I caught my breath and flung the stone down. It bounced on the grass as my mind was flooded with a torrent of phrases which finally slowed enough that I could partially understand some of it … *masculine/feminine, as above/so below, we are one/the king awaits, the ties that bind …*

The words themselves weren't threatening, but it was too much, too fast. I jumped out of the hammock and planted my feet firmly on the ground, forcing it to stop.

"Oh, come on! What is that?" I cried. "What's wrong with me? Twink? Are you there? Pea? Anyone?"

'Wait,' I thought, *'not just anyone.'*

I had learned that one the hard way. Don't invite just "anyone" in, because plenty of trickster spirits and impish jerks were just waiting for an opening like that.

I took it back.

"Twink? Precious Pea?" I asked, "Are either of you there? No one else is welcome."

Both faeries appeared in poofs of sparkly dust, floating above me, Twink shaking with mirth and Pea with her arms folded sternly across her chest, tapping her foot on the air beneath her.

"Aye, we're here," giggled Twink.

"We almost have to be, don't we?" Pea scolded. "When yeh play with fire, yeh're bound to get burned, yeah? Someone's got to watch over yeh."

"Wait," I plopped back into the hammock and stammered. "What do you mean?"

"Yeh're jumpin' in the deep end, without first learnin' to swim!" Pea cried.

"We call her the Sovereign of Similes, we do!" Twink cackled. "The Monarch of Metaphors! Come on, Sissy, give us another!"

Pea turned to her older sister and said, stomping her foot in frustration the way I've seen Twink do so many times, "She's supposed to be preparing for the King, not mucking about like this!"

"Dearie," Twink said in a tone more patronizing than soothing, "I've known this human far longer than you. I promise yeh, that's the only way she'll learn, by bashing her head against a brick wall." She grinned and said, "Ey up, there's a metaphor for yeh!"

"Would you both knock it off," I interrupted, "and kindly educate this stupid human?"

"Look," said Precious Pea, fluttering downward and landing on my knee amid my crystals, half sandwich, and backpack contents strewn across the hammock. "Yeh're obviously trying to put two and two together, and yeh're making a valiant effort at that. There's only so much we can tell yeh … some of it yeh have to work out yehrself."

"D'yeh remember the rules?" Twink asked. "We can't always come right out and tell yeh, but if yeh ask the right questions …"

Yes, it came rushing back to me now, the frustrating first time Twink showed up in my life, smugly laughing at my frantic efforts to take control of the wild and untamed psychic abilities that had hit me like a sandbag in a hurricane … okay, maybe I'm not so good with the metaphors, but the point remains. Twink was a real jerk and would only help me if I asked questions specifically pertaining to what I was so clownishly missing.

I stopped and thought for a moment about what had been happening the past couple of days, to come up with a question that she'd answer. For seemingly no reason, I would be jolted with unexplained dread, a terror that told me to hide under the bed and pray for help—except there may be monsters under that bed.

I thought at first the fear might be connected to tors or ley lines … or even Maddie's book … but, no, that couldn't be right. I was able to be around them and the book sometimes without that pattern showing itself.

Despite my efforts to stay both grounded and uplifted, I was continually hit with these out-of-the-blue jolts of fright that were so powerful I forgot—literally seconds after the discovery—that I could use the quartz sphere to stop them!

During the most recent attack, for lack of a better word, unbidden words spilled through my mind, a torrent of jumbled phrases that overwhelmed me as I gazed into the blue flash of the labradorite.

Yes, that felt on target. There was something there that caught my attention.

"Okay," I said, "a few minutes ago … in fact, the reason I called for you two in the first place … I had this disturbing rush of words running through my head and I was terrified, for no reason I could name."

"What were the words?" Pea asked, sitting cross-legged on my knee with her chin in her hands.

"It was something about masculine and feminine, opposites like that … as above so below …" I said, struggling a bit to recall exactly what I heard. "There was more, but that's all I remember … oh yeah, the two clairaudient messages I heard out loud … 'we are one, and the king awaits.' One more … 'the ties that bind.' I didn't catch the second half of that one."

Twink said, from on high, "None of that were questions, yeah?"

"Hush, Thel," Pea scolded, using Twink's much preferred nickname … a reminder that I was supposed to call her Thel as well, but I kept forgetting due to long habit and finally gave up. She seemed to have made peace with it.

Or had she? Was she toying with me now? She was known to occasionally demonstrate a petty, vengeful streak, so …

"I know you think you're being funny," I said to her, "but you're actually being helpful. If I was in serious danger, you wouldn't be acting like such a butthead, just for your own amusement."

Pea burst out in giggles and said, "Ha! She's got yeh there!" She laughed so hard that she levitated, floating above my knee.

Twink scowled. "Yeh still haven't asked a question."

"I'm going to have to think about this for a while," I replied. "I don't even know where to begin, so I should probably jot down some notes in my journal. I may even figure it out myself."

I resisted the temptation to stick my tongue out at the elder faery, not wanting to push my luck, but she simply said, "Suit yehrself," and flashed out of sight.

Pea stayed around for a minute and said before she, too, popped away, "Yeh'll be okay. Figuring it out is half the fun, yeah?"

I laughed and said, "No!"

"Aye, it is," she said. "And even if not, what choice have yeh got?"

With that, Precious Pea followed her sister and disappeared, leaving me with my thoughts, my journal and my half-eaten prawn sandwich in a gorgeous English garden, complete with a man-made pond and waterfall, in the late morning sun.

I opened my journal and jotted some notes to keep track of the events of this morning … and since we arrived in England, actually. Even Avebury held a few unsolved hints. Yep, it was a good thing I was writing it all down, because it was easy to forget all that had already happened with so much going on.

My final notations were about how powerful the quartz ball could be as a calming tool, but how quickly I forgot what I had *literally just learned* the moment I picked up the labradorite, the darker and denser stone.

Not just forgot but lost it completely.

If I had held onto the quartz, instead of putting it down, would I have still been flooded with fear, or would it have been blocked?

I put my journal down and tried an experiment. Laying down in the hammock, I held one stone in each hand, closed my eyes and tuned into the quartz sphere. Recalling the euphoria I felt earlier when holding it, I was able to easily bring myself back into that state.

Soaking in it, basking in the bliss, I stayed for several minutes, not in any hurry to let it go. The longer I lingered, the brighter I felt. I 'saw' myself floating upward inside an iridescent bubble and heard a faint tinkling of distant bells and chimes, and the sounds of giggling children. I couldn't help grinning. Holy cow, it felt so good.

Upward I drifted—up up up, brighter and brighter, lighter and lighter, tingly and sparkly—breathing easy. Although my physical eyes were closed, I saw coming toward me a similarly bright and sparkly bubble of light and heard a voice so mellifluous that it almost couldn't be perceived, "I'm waiting … I'll be here when you arrive."

Curiosity overwhelmed me so I risked disrupting the moment and asked aloud, "Who are you? Are you the king who awaits?"

The bubble before me popped in a splash of light and I saw, instead of a king, a queenly faery. She was the absolute image of Twink and Pea's Aunt Jennett, Queen of the Night, except where Jennett had black hair and gown, this faery with a similar face had hair and a gown of snowy white. While Jennett shimmered around the edges as if cast in the light of the full moon, this faery radiated pure white light, her edges refracting tiny prisms.

She laughed, her voice like velvet, "Do I look like a king?"

"No, you do not," I replied, careful to not jolt myself out of this exquisite state by exerting too much physical effort.

"You don't have to speak aloud," she said, "I can hear your thoughts."

I sighed with relief and felt myself buoying upward, and thought to her, *'May I ask you a question?'*

"Of course."

"What's happening to me?" I sobbed aloud, overwhelmed, immediately bringing myself back to earth, back to the hammock.

"Damn it!" I cried out.

I closed my eyes again, one crystal in each hand, and focused on getting back to that ecstatic state, to no avail. I was psychically flailing about and, finally losing patience, gave up trying.

Taking another deep breath, I started from scratch using a different tack. This time, making sure I had the quartz in hand, I tuned in to the labradorite … cautiously and slowly. It was such a beautiful stone that I didn't want to believe it was malevolent, but I couldn't help feeling some dread. As a tinge of fear made itself known, I squeezed the quartz and felt it retreat.

I was on to something … like Alice, in Wonderland, taking small bites from either side of the mushroom to balance the effects of the 'eat me' cake and the 'drink me' bottle. As long as I held on to both stones, I might be able to safely explore.

With this in mind, I let myself feel into the darker stone and—just as I had risen higher and lighter with the quartz—I sank downward into pitch blackness. After a moment of terror, *'Am I descending into Hell?'* I squeezed the quartz again. Then I remembered that I don't even believe in Hell … well, not anymore.

This cognitive correction didn't stop my descent, but it did alleviate the fear. I wasn't falling into Hell as I had been raised to believe in—a place where the Devil pokes you with a pitchfork for his own amusement.

Instead, this could be the "lower world" I had learned about in classes on shamanic journeying. That faery of light I just encountered would be in the "upper world."

Exhaling a sigh of relief, I allowed myself to relax and sink further. The velvety blackness was comforting, as if being enveloped in the womb, pure darkness. I felt, more than heard, a throbbing hum and wondered if it was the heartbeat of the Earth.

Then I heard … loud and clear … "Fear not, 'tis but inching lower."

'Inching lower … what a strange turn of phrase,' I thought. *'Is this an olde-world way of saying my vibe wasn't as high as it could be?'*

Feeling so tranquil that I began to drift, I relaxed the hand holding the quartz and it rolled out onto the hammock.

Almost immediately I was pitched into a nightmare scenario: an ancient battlefield—axes and swords, shrieks of terror and bloodlust. I was in the middle of it, hacking and slashing, teeth clenched, a guttural growl emanating from the depths of my soul: *Kill! Kill! Kill!* But it wasn't me.

I screamed and sat up straight, lunging across the hammock to retrieve the little quartz ball and clutch it to my chest.

Fear not??? Inching lower, my ass!

Gasping for air, I forced myself to breathe more slowly. Now was not the time to hyperventilate.

I held onto the sparkly crystal for dear life and decided that was enough psychic exploration for the day. No more playing with fire or jumping into the deep end without first learning to swim, or whatever other metaphor applied.

In fact, I didn't want to think about any of this anymore. I went inside, turned on the TV and distracted myself with British game shows and soap operas for the rest of the day, vowing to let it go and not even bother Maddie with my slow nervous breakdown—if that's what this was.

SEVEN

"You know," I said to Maddie as we zipped along the A39, top down, sun and wind in our hair, "with everything else going on, we haven't talked about the fact that we'll be in Glastonbury—which Twink confirms is Avalon, by the way—on the fall equinox during an eclipse. That's a lot of cosmic alignment. A veritable tinderbox of mojo."

Maddie grinned and said, "Girlfriend, it's always something with you. It's one of the reasons we get along so well. Your storylines rival mine, and that's not easy to do."

Indeed, it was not. The previous night, when we met again in my cottage for dinner, we swapped stories about how we had each spent our day. Mine may have been spent with faeries and fears, but hers was with intrigues and exes. Another antiques dealer from the Cleveland area was at the estate sale, and he recognized her from a tryst they had shared in their much younger years, long before Maddie's cosmetic surgeries to present as a female.

"He's an old queen," she dished, "but he thinks no one knows he's gay. We were both bidding on the same exquisite Victorian-era brooch when he sidled up to me and said, 'Back off, bitch, or I'll spill the beans on you.'"

I reacted appropriately, eyes wide, mouth agape. "Ugh!"

She guffawed. "Right? I told him 'Honey, you go right ahead. I'm not the one in the closet so deep I reek of moth balls.'"

"So, what happened?" I asked.

She reached into her cavernous designer purse and retrieved a hinged jeweler's box. She snapped it open and showed me a beautiful silver pin with a massive, faceted amethyst surrounded by pearls.

"*That's* what happened," she smirked. "He slunk away and scowled at me from across the room for the rest of the day. What made it even better was that the lord of the manor flirted with me all afternoon, and I'm pretty sure he sensed what I have going on under these clothes."

I laughed and asked, "What made you think that?"

"You and I have talked about this in the past," she said. "When you live like me, you've gotta have a double layer of gaydar-radar. Plus, I may not be as hyper-psychic as you, but I've built up an impressive set of skills myself. I mean, I've caught glimpses of your faeries, have I not? Can anyone else do that?"

She had a point. Chuck and Amanda had seen them once, but only after Pea made a concentrated effort to show herself. Maddie, though, could sometimes see them without help.

We'd come a long way since we first met to where we were now, zipping across the English countryside in an expensive convertible. I smiled, recalling the first time Maddie and I met for lunch in uptown Chagrin Falls, after our shamanic journeying class with Glenna. Maddie had seen Twink fluttering around the gazebo but mistook the faery for a hummingbird.

And that was okay because—more important than whether her skill level matched mine—she never doubted it was real.

"What are you going to do about the panic attacks?" she asked, maneuvering expertly around a complex roundabout. "I mean, today we're heading toward the *big* mama jama, the Glastonbury Tor, at the intersection of the St. Michael and St. Mary lines … as you said, during the equinox and an eclipse. Aren't you afraid you'll overload your circuits?"

I didn't answer right away. A ripple of fear passed through me—enough to make me grip the door handle—but it faded almost as quickly as it came.

"I don't know," I finally admitted. "I don't have any meds with me, and there's no rhyme or reason for when they hit, so I'm going to have to depend on my deep breathing exercises, the clary sage oil, and hope that holding my crystal ball will do the trick."

"Is there anything I can do?" She reached over and patted my arm. "I feel so useless, knowing you're suffering."

"Not that I know of," I said. "I don't even know what *I* can do so, until I figure it out, I have no suggestions. Just stick close by. It helps to know you're there to help ground me." The last thing I wanted was to come all this way just to lose it to something I couldn't control.

"Well, that will be easier now," Maddie smiled, "since we're sharing a cottage this time."

My eyebrows shot up in surprise. "We are? I thought you needed your own space."

"I do, in a hotel room" she said, "but this place is large and roomy, with two bedrooms and two full bathrooms. We'll each have our own privacy. If you don't mind, I'll be taking the master bedroom with the ensuite bath. That's my main concern … being able to spread out all my stuff … literally and figuratively."

"No, I don't mind at all," I said. "Of course not." She was paying. How on earth could I object?

We were approaching town, so Maddie pulled into the parking lot of the first grocery store she saw. "Alrighty, let's go ahead and stock up for a couple days."

Once the trunk … or boot … was stuffed with luggage and food, Maddie wove through the utterly charming town of Glastonbury's narrow streets, the High Street of which was lined with shops and restaurants painted in bright colors with artistically decorated windows. It felt almost like uptown Chagrin Falls, but this was the real deal, hundreds of years old. A town like this is what Chagrin Falls was trying to emulate.

So many metaphysical shops, too! I'd have to be careful not to blow my spending budget out of the water. I made a mental note of the places I wanted to come back to as Maddie maneuvered the car through roadways too narrow for two cars because of the vehicles parked on either side.

"Yikes!" I cried. "Boy, back home they wouldn't just get ticketed, they'd get towed!"

"Yep," she said. "The roads and the buildings on either side were built before cars were invented, so the Brits have learned to adapt and drive cooperatively. That's why parking is a nightmare, too."

Before much longer, we were pulling into the driveway of our rental, an old, refurbished farmhouse built of stone. It was a sight for sore eyes, sturdily constructed, meticulously cared for, with flower boxes beneath every window and an expansive well-manicured lawn with inviting patio furniture.

Even more striking, however, was the up-close view of the famous Glastonbury Tor from right there in the yard … the foot of the massive hill upon which the sole stone tower sat began where we stood. I braced for the panic to hit, but it didn't. No overwhelming fear, no chest or gut pains, no hyperventilating. Such a relief, especially being so close.

"Isn't that breathtaking?" Maddie gushed, opening the trunk to fetch her bags.

I gathered my own bags and said, "It sure is. Not just the Tor but look at this farmhouse!"

"Even prettier than the pictures online," she agreed. She typed in the key code and swung open the door to our home for the next couple days. "Oh my! Come and see!"

I joined her inside the living room, with its vaulted ceiling and stone fireplace, the rustic and cushy furniture just waiting to be plopped into. She dropped her luggage and made her way to the kitchen to unpack her groceries and I followed along, doing the same. The kitchen contained the usual appliances but also included an all-in-one washer/dryer unit.

"How the heck does that work?" I asked. "I'd like to do some laundry, but I've never seen anything like that. Is there an instruction manual?" I flipped through the orientation materials on the kitchen table and my shoulders sagged when I saw nothing to tell us how to use the mystery machine.

"Ugh," she said, "I've used them before. They take forever to wash and then dry, so start a load before bed to have dry clothes by morning."

I must have made a face, because she continued in a lighter tone, "It's super easy to get instructions online. Just snap a photo and upload it to Google."

Once unpacked, we had the rest of the afternoon with no plans. We intended to spend the next day climbing the Tor and then visiting the Chalice Well Gardens, and the following day touring the Abbey and the uptown shops but, with plenty of time on our hands right now, Maddie suggested buzzing back into town to see if she could find some blue lotus essential oil.

"I know I told you I have some at home," she said, "but that's miles and days away and I'd like to see if I can recreate that moment at the cottage where Precious Pea was so close I could smell her, especially since we're in this liminal space at such an auspicious time."

"You don't have to twist my arm," I said. "Let's go."

Back on the High Street, the problem wasn't finding an appropriate shop, it was choosing which one. Finally, we saw one just up ahead called Faery Apothecary. No consultation between us was necessary—we both just laughed and said, "That's the one!"

Maddie zipped into a parking space that 'magically' became available just past the shop, as soon as our decision was made. "I like the way this is unfolding," she said, grinning as she climbed out of the car.

We entered the tidy little shop, with its pale wood floors and airy décor—white shelves lined the walls, holding rows and rows of bottles and jars like so many potions, while faery-themed light catchers hung in the storefront windows.

A young man with long, dark hair and a beard greeted us. He exuded a laid back and groovy vibe, down to his tie-dyed T-shirt and leather thong around his neck, upon which hung a huge wire-wrapped quartz crystal.

"Good afternoon, ladies," he said, his English accent reminding us again that we weren't in Kansas anymore. "How can I help you?"

Maddie stood gazing around the shop in wonder, deeply inhaling the fragrant blend of all the scents on offer. "You can help me find some blue lotus oil, please."

"Happy to," he said. "Right over here. American?" he asked.

While he and Maddie chatted amiably and perused the shelves on one side of the shop, my eye caught a display of flower essences on the other. They weren't the standard brand I was used to seeing back home; these were crafted by a local homeopath.

I felt a nudge from one of the faeries—not sure which, but it was no surprise that at least one would be present in the Faery Apothecary—to purchase this brand's version of Rescue Remedy, called *Emergency Essence: Five-Flower Soother.*

'*Brilliant idea*,' I thought, unsure whether my faery companion could hear my silent agreement, but it didn't matter. It *was* a great idea. I didn't have any anxiety meds with me. Sure, this wasn't prescription strength, but I had used Rescue Remedy with good effect. Maybe I could ask Twink or Pea to give it a bit of a magical boost.

"Aye, we can do that," came the reply.

So, they *were* hearing my thoughts. The veil must be especially thin here and now.

We made our purchases and said our farewells to the young man. As we wandered toward the car, Maddie said, "It's too early to go back to the cottage, isn't it? How about if we roam a bit? I haven't yet had my fill of authentic fish and chips. Wanna grab an early dinner?"

Across the street was a classic British pub, the King's Head, with a sandwich board out front advertising fish and chips with mushy peas, so we strolled in and took a seat. Once again, I marveled at how old the buildings were. Nothing in the States could compare. These buildings were older than our country.

"Oh! They have Pimm's!" Maddie cried. "You have to try one. It's usually a summer drink, but we've got two days left so we're squeaking in under the wire."

We both ordered the same meal, and I agreed that the English certainly had a way with this particular dish. I even enjoyed the mushy peas, which I didn't expect. The Pimm's—a cocktail made with Pimm's No. 1 and lemon/lime soda (which they call "lemonade"), in a glass stuffed with orange slices, strawberries and cucumber—was delicious, refreshing and went down way too easily.

So easily, in fact, that Maddie stopped after one and declared, "I shouldn't drive if I drink any more, so let's stop and pick some up to take back with us."

Appreciating her wisdom in not wanting to wreck the Mercedes, especially on the wrong side of the too-narrow road, I agreed.

We stopped on the way back to the farmhouse and bought all the supplies we needed to make our own Pimm's cocktails, conveniently sold pre-made in cans. Once back at the cottage, we popped open a few cans and poured them over fruit and ice—not as expertly as those made by the practiced hand of a British bartender, but pretty doggone good for a shortcut.

And thus, we spent our first night in Glastonbury, stuffed full of excellent food, sipping excellent beverages in the patio furniture on our magnificent, rented lawn, gazing up at tomorrow's big climb … the massive hill upon which sat St. Michael's Tower.

EIGHT

We planned to be up early to climb the Tor and beat any crowds that might be attracted by the equinox and the eclipse vibe, but the Pimm's went down way too easily and were stronger than they tasted, so we weren't exactly bright-eyed and bushy-tailed that morning.

Even so, we were on the other side of the world from home and couldn't conveniently return another time, so we dragged our asses out of bed and convened at the kitchen table for tea and sultana scones, which Maddie had purchased on our way into town.

The kitchen window offered a spectacular view of the Tor looming up there on the hill, partially obscured by morning fog. We sat in silence, gazing at the scenery, until the kettle came to a boil and Maddie set up a pot to brew.

She poured us both a cuppa and offered me some of her clotted cream along with the strawberry preserves she had also bought, pushing the containers across the table at me.

"What is that?" I asked, pointing at the container of clotted cream. "It sounds gross. Clotted? Like coagulated? Like a blood clot?"

"Says the woman who loves blood sausage," Maddie grinned. "It's super yummy, is what it is. It's like if butter and whipped cream had a baby."

"Alright then," I said, mollified.

"Here's how you do it," she explained. "Cut the scone into halves." She demonstrated by cutting her own scone horizontally and laying the two rounds on a dish. "Then, you smear them with jam and top that off with a dollop of clotted cream."

I fumbled with one half of my scone and finally said, "That doesn't make any sense to put the jam on first. It doesn't stick well enough to then smear clotted cream on top of that."

"Well, all I know," she said, "is this is the way Queen Elizabeth used to do it and that's good enough for me." She then bit into her scone with gusto, pinkie in the air.

"To each his … or her … own," I said, doing it the other way with the second half of my scone before taking my first bite. "Mmmm," I said, my mouth full of bliss, "either way, you're right. It is super yummy."

"Yasss, Queen." She smiled broadly and took a sip of tea.

We took our time with breakfast, allowing the healing properties of a hot cuppa to restore us. Once we felt a little more stable and a little less jittery, we got dressed for a day of climbing and a lot of walking: jeans, tennies, T-shirts, pullover sweaters, and hoodies. It was cold out still, having dropped to 40 degrees overnight (or, as they would say, 4 Celsius), but it was expected to warm up to the 60s (or high teens Celsius). Dressing in layers was the way to go.

I filled my backpack with my supplies for the day, including the crystals, the oil, and the *Emergency Essence* drops. Maddie did the same with her own crystals and oils, tucking them into a stylish fanny pack, which she attached around her waist.

"By the way," she said, snapping the buckle in place, "don't call this a fanny pack here. That's yet another word that means something completely different."

I laughed and asked, "What does it mean?"

"They call it a bum bag." Maddie smiled and continued, dryly, "I don't want to explain the word 'fanny.'"

I nodded, as her meaning landed.

She asked, "Do you mind carrying an extra bottle of water in your backpack for me? I wasn't thinking when I brought something so small for our jaunts about town."

"Of course," I said, adding another bottle to the one I had packed for myself.

It was midmorning by the time we set off, the temperature having warmed a bit now that the sun had been up a few hours and burned off the fog. We followed an isolated hedge-lined road near the cottage which, according to the visitors' map left for us on the kitchen table, would take us to the footpath leading up the back side of the Tor.

Although tomorrow would officially be the first day of autumn, most of the trees were still bright green, just a few tinged with red and yellow. The air was fresh and crisp, the birds sang hidden in the foliage, and no one else was around. Pure heaven. At least, until the curving road began tilting upward and it was all uphill from there.

"Look!" Maddie said, pointing up to our left. "I can see it!"

Sure enough, through a break in the hedge, there was St. Michael's Tower clearly in view. We still had a long way to go, but it was looming larger. Up the road we continued to trudge, stepping aside for the occasional car, until we finally reached an enclosed field with a wooden gate, like the one in Avebury that the 'wizard' helped me open.

"Is this it?" I asked. "Thank God. I'm a little winded."

"The sign says so," Maddie replied, pointing at a nearby sign that said *The National Trust – Glastonbury Tor*. She opened the gate and we commenced, now officially on the path.

Across a field fenced off from a herd of sheep and through another gate, the climb began in earnest up a path that followed the curves of the hill. Fortunately, along the way someone had added the occasional set of stone stairs where it was steepest and, once in a while, a bench made of paving stones on which to sit and rest.

I plopped down on one of the stacks, breathing hard, heart pounding, feeling the Pimm's from the night before. Maddie joined me, also winded.

"Let's just sit for a minute," she said. "No shame."

"How about a little hydration?" I asked, retrieving our water bottles from my backpack.

We both chugged about half a bottle before Maddie said, "We might want to save some. We don't know yet what's ahead."

I nodded in agreement and tucked them back into the bag.

Coming down the curving path from the other direction was an elderly English couple, lively and energetic, chatting and laughing. "Lovely day," the woman said to us.

"It certainly is," I replied, sighing heavily. "That's a heck of a climb, isn't it?"

"Oh, you'll be fine," the old man said. "If *we* can make it …"

My head was pounding, matching the beat of my heart, which was finally slowing a bit. "Thanks," I said, cutting him off before he could finish assuring me that we young whippersnappers could surely do as well as the old folks. "How much further?"

"Oh, lass," he said, grinning, "enjoy the walk! You're in Avalon!"

His words sank in. I nodded and said, "Thank you for the reminder. I needed that."

They ambled off down the hill, now on the easy part of their journey. Maddie whispered, "I bet they weren't so spry on the way up."

I laughed. "I bet you're right." I then stood and said, "Let's get it done. We're in Avalon."

The old man's reminder that we weren't just climbing some random hill was like a tonic. I had forgotten that I wasn't just a tourist, I was here on a mission of some sort, even though I had no idea what it was.

After what felt like an interminable hike, past a couple precarious spots where I was concerned about tumbling down the hill—due to my wobbly legs, not because of any genuine danger—we came to the final few yards of the climb, the tower now fully in sight.

There wasn't a lot of flat ground up there. The top of the hill was surprisingly small, only the size of a backyard lawn. We both stopped and gazed up at the stone tower before finally turning around to look at the view.

"I can see our house from here!" Maddie cried, excited as a child. She pointed down the hill at our stone farmhouse and squeed a little before remembering we weren't alone. The hilltop was dotted with over a dozen other people who had just made the same climb, and the vibe was hushed and reverent. She needn't have worried about disturbing their peace, though, as many of them smiled with kindred amusement.

We spent the next several minutes separately wandering the small hilltop, taking in the sights. St. Michael's Tower, the focal point of the top of the Tor, was about two stories tall, erected centuries ago from stone blocks. Arched doorways were built into two sides, facing opposite directions. Inside was a small group of people, so I waited my turn.

Off to one edge of the hilltop was a compass stone, a metal plate set into a low platform, pointing out distant landmarks and showing that I faced northeast. With the arched thresholds lined up directly behind me, those doorways followed a path from the northeast to the southwest.

That felt odd. I half expected the doors to line up with cardinal directions. I wondered, '*Was it built that way intentionally?*'

I tried to get a closer look at the compass marker, but a young couple was there with their two children taking up a lot of space and I didn't want to butt in. Just as well, because it dawned on me then … I didn't need those details.

What I needed was to think about directions in general. Then the remembrance came crashing down … the St. Michael ley line runs along that path and—oh. Right. I'm at the intersection of two ley lines, St. Michael and St. Mary! The realization hit me so hard that I gasped.

I wanted to kick myself for not doing more research before climbing the hill. I knew I'd need this information but noooo … stupid Lola had to blow it off. Stupid! Stupid Lola!

'*What the hell is wrong with you?*' I chided myself. '*Now you've gone and messed it all up! This was the chance of a lifetime, and you came totally unprepared. You could have been learning, but instead you were playing your little faery games with your little faery crystals and your foofoo faery oils!*'

I fought the urge to drop to the ground in a pile and pout, bad girl that I was. Boy, I really screwed up this time. Gritting my teeth and vowing to do better, I stepped away from the young family and the directional marker so my dark mood wouldn't spill over onto them.

That thought caught my attention. '*Wait. What? What dark mood?*'

I wasn't in a dark mood until just now. Up until a minute ago, I was fine.

It was that old, familiar panic manifesting in a new way. Or was it? It didn't feel like me.

I had to think about that.

There was no one inside the tower at the moment, so I stepped through the stone archway and found, go figure, a bench inside. I looked up toward the roofless ceiling at the blue sky above and sighed, hoping no one would join me. I needed to be alone for a few minutes. I then felt Twink's presence and heard, "*I'll take care of that.*"

I smiled, remembering how Twink had 'taken care of' Melinda in the past, so I thought to her, '*Be kind. These are nice people.*'

I sensed more than heard her scoffing, rolling her eyes, "*I know that. D'yeh think I'm daft?*"

Knowing that I had time to let my guard down a bit, I sat and opened my backpack, removed a few things, and set them on the bench beside me. First things first: I opened the bottle of *Emergency Essence* and placed a few drops under my tongue. After giving them a few seconds to soak in, I picked up both the labradorite and quartz crystals, one in each hand.

Closing my eyes, I sat with my back straight and feet planted firmly on the ground. Since the tower was without a ceiling, I focused my attention upward. The top of my head buzzed like I'd never felt before … usually it lightly tingled when I made the effort to connect with higher vibes and I always assumed it was my crown chakra opening and activating.

This was no tingle. This was a buzz.

My feet were also buzzing, like they were blending with the hill beneath my feet at a molecular level. The words then filled my mind: *As above/so below.*

A sharp twinge of fear shook me as I recalled that this phrase was part of the word flood that practically drowned me in the hammock near Brent Tor. The fear didn't last long, thank goodness, because the phrase now made sense: open tower above, sacred hill below. There was nothing frightening about it.

I pushed those thoughts aside. I'd think about it later.

Another part of that word flood then came to mind: *masculine/feminine*

The light dawned. That was it. I sat exactly at the intersection of *masculine/feminine*, right there on the crisscrossing ley lines. The masculine passed through me laterally through those arched doorways, and the feminine ran front to back through my heart. *As above/so below* ran vertically through me, from the earth to the sky, within the tube of this stone tower without a ceiling.

As the realization sank in, I 'saw' my heart blaze with light, the center of my being at the center of it all. There was nothing to fear here at the Glastonbury Tor.

I felt a psychic 'click' as this knowingness locked in place. I would not need to learn this again.

That didn't mean I wouldn't forget about this feeling … after all, I was still in a human suit, and everyday life gets in the way of high vibes … but it would always be a part of me and I could recall it at will.

A handful of folks had gathered outside the tower, waiting for me to move on so they could have their turn. Still tuned in, I gathered my things and put them into the backpack before exiting through the opposite doorway from which I entered.

Ahead of me, down the hill, lay the town of Glastonbury. The path downward on this side was a paved and mostly straight stairway, much easier than the side of the hill we had climbed to get here. Maddie was still wandering, in her own world and obviously in no rush, so I joined a few people sitting on a gently sloping grassy side of the hill.

I plopped down and took off my hoodie. It was warm, here in the sun. I balled it up into a pillow and lay back onto the grass, knees up, eyes closed, still feeling the buzz I carried with me from inside the tower—although, by now, that buzz had settled into a hum.

Smiling and drifting, I let my thoughts wander back to what had just happened, *as above/so below, masculine/feminine*. I floated on the edge of dozing, not feeling my body anymore. I would stay awake. After all the practicing I had done with meditation, shamanic journeying, and psychic readings, I could do that now. I could go deep and stay present without falling asleep.

A sound filtered into my consciousness, a man's voice, lifted in song. The slight echo told me he was inside the stone tower, singing a Pink Floyd song, "*Breathe.*"

'How friggin' appropriate,' I laughed to myself.

Then it hit me. Oh. It was another hint.

So, I breathed. The stranger's powerful, beautiful vocals boomed from inside the tower, his voice bouncing off the stone walls. My deep breathing exercises—at this spot and in this vibe—were enough to launch me upward.

I didn't need to be inside the tower; I didn't need to hold a crystal in my hand. I had made the connection. My essential Isness—my lack-of-body Beingness—rose higher and higher, buzzing all over as I had inside the tower.

Not wanting to lose this ecstatic feeling, I kept my eyes shut, including my etheric eyes. Then it occurred to me: I didn't have eyes in this form, but I could see. And there, before me, was the most dazzling light-being I had ever encountered. This wasn't a spirit guide, like the ones I'd 'seen' before. There was something different.

This wasn't a being of Spirit. This was a faery.

My vision cleared as I adjusted to the light, the quality of which told me she was a different level of reality than me or my spirit guides, another dimension.

The light surrounding her was exactly the same—only completely different—from the way Twink and Pea's aunt, Queen Jennett, *reflected* moonlight even when no moon was visible. This faery *radiated* light instead of reflecting it.

Her face came into focus, so similar to Jennett's … and to Twink, who was the spitting image of Jennett.

I was so dazzled at first I hadn't noticed Twink and Precious Pea there, with their sidekicks Myx and Maj, whom I had not seen in ages.

In fact, I said so. "Myx! Maj! I haven't seen you in ages!"

One of them—I couldn't tell which, from that far away and at that tiny size—spoke up. "Aye, because yeh haven't needed us."

I laughed, then did a double take as it sank in. "Wait. Do I need you now? What's happening?"

Twink floated forward, more serious than I'd ever seen her. "Lola Garnett, I'd like you to meet my mother, Queen Celesta."

NINE

There was that jolt of panic again, but this time it was deserved, not out of the blue. Not only had Myx and Maj implied I'd need help, here was yet another high-ranking member of Fae royalty, this one Twink's mother!

I gritted my teeth as the realization hit—I was entirely unprepared for this.

Although I had been speaking aloud with the twin faeries, I sent a private thought to Twink, knowing she'd 'hear' me, *'Your mother? You couldn't have warned me we were about to meet?'*

Instead of answering my questions, she responded, teeth also gritted and via thought, *'Do not **dare** to call me Twink here!'*

Oh, good. That was all I needed. Even more performance anxiety.

I took a long, slow, calming breath and tuned into the loveliness that got me here, the buzzing, dazzling light. As I dropped back into the vibe, the faeries shifted their presentations to appear at their full sizes, none as tall as me (and I'm fairly short), yet Celesta's presence loomed large.

"It's an honor to meet you," I said, unable to decide between a curtsy and a bow before the luminous faery queen. I ended up offering a clumsy combination of the two.

"Aye," she replied with a simple nod. Just as her form was edged with rainbow prisms, as if she had been sprinkled with diamonds, her voice was accompanied by the faintest essence of tinkling bells. "At last, I am met with the human who has so occupied two of my daughters."

How it was possible to feel dread in the presence of such luminous beauty, I did not know, but there it was again. Like a quick jab to the chest. I ducked my head and almost sobbed with an overwhelming sense of unworthiness.

Emotion overtook me and I fell to my etheric knees on a ground that didn't exist. There was nothing beneath me, above me, or even around me. We floated in an infinite bubble of brilliant light, the six of us suspended and held in midair.

"Oh, do rise, dear Lola," the queen said, her accent similar to but posher than Twink and Pea. She projected a wave of such love and compassion that I wondered whether I had died and gone to the other side of the veil.

"Aye, you have crossed the veil," she said, reading my thoughts, "but not in the way you are imagining."

More panic pushed through as it occurred to me, '*Oh no! She hears you thinking! Watch it! Be careful!*'

She laughed kindly and said, "Oh my, you are in a state! Please, do get up. Seren, help her."

At the mention of this name, a new faery blinked into view. Similarly dazzling, this one was not quite as blinding as Celesta. Instead of her gown appearing to be studded with diamonds, it shimmered like pearls or opals. I couldn't tell which, as the refracting light wouldn't sit still long enough to be sure. And her hair, long like Celesta's, wasn't white but shimmery blond.

The new faery gently took my arm and helped me to my feet, and it finally sank in. "Wait …" I stuttered, "didn't we already meet, when I was lying in the hammock at Brent Tor?"

"Aye," the queen smiled. "I told you then I'd be waiting for you to arrive. And now, here you are."

It all came rushing back—the brief interaction at the cottage in Tavistock, the blissful feeling of touching the light, then crashing into terror as I sank into darkness. That must have been an intuitive warning that this exquisite brilliance was connected to that dreadful abyss.

Once more gripped by fear, I cried out, "No!"

I yanked my arm away from the opalescent faery and turned to run … but where? I was nowhere and there was nowhere to go.

"Calm," said the queen, her voice smooth and soothing. "Calm. Fear not. 'Tis but inching lower."

I reminded her, "You said that last time. Why do you keep saying that? I'm not inching anywhere!"

Celesta furrowed her brow, not understanding the question. "I said nothing about inching."

"You did," I ventured to argue. "You just said I was inching lower."

Realization spread across her face, the 'Aha!' moment plain to see. "I understand now," she said, smiling with pity, "but I fear that you do not." The faeries surrounding us stifled giggles and she continued, enunciating carefully, "I said '*IN-tchin LOH-vuh*.'"

"Okay," I replied, dully. "Sounds like 'inching lower' to me."

Twink kicked me softly in the shin and shot me a stern look. "Mind yehr tone," she said.

"Thank you, Aethelwyne," the queen said to her daughter, "but I understand that the human is quite undone."

I resisted the urge to poke my tongue out at Twink. "Can you spell that for me?" I asked.

Celesta frowned, thinking for a moment, before waving her hand slowly through the air between us, leaving sparkling letters in its wake which spelled out:

Inntinn-lobhadh

She spoke again, as the letters faded, "*IN-tchin LOH-vuh*."

"Okay," I said. "That's very different. What does it mean?"

Not expecting the question ... how can anyone not know this? ... the queen was flummoxed for an answer. She stammered a bit, her mouth opening and closing as she began to speak and then stopped.

"Seren," she said finally, "how does one define these words to a human?"

The new faery spoke, her voice an octave deeper than the queen's, "It means, quite literally, 'mind rot.' I reckon you could say it's fear for fear's sake alone. It's a corruption of the mind, the rot or decay of rational thought."

Celesta nodded, thoughtful, and said, "Aye, thank you Seren." She faced me again and asked, "Is it clear now to you?"

"Clearer than it was," I said. "But let's back up and apply this new knowledge to what you said."

She nodded again, waiting for me to gather my thoughts and continue.

"I've been riddled with this knee-jerk fear for the past few days," I began. "It hits me out of the blue, for seemingly no reason at all. And it walloped me just now, even though I'm here with you in a spectacular and safe bubble of … something. I would be content to rest here forever in this bliss."

Celesta patiently waited as I paused to regroup. Finally, I asked, "How can I feel such intense and random fear, in the midst of such a glorious state?"

"But," she replied, "when you feel that fear, you are *not* in that glorious state."

"Yes," I said. "Exactly."

"Aye," she said. "Exactly."

Both of us stood firmly in our statements. Yes. Exactly.

Finally, the dazzling queen asked, "And? What is the question?"

Making a solid effort to not scoff in exasperation, I restated what I had already asked. "How can I feel such intense fear, in immediate contrast to feeling so sublime? I feel like I could burst with joy and shoot up into the heavens, like glittering fireworks!" I waved my arms about, gesticulating to demonstrate the expansive bliss I could be experiencing, if not for … inching lower.

"Aye," she said, following along, "an excellent question indeed. How can you?"

"No," I cried, "I'm asking you!"

"Oh!" she said, somewhat dumbfounded by my seemingly dumb question. "Well … it's *Inntinn-lobhadh.*"

I sighed and said, "Please explain it to me as if I was a child."

Twink snorted a laugh and I shot her a dirty look.

"Aye," Celesta said, also frowning at her snarky daughter. "I must remember this is a new concept for you. Seren," she said, "you were so skillful at translating the words *Inntinn-lobhadh.* Would you please explain further what they mean, in human terms?"

"You answered your own question," the opalescent faery began, "when you asked, 'How can I feel such fear, in the midst of such a glorious state?'"

I nodded, hoping she would elaborate.

Thankfully, she did. "If you were truly in the midst of that glory, how *could* you feel fear? You cannot feel both at once."

I waited.

"If you were truly in it …" she said, pausing for me to follow along.

"Yes, but then I get knocked out of it," I reminded her.

"Aye, by *Inntinn-lobhadh*. It knocks you out," she said.

"Ooooooooooooh!" I said, finally beginning to see the metaphorical light.

All the faeries nodded, grateful that I was getting it.

"Are you saying this … *Inntinn-lobhadh* … thing is a … a thing?" I had trouble forming the concept in words. "It's not my own mind playing tricks on me? I thought it was mental illness! I thought I needed a pill!"

Queen Celesta clasped her hands together and raised them, saying, "Aye, the light dawns."

"Yes," Seren continued. "It's not you, but masquerades as you. It's a mind parasite and there is nothing tastier than bliss. If you don't interrupt it, it will drain you."

I was silent, listening and soaking it in, but then asked, "How could I interrupt it if I didn't know it existed?"

"Exactly," Seren said, "It does not want to be known or recognized. Hence, it uses the weapon of fear, knocking you off the path of discovery, keeping you afraid of looking too hard for its cause. It has no power of its own aside from deflection. It allows you to rise high enough to be 'tasty,' just high enough, then it bites."

I recoiled, not saying "Ewwww" aloud, but surely it showed on my face.

Seren went on. "Once you're drained just enough to still function, *Inntinn-lobhadh* steps back and allows you to rise again. A vicious cycle."

This time I said it. "Ewwww. And that's not scary to you?"

"Of course," Seren replied. "Hence our recommendation to be one with bliss."

"But," I cried, truly exasperated now, "how can I be one with bliss when this thing keeps taking a bite out of me?"

"Remember it." She enunciated clearly to get my attention.

"See it." She had my attention.

"*Name it.*" She emphasized these words, her patience wearing thin.

"Reclaim the light, where your true essence belongs." As she spoke this last, she lit up like a pillar of glittering, holographic light.

I gasped aloud as another layer of 'Aha!' was revealed. "So, it's what I discovered in Tavistock … gazing into my quartz sphere pulls me into the light."

"Aye!" Seren said, excited, still glowing but less blindingly. "Now you've got it! It's like this," she said, swirling her hand about and finally stopping when a softball-sized crystal ball blinked into view, resting on her fingertips. "When you gaze into the crystal, what do you see?"

I peered into the stone, the light within drawing me deeper and higher into euphoria. On the verge of bursting with ecstasy, I gasped aloud and said, "Enough! I'll die if I go further!"

Pulling myself down into the heightened state with the Queen and her companions, I said, "I think I get it. When I asked, 'How can I feel such fear, in the midst of such a glorious state?' and you said I cannot, you didn't mean that I can't be in two places at once, you meant that it's *false fear* … and I must name it to consciously recall that I'm already where I thought I'd been knocked out of. Right?"

Seren smiled and Queen Celesta said, "Indeed. You humans have a concept you call 'being present,' no?"

I nodded.

"This is the most immediate cure for an attack by *Inntinn-lobhadh,*" she explained. "As Seren advised, name it and it will evaporate, bringing you back to the present moment, expressing the light that is already within you."

Heaving a sigh of relief, I began to ask, "But if the parasite's mode of attack is to literally make me forget … how can I remember to name it?" Before I could go any further, the voice of the man singing within St. Michael's Tower seeped into my consciousness. I was slipping out of the connection.

Becoming more aware of my body lying there on the grass, in the sun, on the side of the Tor, I heard Queen Celesta's parting words, "Go to the well … gather the waters …"

I opened my eyes and sat up. Maddie lay beside me, eyes closed, a satisfied smile on her beautifully sculpted face. At that moment I loved my dear friend so much and was so grateful that she brought me with her on this journey. I lay back down and waited for her to come out of her own reverie.

I only had to wait a few minutes. Once she sat up and stretched, landing back in her body, I said, "Let's get down those stairs," pointing at the path downward before us. "I need to get to the Chalice Well and get some water."

TEN

Down the hill we went, as spry and bouncy as the old couple we saw on our way up. "That was incredible," Maddie said, practically skipping down the stone pathway toward Glastonbury.

"It was, wasn't it?" I said. "A lot happened up there, far too much to share while casually strolling down the streets of Avalon. What about you? You looked pretty serene back there on the hill. What are your thoughts?"

Maddie smiled broadly and said, "I think I need to bask in this for a while before sharing. How about tonight over dinner?"

"Perfect." I grinned. "Well … spoiler alert … I *will* tell you that I was given instructions by yet another faery queen."

I paused for Maddie's reaction and she didn't disappoint. Her jaw dropped open and I continued, "This one is Twink and Pea's mother … Queen Jennett's sister."

"Of course." Maddie nodded. "Let's keep it all in the family."

"Exactly. Anyway," I continued, "Queen Celesta, that's her name, told me to go to the well and 'gather the waters.' I assume she means the Chalice Well. Don't you?"

"I think that's a safe assumption," Maddie said, scooting to the side of the paved path to get out of the way of a couple who were climbing up the hill, winded and in need of a little consideration.

"Remember, you're in Avalon!" I called out to them then continued to Maddie, "Celesta didn't have time before the connection faded to tell me what to *do* with the water, but I suppose that will be revealed in due time. These things usually go like that, don't they?"

Maddie laughed. "They certainly do. Did she say which well? There are two, you know."

"I did *not* know that," I said.

"Should have read my book," she chided. "One is inside the Chalice Gardens. That's the Red Spring, so called because the water is rich with iron. It's associated with the Goddess, the Sacred Feminine, due to the iron content and the reddish hue of the water … equated with blood … and we all know how you love ingesting that."

She winked and I grimaced at the memory of unknowingly enjoying blood sausage earlier in our trip, which seemed like a lifetime ago.

"The other is the White Spring, which runs directly out of the Tor," Maddie continued.

"Let me guess … it's associated with the masculine? Why is it white?"

"Yes and it's mineral-heavy with chalk," she explained. "Not sure why that's associated with the masculine. Bone, perhaps?"

"Yes, and we all know how you love ingesting …"

"Stop right there, missy," Maddie guffawed.

We reached the bottom of the stone walkway and exited through another wooden gate, where the path continued to lead downhill a little further. Before we knew it, we were out on a paved road, still sloping downward.

At the bottom of the hill, the path ended at a wall bordering a narrow side lane. A row of vendors had set up there, their wares on offer, perfectly positioned to catch visitors either starting or ending their climb up the Tor. To the left, a busy street cut across the end of the road, and to the right the lane continued into a quiet neighborhood.

No one had to twist our arms. We gladly wandered down the row of vendors to browse. The table that drew my attention was manned by a darling young couple behind a long folding table draped in colorful cloth. The man had dark and curly hair, with a moustache and goatee, and the woman was a radiant redhead, with the face and smile of a cherub.

More than their wares, it was the beaming couple themselves that caught my attention. They were so shiny, I knew there was something to notice here.

Their display held crystals and handcrafted jewelry, including bracelets made of crystal beads strung on elastic.

He smiled and said, in an accent similar to Twink and Precious Pea, "Ey up, see anything yeh fancy?"

I did, in fact. "Is that made of quartz beads?" I asked, pointing at one of the bracelets with clear stones, about the size of garden peas.

"It certainly is," he said, handing it to me.

As I fingered the beads, the young woman said, "You're American! I love America!"

"Would you like to trade places for a while?" I grinned. "I love England!"

"Ee, I'd love to," she said. "It's my life's dream to visit America."

As we chatted, my eyes scanned the table and were magnetically drawn to a spectacular labradorite sphere, about the size of a tennis ball, sitting upon a small plastic stand to keep it from rolling. "Oh!" I gasped, pointing at the stone, "How much is that?"

"That's thirty quid," she said.

"We also have," her man said, "a labradorite bracelet." He held up a string of dark, flashing beads, similar in size to the quartz beads.

"I must have both bracelets," I said. "How much?"

"Those are seven pound fifty each," he said, handing me the second bracelet.

"Sold," I said, putting the quartz bangle on my right wrist and the labradorite on my left. I wasn't sure why that specific placement. It just felt right.

I turned to the young woman and said, "I'll take the sphere, too, please."

"Of course," she said. She picked it up and turned it to catch the sunlight, the green and blue flash lighting up, and then grinned. "If yeh squint real hard, it looks like the shape of a heart."

I squinted and agreed that, yes, if you use your imagination a little, the flash did look like an elongated heart.

"Excellent choices. That'll be forty-five quid please," the young man said. Meanwhile, she placed the sphere in a metal singing bowl and ran a wooden dowel along the rim, making it tone loudly.

I paid her man and made small talk as she continued to 'treat' the sphere. "Your accent is familiar. Are you from up north?"

"Aye, Yorkshire," he said. "Good ear. Most Americans can't tell one English accent from another."

"I have friends from up there," I said.

"Well, if yeh're ever in York," he said, running my debit card, "come find us at Shambles Market. We don't usually come this far south, but we're in town to visit friends and thought we'd set up shop while we're in Avalon on this magical weekend."

The woman wrapped the sphere in colored tissue paper, sealed it with a sparkly sticker, then popped it in a paper bag along with its plastic stand and handed it to me. "Enjoy," she said.

"I will, thank you," I replied. "When I get home and set it in its new place, I'll think of you visiting America soon. May it act as an anchor object, drawing you further into your dream."

"Thank you," she smiled, pressing her hands together in prayer mode.

Maddie caught up with me then, nodding 'hello' to the Yorkshire couple and said, "One of the vendors told me that the White Spring is just up there." She pointed up the narrow lane and continued, "and the Red Spring is that way," pointing left, "around the corner. Let's go to the White Spring first since we're practically there."

I said farewell to my new friends and followed Maddie up the lane. Before long we found ourselves at a recessed opening in the brick wall lining the right side of the road, tucked away from plain sight. Built into the alcove was a rustic shrine, complete with moss covered brickwork and a series of large earthenware bowls set up in a row to create an artistic waterfall, catching what I assumed to be spring water flowing out of the back wall.

An older woman sat on the rocks next to the wall, reading a book. "It's not open yet," she said, gesturing to a locked, iron-worked doorway to her right.

"That's okay," Maddie said, "we can come back later. We're just here to gather some spring water."

"Help yourself." She pointed past the doorway at a spigot installed into the brick wall about a foot from the ground. Water flowed unchecked into a cement drain basin below it.

"Thank you," I said, retrieving our half-finished bottles of water from my backpack. "Drink up," I said to Maddie, handing hers over. I finished mine, thirstier than I realized, then filled it at the spigot. Maddie did the same.

"Have a lovely day," the woman said, and we headed back down the lane to visit the Red Spring next, inside the Chalice Garden.

Nodding and smiling again to the vendors as we passed—reminding me that I had just been nudged to purchase a labradorite sphere—I mentioned to Maddie, "Remind me when we have our catch-up conversation that I forgot to ask Celesta something."

"Noted," she said. We turned right at the corner of the end of the lane and soon approached the entrance to the Chalice Well.

As we stood in a short line to pay the reasonable entrance fee, Maddie said, "One of us probably shouldn't have filled a bottle at the White Spring. We won't have anything to use here at the Red Spring."

"You can buy a bottle here," the man in line in front of us said, pointing into the little guardhouse where a woman was selling tickets. There, for sale, stood a row of wide and sturdy glass bottles with the words "The Chalice Well" imprinted upon them, along with what I gathered was their logo, a pair of intertwining circles within a larger circle.

When it was our turn, we each bought two bottles, so we'd have one apiece for the Red Spring and another to transfer our already collected water from the White Spring.

After setting our phones on airplane mode, as instructed by the signs, we followed a marked path into the first of a series of eight separate serene gardens, each with their own theme. This first one was sunny and spacious, with the far end bounded by the same wall that separated us from the row of vendors and the lane up to the White Spring.

This garden featured a pair of round, brick-lined pools of orange-tinted water being constantly filled by a trickle from further into the gardens. The two pools formed overlapping circles, designed in the same shape as the logo on the bottles we had just purchased.

Maddie, in tour guide mode, spoke in a quiet and respectful volume, "At the risk of showing off … after all, I did read the book … that shape is called the vesica piscis. It has many meanings, but here it represents two worlds meeting and overlapping, the masculine and feminine. Interesting, no?"

"Interesting, yes," I said.

"Anyway, the pointed oval shape formed by the intersection is said to represent a vulva, or the womb," she continued, a tinge of awe in her voice, "the threshold through which something new can emerge."

She paused as if deep in thought. "Huh," she uttered, then finally said, "Remind me about this when we talk tonight. I need to think on this for a while."

"Noted," I said.

Continuing along the path, we entered the next garden, a space filled with yew trees in shady contrast to the sunny spaciousness of the previous section. Up ahead of us, just passing into the next garden, was someone I recognized.

I nudged Maddie and said, "Look! It's him! The wizard from Avebury!"

He was with the same woman from a few days ago.

"What are the odds? Should I go talk to him?"

Maddie's jaw hung in amazement. After several beats, she gathered herself and replied, "You know what they say, 'there are no coincidences' ... especially when wizards are involved."

I laughed and said, "Well, we don't know that he's *actually* a wizard. We're making that up ... aren't we?"

She shrugged and I went on, "I'll wait and see if we run into them again. Third time's a charm, but I wouldn't even know what to say."

Leaving it up to fate, we continued our stroll through the gardens, but that didn't mean I stopped thinking about the 'coincidence.'

The next section offered a small healing pool, actively fed by a flow of running, rust-tinged water, where a handful of people (not including the wizard and his woman; they had somehow already vanished from sight) had taken off their shoes to stand in the water. Their chattering teeth and breathless gasps told us that the water was far too cold, so we kept walking.

Just as well, because the next section was what we came for: the Lion's Head well spring. Like the White Spring spigot on the other side of the wall, water poured freely, but here it came out of the mouth of a sculpted lion's face. This was where visitors were allowed to collect water, as it was regularly tested for drinkable quality.

"Only take a few sips," warned Maddie. "It's okay to drink, but you don't want to overdo it. Think of it as homeopathic."

We both filled one of our just purchased bottles and took a couple sips. It was icy cold and tasted of iron, like well water back home in Ohio. "No worries about drinking too much," I said. "I've never been fond of the taste of well water."

We screwed the bottles tightly shut and tucked them into my backpack, then continued deeper into the gardens. The wizard and his lady were nowhere to be seen. We passed a cozy little bench draped under cover of ivy off to the side, but neither of us were in a mood to sit, so we continued further until we came upon the spot this place was famous for, the Chalice Well.

Inside a breathtaking little alcove, there it was in the center of a low, circular stone wall, which was about bench height. The wooden lid to the well shaft, a heavy circular covering, was open and upright, tilted back a bit. The vesica piscis was crafted into a wrought iron embellishment and installed onto the wood.

The well itself was covered with a wrought iron grate so there was no danger of falling in. Looking down into it gave me the willies. It was deep, and it was dark. I shuddered and wondered if my reaction was due to a past life memory of falling down a well, or perhaps even something as mundane as remembering the murder story of the well in Avebury.

Either way, I didn't get too close.

Here at the Chalice Well, the vibe was clear: this was a sacred space, and silence was appropriate. Maddie and I each took a seat on the low wall, along with two other women who sat in quiet contemplation.

I hoped they would leave soon and immediately felt guilty about my impatience. They had every right to be there, but the faeries were nudging me. I was there to perform a task. Besides, both strangers exuded a rather sorrowful, pain-filled vibe, and I had to be careful not to empath them and invite their aching to bleed into my field.

I checked myself and took a few deep breaths, wishing love and healing upon them both so that if they did choose to leave now, it was because they felt better.

'*As you wish*,' I heard. I couldn't tell for sure, but I thought it was Seren. Her voice was a lower pitch than Celesta's, and Twink and Pea's voices lilted with a northern accent that was not present now.

Whoever it was didn't matter, as both women soon gathered their things and got up to leave. Once we had the space to ourselves, the voice of the faery continued and, the more she spoke, the more I knew it was Seren.

'Pour a splash of your waters onto your bracelets,' she said, *'the red water on the clear beads and the white water on the dark beads.'*

I reached into my backpack and removed my water bottles, taking this opportunity to pour the water in the plastic bottle from the White Spring into the extra glass bottle I just purchased. Then I held my right arm out over the well and poured out a bit of the Red Spring water onto the quartz, and then a splash of White Spring water over the labradorite beads on my left wrist.

Maddie, following my lead, also took this chance to fill her empty glass bottle with her water from the White Spring. She didn't pour any of her water over anything, but she closed her eyes and held the bottles reverently to her chest, here at the side of the sacred well.

I sat again on the stone wall and waited in silence for any further instructions. After several minutes, it became clear that none were forthcoming. A new stranger entered the alcove and joined us on the wall, so I took this as my cue that we were complete.

I caught Maddie's eye and raised my eyebrows to silently ask, *'Are you done here?'*

She nodded yes, so I put the bottles carefully in my backpack and wound my hoodie around them so they couldn't clink together and break. Then we rose to leave the new visitor alone in her contemplation.

We walked through the final section of the gardens, a beautiful meadow with plenty of benches and a broad, sunny lawn upon which to sit and ponder, but we both agreed that we had done what we came to do. We made a quick stop at the gift shop, where I bought myself a sterling silver ring with the vesica piscis emblem and slipped it onto the middle finger of my left hand, next to my wedding ring.

On our way out, I stopped at the public ladies' room and asked Maddie, "Do you need to go?"

She grimaced a bit and said, "Yes, but I'll wait until we get home. I'm careful to not use public bathrooms unless they're unisex."

"Ohhhh," I said. "You know, this is the first time it's even come up on this entire trip. Don't they have one here?"

"I'll look around," she said. "You go ahead."

I took care of business and, while waiting near the exit for her to return, I turned my left hand in the sun, watching my new ring sparkle next to my wedding ring, considering the symbolism. One ring represented a vow I had made to my husband, while the other signified a new sort of vow that I didn't quite understand yet.

'*Not very wise, Lola,*' I silently scolded as a rush of regret washed over me. '*You're making promises to a spirit realm without even knowing what you're getting into.*'

"Whoops," I chuckled aloud. "I'm inching lower." I could *feel* it—that subtle slide into self-loathing.

I focused again happily on my sparkling rings. My new ring and my wedding ring. Then it occurred to me … my husband! I hadn't checked my messages in a long time.

Close enough to the exit, I took a chance and switched my phone out of airplane mode to check my notifications. Sure enough, there were several messages from Chuck, the first couple cheerful and joking, but the later ones impatient, then worried.

I typed out a quick response, only feeling slightly guilty about lying, "So sorry! I've had a bad connection. All is well. I'll email later. Love you!"

Maddie rejoined me then, appearing much relieved, and we wandered back out into the mainstream world—such as it was here—which was already in progress.

ELEVEN

It wasn't a long walk back to the cottage, just under a mile, but it felt like a cross-country trek after the climb up and down the Tor. By the time we got back, our dogs were barking. We both ate one of our ready-made salads and agreed that it was naptime.

I didn't sleep as much as doze. With a lot on my mind, I spent most of my time reliving the day and rereading the journal entries I had written since we arrived in England. I didn't want to miss any loose threads.

Even so, I was more interested in hearing from Maddie about her experience on the Tor. That enigmatic smile had me wondering. So, as we sat down to dinner and a glass of wine after our naps, I said, "You asked me to remind you about something … we were talking about the intersection of the vesica piscis representing the womb … remember?"

"Yes!" she cried. "I journaled about it once we got home. Let me go get it." She hopped up from the table to fetch her journal while I took a cautious first bite of my steaming hot bangers and mash, fresh out of the oven. Although I burned my tongue, it was worth it. It was delicious. I was blowing on my next bite when Maddie excitedly returned to the table, her journal open to the appropriate page.

Reading from her notes, she said, "My 'Aha!' moment was about being at the intersection between the masculine and feminine, through which something new can emerge." She looked up from her journal smiling broadly, waiting for my reaction. "I underlined that last part, 'through which something new can emerge.'"

I nodded and said, "Okay, I'm following you so far."

She clasped her hands together and held them to her chest. "*I am* that something new, emerging from the intersection of masculine and feminine!" Tears glittered in her eyes. I'd never seen her so emotional.

"I hesitate to ask too many personal questions," I began. "Isn't that something you already knew about yourself?"

"Yes, of course," she said, waving away my question. "That's not even what I'm talking about. You know, everyone who identifies as transgender has their own story and their own understanding of what it means for them. But I still had questions about what it means for *me*. Like anyone might."

"That makes sense," I said. "I've always been baffled by what gender really means, and how it can be so different for each person. I mean, why do I get treated a certain way, simply because of the form my physical body took this time around? Aside from the obvious external features, I've never felt like a girly girl, you know? You're more feminine than I am."

"Yes, exactly, but this goes much deeper," she said. "Up there on the Tor, at the intersection of the masculine and feminine ley lines, yada yada, just soaking in the vibe with my back on the grass ..."

She took a sip of wine and thought for a moment before continuing.

"... it sank in how unimportant it all is, the labels and delineations. We're all so obsessed about gender and how we should behave accordingly," she said.

"Up there, for the first time, I felt completely free of all of it. I am who I am. I'm just me. I embrace my inner masculine *and* my inner feminine. I love dressing up and being girly, but I also really appreciate having male plumbing."

I smiled, watching my dear friend light up as she spoke.

"It occurred to me ..." she paused again to gather the perfect wording, "... it doesn't matter at all if I fit into the cis world or the trans world. I'm finally synced up with who I came here to be. That 'something new emerging' has nothing to do with the outside world. It's who I am inside."

Tears were now streaming down her face and she beamed. I couldn't help feeling equally happy for her, and my own eyes filled with tears. "Oh, honey," I said, leaning over in my chair to embrace her, "I'm so happy for you!"

She giggled and squeezed me tightly before pulling back, sniffling and wiping under her eyes with her finger. "Oh … my makeup … I must look a mess."

"You're beautiful," I said. "You must use waterproof mascara."

"No," she sniffed again, "but it's expensive and high-quality, so …"

I lifted my glass in toast and said, "Here's to life-changing epiphanies."

She clinked her glass on mine and laughed. "Here's to expensive mascara."

"Okay, now you," she said, after we both drank. "You wanted me to remind you that you were going to ask the new faery queen about something." She dug into her meal, pot roast with Yorkshire pudding.

"Right!" I said. "Thank you."

I took a moment to rewind my memory to that point in the day. "So, I was talking with Celesta, Twink and Pea's mother—which still blows my mind—but the connection was beginning to fade. I didn't have time to ask about the way the crystals are affecting me. The quartz sphere apparently lifts me up into this ecstatic, sparkling realm, but something about the labradorite is causing those moments of panic … oh, remind me to tell you what I learned about that, too."

She nodded, her mouth full.

"Anyway," I continued, "I already know it's not the labradorite itself. There's something gorgeous and deeply magnetic about the way it flashes its inner blue and green, drawing me inward. I'm not afraid of the stone. The fear is connected to … but not caused by … the stone."

My backpack was nearby, and I hadn't unpacked it yet, so I reached for it and unloaded everything onto the kitchen table. I found my new labradorite sphere at the bottom of the bag, under the bottles of spring water. I handed Maddie's bottles to her, keeping the red and white water separate, and set my own aside, doing the same.

"We should mark those red and white, by the way," I said. "I had them separated in my bag, but it'll be easy to lose track."

"Look at them," she said. "You can see the difference." She was right. There was a distinct difference in the hue of the bottled water.

"Remember what I did with the water at the well?" I asked, and she nodded. "One of the faeries told me to pour red water over the quartz beads, so let's assume that's related to the feminine. After all, it's the quartz crystal ball that helps me connect with Celesta."

"Makes sense," Maddie said, taking another bite of pot roast.

"She also told me to pour the white water over the labradorite bracelet," I continued. "So, ipso facto, the masculine."

"Ooooo, listen to you with your fancy shmancy jargon!" Maddie grinned. "Looks like we're playing girl detectives again," she said, reminding me of our previous adventure helping Seth to return from the land of the Fae at Jennett's Foss.

"Looks like it." I grinned and said, "We should have our own TV show. Anyway, Google is our friend. Let me do a quick search …"

I typed some relevant keywords into my phone: labradorite, sacred masculine, Glastonbury. I gasped when I saw one of the top results: *King of the Fae and Glastonbury Tor: the Divine Masculine.*

"Oh my God, Maddie, look at this!" I said, showing her my phone.

"Holy crap!" she cried.

"I know, right?" I clicked on the link and scanned the page, reading aloud the relevant passages. "Legend holds that beneath the Glastonbury Tor lies the gateway to Annwn, the Celtic Otherworld. There lives the King of the Fae, Gwyn ap Nudd." Fortunately, the page included a phonetic pronunciation guide, so I was able to say the names properly, *Annwin* and *Gwin ap Neeth.*

"This must be the king I've been getting messages about," I said. "Don't you think so?"

"Who else could it be?" she asked, matching my excitement.

"Oh no," I said, my breath tightening. "Here it is again … that panic." I pressed my hands to my chest, which did nothing to quell the pain.

"Calm down," Maddie instructed. "You're fine. Take slow, deep breaths." She breathed slowly in and out.

I followed her lead and gradually regained control of my breathing. "Thank you," I said, still a little breathless. "So glad you were here. That was a doozy."

"Weren't you just saying something about wanting to be reminded about these panic attacks?" she asked.

"Yes, of course!" I said. "Gimme a sec." I took a few long, slow deep breaths, practicing the exercises that had helped me previously when this happened, then took a bite of food. Finally, I felt grounded enough to continue.

"That was something else I learned from Celesta," I began. "I'm not having panic attacks, like I assumed."

Maddie raised her eyebrows, her question implied.

"No," I continued. "Apparently these attacks—I don't know what else to call them yet—there's this sort of dark, external force. It makes me want to curl up and hide. Celesta called it *Inntinn-lobhadh.*"

"Inching lower?" Maddie asked.

"Nope. I made the same mistake. It's *Inntinn-lobhadh.*" I enunciated clearly. "Those words translate as 'mind rot.'"

"Go on."

I did. "It's not my own mind messing with me, like I thought. It's something outside of me trying to keep me from learning the truth. So, it makes me afraid whenever I get too close to … whatever it is. Apparently, it has something to do with this king I keep hearing about."

"So, why didn't you feel the panic just now, when you mentioned him?" she asked.

"That's the thing," I explained. "The cure, for lack of a better word, is to remember that's what it is. It has no true power, aside from terrifying me enough to look away. It can only distract and deflect and, as long as I can remember to do so, naming it makes it go away."

"Oh!" Maddie said. "That sounds easy enough. Not much of a foe, is it?"

I laughed a little and said, "You'd like to think so, wouldn't you? But that's the problem: remembering to remember. If you hadn't brought up the fact that I said something earlier, I might still be freaking out and hyperventilating."

"Maybe that's why you were led to buy and then anoint that bracelet," she said, pointing at my left wrist. "Your reminder is right there."

"Yes, must be," I said, fingering the beads, grateful for their presence now. "Funny, isn't it, that the first labradorite I bought was in Avebury, and that's where I first heard the message '*the King awaits.*'"

"And we were leaving Avebury the first time you had one of your attacks," Maddie reminded me.

"Right," I said. I took a sip of wine and noticed both of our glasses were nearly empty. I topped us both off and said, "That's also the first time I saw that intense light connected with the quartz sphere. I saw it again in Tavistock and here today, but Avebury is where it began."

I didn't hear any of the faeries, but I distinctly felt Twink's impatience at waiting to be invited into the conversation. I raised a finger to Maddie, a silent wait-a-minute, and said aloud, "Yes, Twink? What is it?"

"That's not where it began," I heard. *"That's where yeh first noticed it."*

"Does that matter?" I asked. Maddie's puzzled frown told me she didn't hear Twink's side of the conversation, so I told her, "Twink says Avebury isn't where this all started."

"Aye, it started centuries ago," she said. *"And that's all I can tell yeh."*

I scoffed and said, "That's not helpful." I rolled my eyes at Maddie and filled her in, "Little Miss Enigma Pants says it began centuries ago."

She laughed and said, "Well, if there's one thing I've learned, it's that Twink would tell you more if you needed to know right now."

"Isn't she a brat?" I asked, then ducked my head a bit, remembering that Twink could haul off and kick me if she wanted to. When I heard Precious Pea giggle I relaxed, assured that this wasn't a serious situation, just an interesting one.

"So," said Maddie, "this king is apparently a mythic character who *isn't* so mythic, and he lives under the Tor. The labradorite is somehow connected to him, and he's waiting for you … for some reason."

"How can anyone live under a hill?" I asked, digging into my food. "I can't wrap my head around that idea."

"How can you have faeries floating around, always listening to you?" Maddie asked.

"Well, that's a good point," I said. "So, yes, I have both quartz and labradorite, each apparently connected to Fae royalty. I've met one, but not the other. One is joyous and blissful and sparkly, and the other is scary as Hell."

I paused, my fork stopped halfway to my mouth. "Literally. He lives in the Underworld!"

"Now wait," Maddie said, "that article you found said 'Otherworld,' not Underworld. I think that's an important distinction."

"Okay," I agreed. "Another good point. Why do you suppose Seren had me pour water over each of the bracelets today?"

"Ooo! Ooo! I know that!" I heard Precious Pea, unintentionally doing a great impression of Arnold Horshack. I tilted my head up toward the sound and waited for her to continue. *"Yeh wouldn't understand our word for it, but it's somewhere between a blessing and an activation. Yeh did this at the wellhead, yeah? That were a point of power, and yeh were using power tools ... the waters at the well, and the corresponding stones."*

My jaw dropped and Maddie waited, albeit impatiently, for me to fill her in. "This is fun," I said. "Pea says the bracelets were activated by power tools!"

Maddie's face lit up with laughter and she said, "I've said it before, I'll say it again, this is why I love hanging out with you. This kind of stuff doesn't happen to just anyone."

"No, it does not," I said, "and thank you for being the kind of friend I can share it with. Can you imagine trying to explain these events to anyone else? Well," I said, raising my glass once again, "here's to friendship."

Maddie clinked my glass and said, "Here's to celebrating the equinox in one of the most magical places on Earth."

We sipped and each took another bite or two of our meals, which were getting cold as we talked.

"We're only here for another full day," I said, "and tomorrow is the eclipse. I wonder if we'll complete what we came here to do. Feels like a lot of unfinished business in a short period of time."

Maddie reached into her massive bag, which hung over the back of her chair, and pulled out her planner. "Tomorrow morning we're going to tour the Glastonbury Abbey, where King Arthur and Guinevere are supposedly buried, and the eclipse is later in the afternoon. We could climb the Tor again, if you want to be up there when it happens. And we don't have to leave for London at any specific time the next day. We can check in to the hotel at any time, because we're not flying out until the following morning."

I nodded, thinking about our itinerary and said, "I like the idea of being up there during the eclipse, even if I don't relish doing that climb again. It feels right to be there."

"It's a plan," she said, and once again we raised our glasses to clink them together. It was a plan, indeed.

TWELVE

I was sound asleep when Maddie banged on my door and shouted, "Hey, get up! Are you going to sleep all day?" I pulled my head out from under the covers and checked my watch. It was already 9:30, and we had planned to head into town to see the Abbey at 10:00.

"Sorry," I called out. "Be up in a sec."

"Okay," Maddie said through the door. "I'll make you a cuppa."

I had showered the night before, so all I needed to do was get dressed, brush my hair, and throw on a little makeup. I wasn't hungover from our glass clinking at dinner. I didn't drink enough for that, but I was feeling—and looking—a little ragged.

Jeans on, I pulled my sweater over my head before having second thoughts. It might be too warm later. I should dress in layers. I pulled the sweater off and tossed it on the unmade bed.

I searched through my suitcase for a clean T-shirt and discovered, to my dismay, that all my favorites were dirty. I'd have to throw in a load of laundry. Ugh.

All this just to go look at some old ruins. Who cares?

This was beginning to feel like a chore.

My bed looked so inviting, with its tousle of still-warm sheets. *Come to me*, it sang in the language of its people. *I'm so cozy and comfy, and you'll be soooo happy here.*

I had to come up with a good story if I was going to get out of Maddie's plan to go into town. I could already hear her rebuttal to anything I might say. I wouldn't be able to argue with her because she would be right. We may never pass this way again. Suck it up buttercup, get your ass in gear and get out there.

But seriously, I just didn't *want* to. I was tired and she was the one who wanted to visit Glastonbury Abbey. I mean, yeah, if I was up for it, it might be interesting, but I wasn't.

Either way, I had to get out there to the kitchen, if for no other reason than she'd made me a cup of tea. I grabbed the last clean shirt from the suitcase and pulled it on, leaving the sweater on the bed.

"Would you mind terribly if I didn't go with you?" I asked Maddie, joining her at the table.

"I certainly would mind," she said, arching a perfectly stenciled brow. "Why on earth would you even ask?"

I sighed. "I'm worn out. I have laundry to do and I'm not all that interested in seeing the Abbey, to be honest."

"Girl, get yourself dressed and throw a load in before we leave the house," she sassed. "We're in England … Glastonbury, England to be precise. If you think I'm going to let you drag ass around here all day, you've got another think coming."

Of course she was right. I knew she would be.

Even so. I don't think I've ever been angry at Maddie—she's one of those people you just love no matter what they say or do—but I was starting to get pissed.

I had to bite my tongue to keep from saying what I was really thinking and said instead, "I don't feel like going. I have a lot on my mind, especially with the eclipse tonight and all that. Isn't it bad enough I have to climb back up that hill just to meet …"

Throwing my hands in the air with disgust, I got up and walked back to my room before I said anything really nasty to my best friend.

Maddie was silent as I stormed off, but I could feel her eyes boring holes into my back. Just as I was about to shut my bedroom door behind me, I heard her say, "Lola, look at your left wrist."

I closed the door, taking care not to slam it, although it's what I really wanted to do. She was paying for this trip, and we still had a long way to go before heading home, so it would behoove me to keep my cool.

I stood with my back against the door and took a couple of breaths. *'Calm your ass down, Lola.'* I stayed there until my pulse stopped pounding in my ears.

The owner of the rental had kindly supplied laundry baskets, so I gathered the clothes I wanted to wash, trying to decide if they needed to be separated by color, or if I could get away with one big load.

Reaching into the basket to grab a shirt that needed to be turned right side out before washing, my quartz bracelet caught on the handle and stretched so far I thought it would snap and send beads flying. Thank goodness I saw it in time, because I was able to unsnag it before disaster hit my right wrist.

Then it registered what Maddie had just said … look at my left wrist.

The labradorite bracelet. *Inntinn-lobhadh.* Of course.

And just like that, it was like a spell snapped—like an overstretched elastic bracelet.

I dropped the T-shirt and rushed out to the kitchen. "I'm so sorry," I said. "Thank goodness you realized what was happening! I didn't even see it."

She laughed with relief. "Thank goodness I was right!"

"Man, that is some tricky stuff," I sighed. I sat down at the table and doctored my tea. "What was your first clue?"

Maddie thought for a moment and finally said, "Well, at first I was surprised that you didn't want to go to the Abbey, *and* that you were offering some pretty lame excuses, but I thought … maybe she's just travel-weary. It happens."

I nodded, appreciating the compassion in her words.

"What really tipped me off, though," she continued, "was when you started getting mad. That was a bit of an overreaction. And then you got all snippy about having to climb the hill again just to meet …"

She paused for a couple of beats, letting it hang.

"You stopped talking and left the room before you could even say 'the king.'"

My jaw dropped open. "Wow." I took a few seconds to let that sink in. "That's not even subtle. How could I have missed something so obvious?"

"Must've been inching lower," Maddie said with a grin. "Now go start a load of laundry. Time's a wastin' and we have a lot to do today. I want to have lunch at place in town that gets great reviews."

"You're a dear." I stood and impulsively kissed her cheek. "I'll just be a minute."

Before long we were driving into town, past the High Street shops and around the corner at the Market Cross, to the car park just past the entrance to the Abbey. The Abbey itself wasn't visible from the road. It was obscured by several buildings in the way.

The sidewalks were scattered with residents and tourists, and lined with metaphysical shops singing their siren songs. I could justify my purchases so far—they had turned out to be useful tools, not just trinkets—but I would have to be careful not to go off half-cocked with my debit card. One of Chuck's messages from yesterday, once he grew impatient with my lack of response, was: "I hope you're not spending all my money!"

He was lucky I wasn't in the same room with him when I read that, because that was over the line. I was spending my own damned money, and he needed to mind his own beeswax.

Just thinking about his message, I felt myself getting worked up as we walked past a particularly lovely shop. I could easily drop a load of cash in there, but I was choosing not to. It pissed me off that he would treat me like a child and scold me like that.

But then I caught myself. I darted a glance at my left wrist … *'Am I inching lower again?'*

Nope, I was still irritated. Maybe this was genuine anger, not a distraction. It was interesting to see the difference, and I laughed to myself as I forgave Chuck for being a butthead—and for helping me to learn something I needed to know.

Finally, we arrived at Glastonbury Abbey and paid the entrance fee. Stepping out the door from the Visitor Centre, our eyes were met with a massive expanse of ruins dotting a huge green lawn. Where once was one of the largest monastic churches in England now only stood some leftover walls and soaring arches, and the ruins covered almost 40 acres. As with many of the sights on this trip, it took my breath away.

"Did you happen to learn anything about this place in advance?" I asked Maddie, since she usually did before we visited anywhere. "I await words of wisdom from my tour guide with 'bated breath."

"You know what?" she said, somewhat nonplussed, "I didn't!"

"Really?" I laughed. "That's a first!"

She shook her head with wonder. "I know, it really is," she said. "I guess I was busy doing other things. Fortunately, we have our little maps."

Indeed we did, handed to us at the ticket counter, along with our entrance receipts.

"Let's just wander," I suggested. "I'm mostly interested in seeing King Arthur's tomb anyway."

"Now *that*, I did look up," Maddie said as we strolled across the lawn to the first set of ruins, the Lady Chapel. "It turns out that he and Queen Guinevere might not actually be buried here."

"I wondered about that," I said. "I always thought he was mythical, not a real person, so I was surprised to hear that he was buried here, in what is supposed to be Avalon. I mean, is Avalon even real?"

I stopped myself before getting sidetracked down that rabbit hole. "Sorry, I digress. Tell me about Arthur and Guinevere not really being buried here on the grounds."

"Good thinking," Maddie agreed. "Avalon is a conversation for later. Anyway, the graves were 'discovered,'" she said, using finger quotes, "on the grounds after a huge fire nearly destroyed the place, and the Abbey needed money for repairs. Their claims that Arthur and Guinevere were buried here brought a lot of visitors—and their dollars—not to mention royal interest."

She looked at her map to orient herself and pointed up ahead. "That's where they're supposed to be buried."

We walked further up the lawn band found, very plainly planted in the grass, a couple dozen cement steppingstones formed into a rectangle, next to a small section bordered by a row of bricks. In the center stood a very ordinary sign that read, "Site of King Arthur's Tomb."

The sign went on to explain that Arthur and Guinevere were discovered buried elsewhere on the property in 1191 and moved to this spot in 1278, in the presence of the then-current king and queen.

"I expected a little more pomp," I said.

"Maybe their original graves were more ornate," Maddie said, scanning the sign. "This spot is supposedly where they rested until the Abbey's dissolution in 1539."

"So, what happened to the bodies then?" I asked.

"Honestly, I don't know enough about British history to answer that," Maddie said. She glanced at the pamphlet to see if any information could be found there. No joy. She continued, "I do know, from what I could gather online, that the Dissolution happened when Henry VIII declared himself head of the Church. After having the abbot here executed for refusing to cooperate, he had the place torn apart. He might have considered Arthur's bones religious relics of the system he was dismantling. If there were any bones, they were probably scattered."

"Oh, that's messed up," I said.

"Yeah, it is," Maddie said. "We'll never know what happened. It's lost to history."

I let my eyes wander across the structures rising skyward around us. The ruins of the former abbey were breathtaking. The stone walls were several feet thick and the remaining arched doorways gave a sense of how enormous this building must have been. I wished that my sometimes-overpowering psychic abilities would let me glimpse into the past to see what it looked like when the walls and ceiling were intact.

Plopping down on the grass next to the maybe-tomb of Arthur and Guinevere, I waved Maddie down to join me there. "Let's get back to the question of Avalon. Do you think it's real? I mean, King Arthur and Camelot may very well be mythical. I've read that much of the land around where we're sitting used to be under water and the Tor, that massive hill, was once an island where the Fae were rumored to live."

"I've read the same," Maddie said, "and that St. Michael's Tower was part of a full church. They used to build churches—especially those dedicated to St. Michael—on top of sites that had long been considered pagan to …

overwrite the energy. It is interesting, most of that church was destroyed in an earthquake and all that's left is the tower."

I pulled a piece of grass and chewed on it. "Hmm," I said. "There's no doubt about the Fae presence. We've already witnessed that."

"You said a mouthful!" Maddie said. "Speaking of mouthfuls, what are you doing? Eating grass?"

"One would think you didn't grow up in Ohio," I replied. "Have you never chewed on grass before? Look …" I said, pulling up another piece and exposing the soft, white inner sprout near the root. "It's kinda sweet. Next, you'll tell me you never sucked on a lilac."

She rolled her eyes and laughed. "Whatever you say, Miss Thing."

We sat quietly for a minute or two, breathing the fresh air and enjoying the silence, until it hit me.

"Hey …" I said. "I forgot about this. Remember when we were in Tavistock and I had what I thought was a panic attack and heard that flow of paired phrases?"

"Of course."

"Remember that there was one set that wasn't paired?"

"Not really," Maddie said.

"There was 'As above/So below,' 'Masculine/Feminine,' 'We are One/the King awaits' …" I recited them in a singsong cadence … da da da / da da da.

"Right, I remember," she said. "And they came up yesterday, on the hill."

"Yeah," I said, "but there was one phrase that didn't have a pairing, that hasn't come up yet. Remember? 'The ties that bind …'" I said this last in its own cadence: da dum da dum. "Doesn't that sound familiar? Like it's a line from a poem or well-known expression, like the second half should easily roll off the tongue?"

Maddie repeated it. "The ties that bind … da dum da dum … it does sound familiar."

"Yes, like a lyric or saying I've heard before," I said, squeezing my eyes shut as I tried to force my brain to cough up the rest of the line.

"The ties that bind," Maddie mused, "the claws that catch." She laughed like it was nothing.

"What? Ew!" My eyes were wide as I stared at her in horror.

Maddie chuckled again and waved dismissively. "It's from Lewis Carroll's poem, *Jabberwocky*. I know it by heart. That's not really the second half of your phrase. It just fits the cadence … da dum da dum, da dum da dum … the jaws that bite, the claws that catch."

"Well, let's *hope* that's not the second half of the phrase," I insisted. "Seren was just saying yesterday that *Inntinn-lobhadh* waits for me to be tasty before it bites."

"Ew." Maddie recoiled.

"Right?"

Both deep in thought, we sat in silence … pensive … until I broke the hush with a question.

"How on earth do you know Jabberwocky by heart?"

Maddie burst into giggles. "Oh, you're going to love this." She paused dramatically, eyeing my level of anticipation for the right moment to finally begin.

"Well, as you know, I used to perform in drag shows. My former life, but some of the most fun I've ever had. I was rather notorious for my bang-on impressions of Bette Midler and Cher."

"Ha!" I leaned in, all ears. "You have to show me sometime."

"We'll see." She winked. "Anyway, I was performing at a club, a little shithole in Wooster with no advertising budget, so there was no audience when I got there. Completely empty. Just the bartender and the owner, and a couple of servers. One of them was sitting in the back of the room, reading a book. *Alice in Wonderland.*"

Another dramatic pause later, Maddie continued. "So, this cretinous little club owner demanded that the other performers and I put on a show anyway. After all, he had to pay us one way or another, so we were gonna put in our time on stage."

Her eyes twinkled as she launched into the next part of her story. "He didn't say what kind of show we had to put on, so I borrowed the server's book and read *Jabberwocky* over and over for twenty minutes, dressed as Cher, fulfilling my contractual obligation for stage time."

She grinned, and I laughed long and hard. "I can totally see you doing that," I finally said, still giggling.

"You shoulda seen me," she vamped, snapping her fingers, "Twas brillig, and the slithy toves … HO!" She tossed her hair, Cher-mode on.

We burst into hoots of laughter again, appreciating the moment as joy settled, chuckling until we finally relaxed into smiles, then once again enjoyed the silence.

Gazing at the spectacular display of history around us, I wondered why we were drawn to come to the Abbey. The ruins were amazing, no doubt about it. I was glad Maddie pushed me through inching lower that morning. Otherwise, I never would have seen them, with their awe-inspiring historical significance.

But what was the point of being here? Surely there must be a reason … something to do with the deeper reality of Avalon.

Then it hit me.

"Oh! I get it …" I said, startling Maddie out of her reverie.

"Yes?"

"We were … er, I was … wondering if Avalon is real but it just sank in—Avalon is as real as you make it."

"Go on," she said.

"Okay, plenty of people visit Glastonbury for the kitsch, and plenty come as witchy folk. But I've noticed people here just blend in with the vibe. You know? They belong here. They're not poseurs. We noticed the same thing in Avebury."

"You mean they're not Cone Lickers?" Maddie said, invoking the name we locals in Chagrin Falls affectionately call tourists who visit our town for an ice cream at the Popcorn Shop. "I did notice that, now that you mention it. Up on the Tor, those people were tuned in. There wasn't any performative phoniness."

"Nope, not at all," I agreed. "Not even the guy singing *Breathe* inside the tower. He wasn't showing off, he was there exactly when he was supposed to be, doing exactly what he was supposed to do. I can still 'see' the ripples his voice created in the air. Look," I said, holding up my arm and pulling back my sleeve, "I have goosebumps just thinking about it."

I closed my eyes and felt into the moment, my butt planted on the grass next to where one mythic king was supposed to have been laid to rest, knowing another king was waiting for me inside that giant hill across town.

An inner nudge told me to cross my hands, one over another, to grasp both wrists. With one bracelet in each hand, the left wrist in the right and the right wrist in the left, a circuit was completed. Light then streamed up into my tailbone from the ground beneath me, up into my shoulders and down each arm.

The flow circled and met again at my spine, then shot up into my head and out the top. As if being dispersed by a round sprinkler, that light fell all around me to the ground, where it was then pulled back up into my tailbone. I looked like a glowing donut, with my spinal column as the donut hole.

"*Remember this,*" I heard Seren say.

As quickly as the moment began, it ended and I opened my eyes to see Maddie watching me, smiling.

"I'm getting better at this," she said. "Either that, or this place is rubbing off on me. I could actually see your aura light up and all sorts of energy moving around in there."

"That's so freakin' cool," I said. "Now, if you've had your fill of medieval ruins, I'd love to have my fill of fish and chips. Grass is only so filling, you know."

THIRTEEN

Maddie was right when she said English fish and chips beat the Yankee version, hands down. The place we visited after the Abbey was just as good as, if not better than, the pub where we ate the first night here.

It did rest a bit heavy in my stomach, though, as I sat cross-legged on my bed that afternoon, gathering my thoughts before the big event of the day. I was scared, and it wasn't just *Inntinn-lobhadh*. This was legitimate fear.

What had I gotten myself into? I was about to climb one of the most famously magical hills on earth, during a live eclipse, on the equinox, on the other side of the world from home, to meet the King of the Fae.

And, possibly, the claws that catch.

Who did I think I was? I'm just Lola Garnett from Chagrin Falls, Ohio, who gives helpful little psychic readings in a cutesy little tourist shop.

Sure, I've battled a vicious arsonist who used black magic to try to destroy my family. Then she whacked me in the head with a real-world 2x4, putting me in the hospital—and that was only halfway through that adventure.

And yes, I've visited a Faery Queen at her waterfall, and now have four faery sidekicks, if you count Myx and Maj who recently showed up again.

True, Maddie and I helped Seth—my little sister from a past life, who was trapped on that side of the veil—to get back to the human world, where he now thrived as Maddie's shop manager.

So, no … maybe I wasn't just little old Lola from Ohio.

But this was different.

It almost felt like those events, while huge at the time, were like reading a cozy mystery novel in comparison. When Maddie called us "girl detectives," it's because those events carried a fun and adventurous vibe.

What I was about to do here felt more foundational, like I was going to come out the other side a completely different person. It reminded me of what Paul McCartney once said about hesitating when the rest of The Beatles took LSD, something along the lines of "I'd heard you would never be the same again and I wasn't sure that was such a terrific idea."

Maybe I shouldn't rock the boat. I was already doubting my marriage, and I hadn't missed Chuck at all while on this trip. I was in no hurry to go home, aside from Amanda needing her mom. After all, I was with my best friend, having an interesting time, eating new foods, buying sparkly crystals … and next I was about to embark on a journey that might just snap any attachment I have to going back to Ohio.

I glanced at my left wrist. Nope, I was not inching lower. This was a legit concern. The fear shivers were real.

Reaching into my bag of mental tools, I pulled out the old standby: bring myself back to center and connect with my heart. I took several long, deep breaths, exhaling longer than the inhale to activate the vagus nerve and release anxiety.

Usually that would be enough, but something nudged me to take it further. I felt Seren's presence, bringing the memory of my glowing donut to mind.

Breathing in through my nose and out through my mouth, I sat tall, spine straight, legs in lotus position, and crossed my hands to grab my wrists as I had at Arthur's Tomb. As soon as that physical contact clicked into place, the connection lit up the donut. It had already been there—I realized now that it always was—but now it was clairvoyantly visible, so I was conscious of it. Somehow that contact ramped up its power.

'*This is fun. I could do this all day,*' I thought, as I felt myself levitating off the bed. Did my physical body actually leave the duvet? I doubt it. But my etheric body certainly did.

As I floated, I instructed the glowing donut: stay lit until I say otherwise—no inching lower. With that psychic guidepost locked in, I let myself go.

The first place I drifted was into a cloud of intense gratitude for even learning about *Inntinn-lobhadh*. Then I laughed aloud. If this was what "never being the same again" felt like, then Paul McCartney and I had nothing to worry about.

That train of thought was followed by more gratitude, this time for my path being led here in Glastonbury—apparently by Twink, et al—into the various shops for my 'power tools' and to the locations where epiphanies could land.

In this expanded state, where everything felt exactly right, there was no question that I was precisely where I was supposed to be. Not as a cliché or a platitude, but as a complete lack of resistance.

I drifted lazily in vibes of contentment, feeling yummy overall. No question at all.

I guess I shouldn't have been surprised that focusing on the very idea of no questions would go ahead and produce one. Now I was faced with the visual of a big ol' pink question mark a few yards in front of me, floating before my eyes.

I chuckled. '*Go figure.*'

The question mark was about four feet high and shimmery, as if covered in sequins, and surrounded by puffy, baby blue clouds. As pretty as it was, a random question mark wasn't all that helpful. I still had to wonder: '*What's the question?*'

There were too many to choose from, so I started with the most pressing:

What's up with this weird story that my life has become?

What is this all leading up to?

Why me?

My first thought was a sarcastic quip—'*Why not you?*'—and I tucked that away. Valid question. Why not any of us? But that wasn't the $64,000 Question. Since I couldn't come up with anything more specific, I fell back on the old standby:

What do I need to know?

As if on cue, my field of clairvoyant vision was filled with a panoramic view of all that Maddie and I had done since we arrived, sort of a mini-life review showing me all the loose threads of what we'd said and done since we left London and our metaphysical adventure began.

Now, those loose threads were woven into place in the tapestry of my life, before my eyes, showing me they were never loose to begin with. I just hadn't seen yet where they would be woven in.

My presence there, at this exact place and time, was just as it should be—just as it had been planned before I was even born. I couldn't see the full shape of it yet. The whys and wherefores were still out of reach.

What was about to happen might not be pleasant. It might not be easy. But it was inevitable.

This is where *Inntinn-lobhadh* would normally take a bite, but I felt not even a flicker of fear. Here, I was held. I was safe.

While in Big Picture mode, I was shown that Maddie, Seth and Raven … Twink, Pea, Myx, Maj … even Jennett and Celesta … had all entered my life at exactly the right time, as if on cue. It had all been prearranged by soul contract, agreed to before any of us were born.

The most surprising was Melinda—that bitch from across the street who, for a while, made it her life's mission to try to take me down.

"Yeh can still hate her," I heard Twink say. *"She's a mare. But at least recognize that the two of yeh agreed to play these roles."*

I laughed, appreciating Twink's permission to carry on with my very human disdain for that creature. What she had done wasn't an easy forgive-and-forget scenario.

Allowing myself this bit of grace let me see what Twink was pointing out. Yes, Melinda had played an important and necessary role in my life. It was no accident that I happened to fall asleep while she was across the street fooling with powers she didn't understand. It was an agreed-upon point in both of our timelines.

I was *supposed* to wake up with out-of-control psychic abilities. I was *supposed* to be so desperate for help that I cried out for it. And Twink … she and I were *supposed* to be matched up like this, even if she didn't like it much, either.

And yes, Chuck was supposed to be there also, to ground me and keep me from going too far into the world of woo. This dynamic made for some aggravating arguments, but I could see now that his skepticism was actually helpful. It forced me into frequent reality checks. With him in the picture, I was in very little danger of falling down any conspiracy theory rabbit holes.

I had to wonder, though, how he was going to keep me down on the farm after I'd seen Paree.

And, more importantly … did I even want to be kept?

That question pulled my floating, glowing donut back down to rest on the bed. I felt the duvet beneath me, and one of my feet had fallen asleep—not the pleasant, tingly kind, but the full pins-and-needles assault.

The stinging pain was too distracting to tune back in, so I released my donut's instruction to stay lit. I stood and shook it off, stomping on my sleeping foot.

Just as well that I was brought back down to earth. It was time to head back up the hill. The eclipse was set to begin soon, and I wanted to get there in time to secure a good spot. I had no idea how many … if any … other people would be there. After all, the weather conditions weren't ideal; it was getting a little chilly as spotty, afternoon clouds had rolled in. Plus, because it was afternoon, the sun wasn't as high and warm.

Fortunately, the eclipse would end before the sun set, so we wouldn't be climbing back down in the dark, but even so it wouldn't be as sunny and idyllic as it had been yesterday.

All these conditions could mean that your average tourist probably wouldn't be up there, only the die-hards. Come to think of it, though, the die-hards were probably already there, staking out the best places to sit. The chances of having the tower to ourselves were slim to none.

Then I heard Precious Pea's voice, *"It doesn't matter where yeh sit. You could even visit the King from where yeh are now … heck, yeh coulda done it from yer living room sofa back home … but anywhere atop the Tor is good enough."*

"Wait," I said, "if I could have done this from home, then why jump through all these hoops?"

"If yeh're going to nitpick," I heard, *"aye, yeh could journey under the Hill from yehr home, but yeh needed to walk the path yeh've taken these past few days."*

That made sense, so I let it go. It was going to be what it was going to be.

I stuffed my backpack full of everything I'd gathered over the past few days … crystals, spring water, clary sage oil, Maddie's book—still unread—

and put my shoes on. I grabbed my hoodie and headed out to knock on Maddie's door to let her know I was ready.

If only I was.

FOURTEEN

Unlike our first trip up the Tor when we climbed alone, this time we encountered several people making their way up the twisting path on the back side of the hill. As I had feared, we would not have the place to ourselves. Not only that, but many of them carried drums.

The closer we got to the top, the more apparent it became that a full-blown drumming circle was gearing up.

"Oh no," I moaned to Maddie. "How am I going to concentrate with all this brouhaha?"

She shook her head and said, "I don't know. This could be a real challenge. Do you think this is a distraction created by *Inntinn-lobhadh*?"

"Oh, I hadn't thought of that," I admitted. "I don't know enough about how it works. I thought it just messes with my head, not that it can gather a couple dozen people to bang stuff together."

"I know less about it than you," Maddie said. "But even if it can't create a drum circle, it sounds like it can skew your reaction to it."

I nodded, wondering.

"Either way, too late now to even ask," she said, gesturing behind us at how much hill we had already climbed. We were almost all the way to the tower, and we could now see even more people climbing up the paved steps on the other side of the hill.

"Well," I sighed, "it's gonna be what it's gonna be. Might as well stake out a spot."

The tower was surrounded by a ring of people, some wearing festive garb with flowers in their long hair, lots of tie-dye and jeans, most carrying some sort of percussion instrument. Inside the tower were several women. I couldn't see what they were doing, but they were gathered around something on the ground in the very center of the stone structure.

"Looks like we're interrupting something," Maddie said, eyebrows raised.

"Of course, you're not!" cried a young man who overheard. "All are welcome. Join us! We can even find an extra drum, if you'd like."

"Thanks, no," I said, my eyes scanning the crowd. "We're here to do something else."

He nodded, smiled, and said, "As you wish," before bowing and stepping back into the crowd.

"Maddie!" I gasped, pointing to the far side of the hill by the directional marker, "Look … it's him. The wizard!" I'd seen him too many times now for it to feel accidental.

Maddie's jaw dropped when she saw that, sure enough, there he was with the same woman we'd seen him with both times before. They were talking to the Yorkshire couple from whom I'd bought the bracelets. That young woman caught my eye and waved, offering a broad smile. She said something to her friends, then crossed the hill to join us.

"So good to see you again," she said, giving me a big hug, a warm and welcoming embrace, and I returned it. "Are you joining the drum circle?"

"No, I'm here to do sort of a shamanic journey," I explained, for lack of a better way to describe why I was there. "We're just looking for a good spot to stay out of the way."

"Oh, that's lovely," she said. "We'll be over on that side of the tower, where there's a bit more flat land, so this side will be perfect for you. And the drumming'll fit right in!"

"She's right, you know," Maddie said. "That drumming might have been 'planned' by someone in the other realms, but not for inching lower." She used finger quotes on "planned" and gave me a wink on "inching lower."

"Ha," I laughed. "Maybe you're right."

I said to the young woman, "Who were you talking to over there, the guy dressed like a wizard? I've seen him a few times already. That feels like more than a coincidence."

She winked. "There are no coincidences, you know. That's our friend Gareth, the one we're staying with here in town who I mentioned the other day. He's leading the drum circle, and his wife is performing an equinox/eclipse ceremony. It's quite an auspicious cosmic event. You're here at a perfect time."

One of her friends called her name, but I was unable to hear what they said. She turned and raised a just-a-minute finger to them and said to me, "I'd better get back. See you after?"

"Of course," I said. She blew an air kiss to both me and Maddie, then returned to her group.

Maddie and I scoped out the side of the hill facing Glastonbury, the side of the tower away from the revelers, for the best place to park our carcasses. "How about right here?" Maddie asked, pointing to a spot on the other side of the walkway where I lay just yesterday, soaking in the sun and the sparkly vibes. "You can see the town from here, and the Abbey is in that direction. That way we're right between the two ruins."

That made so much sense. As she spoke, I clairvoyantly 'saw' the truth in her words. If I sat here on the hill, there could be a straight connection to me … through me … from Arthur's Tomb at the Abbey, down into the Tor and what I assumed was the realm of Gwyn ap Nudd.

As I focused on this inner vision, I felt the line of connection shifting— arching up from the Abbey, passing through me, then curving down into the hill. It continued beneath the earth, completing a glowing circle before rising again toward the Abbey.

As above, so below. I felt these words ringing in my ears.

Before I could sit, though, Maddie pulled a rolled afghan from her voluminous bag. "Snagged this from the living room couch," she said, "just in case the ground is cold. We may be sitting here a while." She unfurled it with a flick of her wrists and spread it out on the grass.

"Good thinking. Thank you." I plopped myself down, leaving room for her, with my back to the tower and the drum circle, facing out over Glastonbury. Maddie sat beside me as I unpacked my bag. I had no idea what

I might need—after all, I had no clue what I would be doing—so I laid everything out next to me.

"Hand me the book, would you?" she said, reaching for her paperback. "I don't know what you have planned, but I thought I might just sit here and read ... keep an eye on you, kind of like an ayahuasca guardian."

Heaving a sigh of relief, I handed her the book and said, "I'd appreciate that. I don't know if any of the faeries will be here, so it's good of you to offer."

Maddie's eyes darted around above me, clearly seeing something I wasn't. "I think you spoke too soon," she said, pointing. "I think they're here."

"Really?" I asked. "Why don't I see them?"

As I spoke, four of them popped into view, Twink, Pea, Myx, and Maj. "Told yeh yeh'd need us," one of the twins said, a wink implied in her tone.

I still couldn't tell them apart, particularly when they were in miniature mode. Not only did they look alike, they inherently presented a chameleon-like quality, making them hard to see. This they shared with Olfen, the wizard I had met when Seth was trapped in Jennett's realm. They didn't so much change color as much as they just ... blended in. Hard to explain.

"Why didn't I see you, but Maddie did?"

"Dunno why *you* din't," said the other twin, more matter-of-fact, "but she couldn't help seeing us, in this liminal space at this magical time."

"Can they see you?" Maddie asked, indicating the drummers behind the tower.

"Dunno," the first twin said, with a shrug.

Pea interjected, "They can't. After all, yeh've both already seen us before, so yeh know to look. They're not even looking this way."

"Even so," Twink finally spoke, "we're here to stand guard. We're making a ring around yeh so yeh can concentrate without fuss. Yeh don't want to bung this up."

"Hey," I said, "that doesn't help. I'm already nervous enough."

Although Twink was also in mini-mode, I could see the smirk ... it changed her entire demeanor.

"So, what am I supposed to do?" I asked. "As usual, I'm not being given an instruction manual."

"How should I know?" Twink shrugged. "I'm just a brat, remember?"

"Ye gods!" Pea cried, stomping her tiny foot in the air. "Would yeh stop? This is important. Mum would skelp yeh if she saw …"

Seren then faded into view, full-sized, and Maddie gasped. This was her first time seeing this faery and she could barely contain her awe. Seren was, indeed, exquisite in her opalescent garb.

"You're correct, sister," Seren said to Pea, "Mother wouldn't like for Aethelwyne to act up at a time like this." She shot Twink a look, and I felt sorry for my little friend … then I remembered how much Twink HATES pity, so I stopped immediately before she caught me.

"Wait," I asked, "you're sisters?"

Twink was too busy fuming to respond.

"Aye," said Pea. "Celesta is our mum, and Auntie Jennett is Mum's sister. Our father is in Jennett's realm and that's why we mostly live there, in her service. Seren has a different father, so she stays here in service with Mum."

Too dense to follow along, I asked Seren, "Why would having a different father mean you would stay here? Who is your father?"

Seren offered an enigmatic smile and said, "You're about to meet him. Are you ready?"

FIFTEEN

Ready or not, here I come! And really, did I have a choice at this point?

I mean, of course I had a choice. I could say "screw this" and go back down the hill, pack my suitcase and get on the plane home without ever finding out what would happen if I went ahead with this crazy idea of visiting the King of the Fae under the hill upon which I currently sat. But the momentum was too strong.

So, I gave Seren a nod and asked, "What now?"

"You've already discovered the way to communicate with Celesta, using your quartz ball," she said, pointing at the crystal sphere that lay beside me on the afghan. "Might I suggest using your other stone the same way?"

"Which one?" I asked. I had two labradorite stones, the sphere and the UFO-shaped one. I even had the bracelet on my left wrist.

"I don't suppose it matters," she replied. "Whichever feels appropriate. Of course, you realize that you don't actually *need* any of them, yes?"

I picked up both stones, one in each hand, and felt into each one. I said, "I know I don't *need* them, but training wheels are nice when you're learning to balance."

Seren wrinkled her brow, puzzled. I realized my metaphor might only make sense to humans.

"Sorry," I said. "I meant that tools can be useful while one learns how to do without them."

"Ah," she nodded. "In that case, I don't see a need for any of your other tools." She gestured at the collection I had brought just in case.

"Simply follow the same method you used when you discovered Queen Celesta, but focus your attention downward. As you know, my father resides below this hill in Annwn, the Otherworld, not above like my mother."

"Can I ask," I interrupted, "something that has been vexing me?"

"Certainly," Seren replied while Maddie gazed wide-eyed, watching our conversation.

"How can he live under the hill?" I asked. "How can he breathe? How can he move around?"

The faery thought for a moment then finally said, "Do you think Queen Jennett actually lives in a hole behind a waterfall?"

It all made perfect sense now. Of course, Jennett didn't live inside a hole beneath a watery outcrop. That hole was a portal. When I visited her realm, I sometimes traveled psychically through it, and on the other side was a whole 'nother reality.

"Got it. Let me ask, then," I continued, "what I'm looking for so I know when I'm there."

Seren's eyes grew dreamy and she sighed wistfully. "Annwn is so beautiful," she said, "so green … so alive. If you listen properly, you can hear the grass singing."

"Really?" I asked, stunned to the point of rudely interrupting. "I'm sorry, but I expected it to be caves or tunnels."

"Oh, aye," Seren said, unfazed by my interjection, "there be tunnels and caves, but no more than here in the middle world."

So swept away by our discussion, I had almost forgotten that Maddie sat next to me until she asked the faery, "Will she be safe?"

"I will accompany her," Seren replied.

"That's not what I asked," Maddie said.

The terror struck then, harder than ever before. A shard of pain stabbed me in the gut. I had to find a bathroom *right now* or we would all be sorry. There were no toilets up here. The closest one was either back in our cottage or down the other side of the hill at the Chalice Garden.

I doubled over, holding my lower abdomen in both hands, and tried to control my breathing. The fear surged and my gut hurt so badly that I began to hyperventilate.

"Ow," I wailed. "It's the claws that catch!"

"Lola!" Maddie cried, grabbing my upper arm. "My god, are you okay?"

"No," I moaned. "This really hurts. I have to find a bathroom."

"Oh no," Maddie said. "I hope the fish and chips for lunch wasn't too heavy."

"That's not it," I groaned through gritted teeth. "This feels different."

Maddie scanned the hilltop and below for the nearest facility and saw none. She pleaded with Seren, "Is there anything you can do to help?"

Seren took a step forward and placed the palm of her tiny hand on my forehead, her fingers in my hair. She hummed a low tone and I felt buzzing throughout my entire body. As she continued to hum, my agony faded. Finally, the pain was gone and I could breathe again.

"What have we learned?" she asked.

"That she's not safe?" Maddie insisted.

The pain began building once more at Maddie's words and I grimaced, gritting my teeth again, fighting against being taken over … again.

"Lola Garnett," Seren said, "I want you to stop the pain yourself this time. But first, look at your left wrist."

Gasping for air, I followed her instructions and glanced down at the bracelet I wore. Just like that, the pain stopped.

"Holy cow!" I cried. "Was all that just *Inntinn-lobhadh*?"

"You tell me," the faery replied.

I caught Maddie's eye and we stared at one another in disbelief.

"How does it do that?" I asked. "More importantly, *why* does it do that? It's as if it wants to stop me from meeting your father."

"You've answered your own question," she smiled. "As far as *how* it does that, it finds your weaknesses and amplifies them. With another person, their symptoms would be what most cripples them."

I heaved a sigh of relief and asked what I hoped would be my final question so I could get this over with. "Why does *Inntinn-lobhadh* want to stop me from visiting Gwyn ap Nudd?"

She laughed lightly and said, "I believe you'll discover that along the way. Now, shall we?"

"About time," Twink muttered, and Seren glared at her, silencing her younger sister … or was Twink older? I couldn't tell.

"Let me get comfortable," I said, tugging my sweater closer over my T-shirt. I lay back on the grass, like the day before when I first met Celesta, with the afghan and my sweatshirt beneath my back to keep the cold from seeping into my bones. It was, after all, the first day of autumn. The eclipse was already in progress, so the moon would soon cover the sun. The temperature would dip as it got darker.

The drummers in the circle were just beginning to tap on their instruments, finding a common beat. "Excellent timing," Maddie said.

I nodded and grinned at her before closing my eyes. Gripping both labradorite stones, one in each hand—I had decided to use both because, why not? —I crossed my braceleted wrists over my chest, holding the stones over my heart and taking some intentional breaths.

The drumming was distracting, at first. I always used a monotonous, steady beat for shamanic journeying. That's the way I learned it from Glenna. But she had also taught that we could use external, disruptive sounds as tools, instead of fighting their existence: every noise you hear takes you deeper.

So, I tuned in to the beat the drummers had fallen into. Much more musical and rhythmic than I was used to, riding the waves of their tempo took me to another place … somewhere I had never been.

I felt myself sinking into the Tor, glad I had asked Seren what to expect. Otherwise, *Inntinn-lobhadh* might have used the fear of literally "inching lower" into being buried alive. It would have stopped my consciousness from sinking into what I would have assumed was just dirt.

It wasn't dirt … I mean, it was at first, but I was oddly okay with that. As I let go of my preconceived notions, it was like drifting downward through sand, and then the sand gave way to fine powder and finally a light fog. At length—with the drumbeats still in my ears but distant now —my back gently touched down onto the earth that was now beneath me.

I opened my etheric eyes and sat up. What Seren had called Annwn was, indeed, breathtaking.

Funny, though, it was just a meadow, with a line of trees off to one side in the distance, a row of mountains off to another side. The distance from here to there seemed to shift, as if the features on the horizon were moving.

It wasn't the scenery that took my breath away though, it was the quality of the light, the fresh, springlike fragrance in the air, and the brightness of the colors.

I'd heard people describe Near Death Experiences, saying they witnessed colors that didn't exist in the "real world." It was exactly like that, only completely different.

The light here wasn't white, sparkling, and coming from above as it was in Celesta's realm. Here it was bright and glowing, but more an extension of the greenness around me, as if my eyes were filled with tears and I was viewing the landscape through a curtain of water and inner light.

I couldn't see the sky. There was no blue up above. There was no … anything, as if my eyes simply stopped working when I looked upward, as if my peripheral vision ended at the edge of the sky, even though I was directly facing what I was trying to see. I wish I had the words to explain. I could describe it as like a migraine aura … not the sparkling visual disturbances but the blank spot they leave behind. There's just … nothing to see.

Somewhere far off, the rhythm of the drumming switched as the revelers evolved their tempo to match the next phase of the eclipse. I was barely aware of them and their purpose, but the sound did bring the eclipse to mind—enough so that it made me wonder if the shifting of the sun and the moon was causing the otherworldly lighting.

But then the word "otherworldly" caught my attention and the question answered itself.

With the new drumming pattern, the landscape shimmered and shifted a bit and I saw—about a quarter mile before me, if distance meant anything here—ripples in the air, as if someone had thrown a stone into a vertical pond. The ripples continued outward and then faded at the edges, but at the center the ripples vanished to expose another layer of reality behind them.

The opening grew and expanded until eventually the curtain of … whatever was there before … vanished and a new scene lay before me. Same meadow, same horizon, except now there was a stone circle similar to Avebury, but nowhere near as large.

Directly in front of me, yet some distance away, was a massive diamond-shaped stone, maybe ten feet high and twelve feet wide, the corners of which pointed upward and to either side, with the bottom corner buried in the earth. In front of it stood what I could only call a man, although he was not a human male. Like the rest of my surroundings, he was difficult to focus on and see clearly, but parts of his form were becoming visible.

Then Seren was at my side. I hadn't noticed her absence until now. She had promised to accompany me and I had forgotten.

"Where were you?" I asked, a little concerned.

"I've been here the entire time," she replied. "You simply needed to adjust your perception. Can you see Aethelwyne and the others? They are here as well."

"No," I said, looking around. They, too, had promised to stand guard around me. I allowed my gaze to soften as if I was trying to see the hidden shape in a Magic Eye 3D image.

I was soon able to see them—as if a fogged surface had just been wiped clean, revealing them in a circle around me. They stood in their full sizes facing outward at the world surrounding my physical body, which lay on the Tor with Maddie sitting beside it, her brows furrowed with concern.

"Okay, there's Twink," I said. "I can see them now."

Well, apparently Twink could hear me because her reaction instantly reminded me of her stern warning to not call her by that nickname in front of her family. She stiffened her posture and scowled, narrowing her eyes into slits, while Myx and Maj burst into disrespectful giggles.

"Twink?" Seren asked.

"Never mind," I quickly said. "Let's focus on where we are now."

"As you wish," she grinned, her ethereal face lit with glee. "Father awaits, yonder."

Seren strode across what seemed like a great distance in the blink of an eye, taking me with her. Before I knew it, we were facing the King of the Fae.

Now that we were up close, I could see his face clearly, no longer through a fog or filter. Seren resembled her father more than her mother Celesta. They had the same firmly set nose and chin, although his graying auburn hair was much darker than hers. The female faeries I had met came up to my chest, but Gwyn ap Nudd was my height—I was short, as humans go.

His face was about the only thing I could clearly see, though. As with the sky, his physical form was difficult to focus on, no matter how I tried. Like Celesta and Seren, his garb—a long-sleeved tunic, leather breeches, and tall boots—appeared to be woven with jewels, and his jewel was emerald. Like Annwn itself, he radiated the essence of *green*. If I'd had the time to think about it, I might have wondered if the luminous green of Annwn originated within him, or vice versa.

I hadn't even thought to ask Seren what I was supposed to do once I was here. How do I address him? Should I use an honorific like Your Majesty? Your Highness? O' Ye Great and Powerful One? With no better option I stayed silent, allowing the two faeries to lead the conversation.

"Hello Father," Seren said, standing on her toes to kiss his cheek.

His eyes crinkled and he pulled her into a quick one-armed embrace before releasing her. "And who do we have here?" he asked her, his voice deep and melodious.

His accent was different from the faeries I had met so far. Most had a Yorkshire lilt. I hadn't spent enough time in the United Kingdom to pinpoint it, but I took a guess … Welsh? Was that a Welsh accent? That would make sense, given the spelling and pronunciation of his name.

"This human is Lola Garnett, the one you called for," explained Seren.

"Did I?" His brow furrowed. "Remind me, child."

His demeanor reminded me of Olfen, the wizard who shared the northern realm with Jennett and had been instrumental in rescuing Seth. Olfen was more grandfatherly and loving, but otherwise similar. They both seemed distracted—as if small matters held little interest for someone with greater affairs to attend.

"She's the one my half-sisters have been watching over," Seren explained. "Aethelwyne and Precious Pea, daughters of Brannoc. This is the human who was swept into the vortex by accident—her buffer was partially stripped away, exposing her to more than she was ready for."

"I see!" he said, eyebrows raised. "Yes, I do recall this now. She and I need to have a word. Thank you, daughter."

'Oh shit,' I thought. '*He knows about me? He called for me?*'

My blood ran cold with panic until I realized it was *Inntinn-lobhadh,* having a field day. I bit my lip, took a deep breath, and steadied myself by planting my feet firmly on the bright green grass.

The King examined my face intently and finally said, "Fear not, my dear, you haven't been called on the carpet."

After I sighed in relief, he continued. "I became aware of you at the time of the vortex incident and I have been updated on your progress, now and then. My dearest Celesta commissioned and dispatched an assistant to you after you wisely requested help. It was she who assigned her ... spirited, I suppose is a good word ... daughter, Aethelwyne, to come to your aid."

Seren giggled and said, "This one calls her 'Twink' ... hee hee ..."

Gwyn ap Nudd burst into a broad grin and declared, "Well, I'll wager that this does not please wee Aethelwyne!"

I sank my face into my hands and shook my head with remorse. "Please don't tease her about that slip of the tongue. She will be so, so angry with me."

"Your secret is safe," the King said. "One doesn't want to anger ... 'Twink' ... does one?"

'She hears us! Can we get on with this?' I thought, not daring to ask it aloud as I lifted my head to face him.

He must have read my expression ... or my thoughts ... because he said, "Aye, let us move on."

I would have thanked him, but he now meant business. He locked eyes with me and continued. "You may have believed, when you ripped into the fabric of the veil, that it was only eventful for you, but we felt the disturbance and repercussions here as well."

"Oh!" I said, "I had no idea! In fact, I've never understood, really, what happened that day. I didn't mean to rip anything. I was just taking a nap! Could you ... *would* you ... tell me what you know?"

"Of course," he said, his tone a bit softer now. "You deserve to know. I must say, I've never seen aught like it in all my time. This is a bit of a tale, though, so let us sit."

At his words, the entire scene around us shifted and we were comfortably seated in a huge, high-ceilinged room that appeared to be built into a living forest. Its ivy-covered walls were pillared with massive tree trunks, their canopies forming the ceiling. A small stream of water ran through a channel carved into the stone floor, narrow enough to step across easily, adding to the chamber's living ambience.

He steepled his fingers and thought for a moment, before finally saying, "The veil between our world and yours is thinning, as you may know."

I nodded and said, "I've heard rumors to that effect. The metaphysical community in the human world is all abuzz, but I don't really know what that means, if I'm honest."

"Oh aye, do be honest," he said. "Being plainspoken is vitally important, given the work we're to do today."

The work we're to do today.

That phrase gave me pause—and a brief flare-up of *Inntinn-lobhadh*. I glanced at my left wrist to chase it away.

The King continued. "So far, you are the first living human to burst through. I am not including those who die and reincarnate, as your Afterlife is not the land of the Fae. Others, with their spiritual practices, do make their presences known here by sometimes creating substantial dents in the veil. The only breakthrough similar to yours was that young man, Seth, who you came to know. His situation, however, involved magical interference and intervention by someone native to our world ... the one you call 'Twink.'"

I nodded and hid a grimace. He was no longer joshing.

"That these events happened at all was cause for concern," he said. "Or, at the very least, our attention. We cannot prevent the veil from thinning. It is not our task to do so. It is our task, however, to observe and minimize the damage. Not just our task, but our right."

I didn't like the way this was heading.

"Whether it pleases us or not," the King said, gaining momentum, "the veil *is* thinning, and time is at hand. We are past the tipping point, or you and that young man could never have entered our realm."

Gwyn ap Nudd stopped speaking and watched my face for any reactions or signs of confusion. Seeing no reason to explain further, he went on.

"You are an anomaly," he said. "Ponder this for a moment ..."

When he spoke again, his voice thrummed: "You have the attention of the King of the Fae."

The force of his words took my breath away.

He sat forward, elbows on his knees, and held my gaze before continuing in a softer tone, "This is not to say you are special or a 'chosen one.' It means you play a role in a much bigger picture than you had imagined."

He let the words settle.

"At the time of your incident, I had to ask …" he said, turning his eyes upward, as if recalling something from memory, "what is the meaning of this event? How did this occur?"

He looked at me again and continued, "I consulted with others, including Celesta, who has a broader view of the human world than I. It was she who rewound the spool of time to witness your transformation. It was unprecedented and entirely unexpected."

As he spoke, I was brought back to the memory of that moment—the burst into brilliant light and blissful expansion—which left me forever changed, with psychic abilities beyond my ken. While the experience was magnificent, it threw my everyday life into turmoil.

"It was Celesta who pointed out the coincidences," the King continued. "She noticed, within your timeline and Akashic records, that you and this man, Seth, have shared many lifetimes together—as have both of you with the woman Melinda. She is the one who launched the power grab at just the right moment."

I nodded vigorously while forcing down the need to argue the point. *I thought there were no coincidences!* Instead, I said, "Yes! I've noticed the 'coincidences' too! What do they mean?"

He held up his hand to indicate I should be patient … he'd get to that. "This piqued our curiosity, so we asked Aethelwyne and her wee sister to gather more information as their father, Brannoc, holds charge over all family records. And he was able to find an interesting seed."

Gwyn ap Nudd then stood and strode across the space we inhabited—it felt odd to call it a "room"— and took hold of an elaborately carved wooden staff with a massive, flashing labradorite sphere installed at the top.

Now my attraction to labradorite stones made sense. I recognized this staff immediately, although I couldn't say from where. Its sphere was the size of a softball and, even from where I sat, I was drawn in. I had to make a deliberate effort to not be pulled into yet another apparent layer of reality … I mean, how many layers are there?

"This staff," he said, his voice bringing me back to the present moment, "belonged to someone in your lineage, centuries ago in human terms."

As he spoke, a phantom kick in the chest stole my breath and terror overtook me. When as I could breathe again, I dissolved into a puddle of tears.

"Seren …" he began, but he didn't need to say more.

She stepped up and, as she had earlier, put her hand on my forehead and hummed. This time I didn't feel the buzzing, but I heard it … it was far away.

"Breathe," she commanded.

I struggled to remember the process, but it slowly came back. Deep inbreath, hold, then exhale longer than the inhale. Vagus nerve. Breathe. As I did so, the buzzing became louder and closer. Finally, I felt it in my body so I touched her hand to let her know it was enough. Any more and I would end up back in the physical world.

"Well done," she said. "That takes a level of expertise that you do not give yourself enough credit for."

My heart lifted at the compliment, and I felt a moment of guilt for wondering if she could replace Twink as my sidekick. Seren was so much nicer.

"Perhaps we should allow you a bit of rest before we go further," the King said. "I want you clear headed, as you have a decision to make. One that will change the future, and more than just yours."

Yes, a bit of rest sounded like a good idea. The distant drumbeat was shifting again and the eclipse was deepening. Something big was about to go down and *Inntinn-lobhadh* was right there with me.

SIXTEEN

Seren and the King stepped aside for what seemed to be a private conference, leaving me seated in the deeply comfortable chair that I couldn't see—just like the sky earlier. I could only sense something beneath my body weight, holding me.

I wanted to walk over for a closer look at that wooden staff with the labradorite sphere that had called so loudly earlier, but I didn't know if I was allowed. I'd watched enough British TV dramas to know that there was a strict protocol when dealing with the Crown, but I had no idea if those same rules applied to Fae royalty.

Before attracting King Gwyn ap Nudd's attention to ask permission, I needed to know what to call him. I must have thought this loudly enough because I received a response from Pea, who picked up my signal.

"You may call him Lord Gwyn," she whispered.

"Thank you," I whispered back, then said aloud, "Lord Gwyn, Seren, I'm sorry to interrupt …"

They both turned to me, expectantly waiting for me to continue.

"… might I see the staff?" I asked. "The one my ancestor used to own?"

"Of course," the King said. "By all rights it belongs to you."

He and Seren then dropped all notice of me, so I got up and crossed the room to where the staff stood, leaning against one of the ivy-draped walls.

To get there, I had to step across the small stream running through the narrow stone channel, and that's when it hit me. This stream was decoratively landscaped like the flowing water in the Chalice Garden, where the Red Spring runs. This must be the corresponding White Spring, flowing directly from its source beneath the Tor into the human world.

The magnitude of the realization almost sidetracked me, but I focused on what was right before me—the wooden staff. I reached for it and it practically leapt into my outstretched hand as if finally coming home.

I felt it too … home … even though I stood in the chamber of the King of the Fae. All fear was gone and I *belonged* in a way I'd never understood. In an instant, I became the essence of the word '*Yes!*' Language fell away— only an angelic tone aching to escape remained.

Instead of voicing the tone aloud, I internalized it and it lit me up to my very core, taking my consciousness to a place where I simply was and forever would be. I closed my eyes and allowed myself to just … shine.

I felt a hand on my left shoulder and opened my eyes. There before me stood the glowing figure of a silver-bearded, teddy-bear of a man in what looked like a Druid's robe.

"Well met, lassie," he said in an accent from even further north than anyone I'd met on this journey. "It's been a long wait, aye. Centuries at least."

"You've been waiting for me?" I asked. "You know me?"

"Oh, aye. Since the dawn of time," he said, beaming. "We are One."

At the edge of my vision, Gwyn ap Nudd stepped forward and removed the staff from my hand, gently and respectfully, breaking the connection.

The glow vanished. I became painfully aware of being back in my etheric body as it existed on this plane, and I shuddered with the discomfort that came with the crash.

Seren darted behind me to catch me as my knees gave out. She led me back to where I'd been sitting and settled me there. Lord Gwyn again sat opposite me and peered into my eyes, grave concern etched into his face.

"Aye, not a moment too soon," he said to Seren. "Well done bringing her here."

I shook my head to clear it and push back the fear that stood at the edge of my thoughts. *Inntinn-lobhadh* was now a palpable presence, like a giant creature poised to sink its claws into me. The claws that catch.

"Why did you do that?" I asked, still dazed. "Why did you take it away?"

"Clearly, it is not yours yet," the King said. "Aye, the staff belongs to your lineage but there is work to be done before you may hold it again."

My head was finally clearing, so I straightened and met his gaze. "What work? You mentioned that before, 'the work we're to do today.'"

"As I began to tell you," he explained, "it is written in the records of your lineage. You are descended from the man you just saw, your grandfather from many generations back. He was a human, but a friend to the Fae. His name was Padraic, and he was a greatly skilled…" He ended with a word I couldn't understand.

"What was that?" I asked. "That word you said just now."

He enunciated more clearly, saying "*Ah-SHAH-pukh*. Seren, help me, dear."

"Of course, Father." She smiled, her eyes shining with the joy of being useful. "Lola, it means something like 'shapeshifter' in the human tongue … the words translate as 'one who reshapes themselves anew.' Your distant ancestor walked in beauty … his surroundings instantly reflecting his inner self, which he could change at will."

As Celesta had done just yesterday (God, was it only yesterday?) Seren waved her hand in the air between us, creating sparkling letters which spelled out *ath-shapach*.

"Can we just use the word 'shapeshifter?'" I asked.

"It is of little consequence which word we use," Lord Gwyn said, "so long as you understand its meaning."

"Yes, I believe I do," I nodded. "It feels … natural, especially after those brief moments of connection with him."

I yearned to relive those moments, so I tried to mentally call them back. Surely it would be simple to just … remember … joy and light and expansion and all the things and bring them into my present moment.

It didn't work. Yes, I could remember, but thinking wasn't enough to click it into full expression.

I *knew*, in my bones, how to do it. But no matter how I tried, I could only catch a faint glimpse of that Isness, the way he embodied that splendor without effort.

As it became clear I couldn't reach it, fear overtook me. I'd never feel that way again. It was gone. I screwed it up. *Inntinn-lobhadh* was there instead, the predator, using the ties that bind. I was useless.

With the word "useless" echoing in my brain, I sobbed and Seren's voice broke through, as if from very far away, "Lola Garnett, look at your left wrist."

Like that, I snapped out of it. "Damn it!" I cried. "How can it keep doing that? Why am I not safe here, of all places, from inching lower?"

"This is important," Gwyn ap Nudd replied, his tone stern. "There is more that you do not yet know, and it must be made clear before we commence." He steepled his fingers again and thought for a moment, as if deciding how far back in the story to go.

"I knew Padraic well," the King finally began, "and held him in the highest esteem. Few humans existed then who walked with a foot in both worlds. Many had been killed off by jealous, power-hungry leaders. Others went into hiding. And now, in your human concept of time, those who carry these lineages in their bones have mostly died off or gone dormant."

"That means you, Lola Garnett," he said, looking directly into my eyes.

I gulped and met his gaze, not daring to interrupt.

"Padraic had a son, also one of your distant grandfathers," Lord Gwyn said. "And like his father, he also walked in beauty, leaving tranquility in his wake. But, like many youngsters, he grew restless and wished for a great challenge. Does this sound familiar?"

I blushed as he named it. This was exactly what I had done right before my boring little Midwestern life exploded.

The King went on. "Between his well-honed *ath-shapach* ability and his desire for something new—with those forces in tandem—he began to be seen by the right people. The military took notice and called him to fight in the wars. He readily joined them."

Wincing as I saw what was coming, I nodded for Lord Gwyn to continue.

"He became a great commander, a leader of men. But in turning away from peace and tranquility, his outer world quickly changed."

I held my breath, bracing for what came next.

"He became power mad and began to behave abominably. He had to be stopped. His father, Padraic, came to me," Lord Gwyn said as he rose to retrieve the staff, stepping across the flowing White Spring waters, "and asked the Fae for assistance. It took more than his own effort to disempower his son, for their skills were equal."

The King paused, gazing into the labradorite sphere, then returned to his seat and continued his story. "Padraic and I worked together to draw in his son's magical authority. His inherited *ath-shapach* power was removed entirely and bound within this stone, leaving him to function as an ordinary human with far less ability to do harm."

He held the staff before me, directing my eyes toward the sphere attached to the top. It was then that I saw that this stone's flash was in the shape of a distorted heart, not unlike the smaller sphere that I had purchased yesterday from the vendors from York.

"And now, Lola Garnett," the King stated, his voice filled with gravity, "you have come along, having ripped into the veil releasing untamed abilities for which you were unprepared."

My jaw dropped as the implication settled. I was beginning to understand … or was I? No, I wasn't.

More confused than ever, I asked, "Did I do something wrong? I didn't mean to!"

'*Oh no,*' I thought, '*I'm in trouble now—what have I done? Oh no. Oh no. Oh nooooo.*'

"Lola Garnett," Seren said sternly. "You're doing it again. You asked why you are not safe here from *Inntinn-lobhadh*. You are inviting it yourself."

Eyes wide, I waited for her to explain, but instead she asked, "What do you need to do instead?"

"Look at my left wrist?" I asked, my voice barely a whisper. Just the reminder of the bracelet cleared the spiraling thoughts.

"Aye," said her father. "*Inntinn-lobhadh* is a parasite moving unseen through the human world, responsible for much of the turmoil there. In your case, as you began honing the abilities you have awakened, it unsheathed its claws to keep you down. And because you continue to push back, it has become a danger not just to the human world, but to ours as well. And that is why you have been called here."

"Wait," I said. "I feel like I'm missing part of the story. Please give me a minute."

I closed my eyes to gather my thoughts and replay what I had just been told. My distant grandfather from centuries ago was what? A wizard? A druid? *Ath-shapach*? Whatever it was, it meant a magical lineage.

This ancestor abused his power, so his father, Padraic, and this King of the Fae, Lord Gwyn, removed his magic and bound it into a labradorite sphere at the top of that staff. And now, centuries later, here I was, completely unaware of any of these people, being fed on by a mind parasite. I shuddered at the thought.

Yes, I was definitely missing something.

"So …" I began. "How do I fit into this? I didn't even know any of these people existed. I'm pretty sure they wouldn't come up in any genealogy search. I was just minding my own business, and now I'm posing a danger to two worlds?"

"Aye, a great deal of this tale has been left out in my haste," the King said, a hint of impatience in his tone. "It is, after all, the culmination of centuries."

"Okay," I said. "But essentially, what you're saying is that *Inntinn-lobhadh* is always there as a human world undercurrent, wreaking havoc, and doesn't usually single anyone out—but now it's going after me specifically. It's feeding off something that woke up when I did."

Seren and Lord Gwyn exchanged a glance and both nodded. "Aye," said the King. "You have the essence of it."

After a quick glance at my wrist, I asked, "What do you want me to do?"

"You must choose," he said, pausing to ensure that he had my full attention.

"You cannot continue in this fashion," said Gwyn ap Nudd. "It is unsustainable. It will not be long before your own powers grow strong enough for *Inntinn-lobhadh* to twist your creations sideways, and you have not yet learned to control them. Therefore, you may choose to relinquish these newly awakened abilities and go back to being as you called it … boring. Ordinary. I cannot say if you'll have any memory of what has occurred since, and I do not know which is worse, remembering or not."

He waited while my mind reeled. Go back to that miserable existence? And what if I couldn't remember anything since then? I'd experienced that when Melinda made the poppets to control me and my family. We all had distorted memories, unable to keep track of what was real, or who remembered what. It was wretched, like a horrible, looping dream from which I couldn't wake.

Fury rose within me as I recalled what she had done—righteous anger blazed. That damned Melinda! Would the fallout from her selfish madness never cease? And why do *I* have to make this choice? Why don't they take *her* power away? I didn't ask for this, I just wanted something interesting to do!

This was beyond unfair. So messed up. Hadn't I suffered enough?

My God, what more did Spirit or my guides … or whoever was making decisions about my life from the 'other side' … expect of me? If I had to be stuck in a looping dream, why couldn't it be a *good* one?

Then it occurred to me—what if this *was* all a dream?

I mean, what were the chances that this was real—me sitting on a chair that wasn't there, beneath an English hill, chatting with a faery king about one of my ancestors having his dangerous powers taken away?

The King watched my face closely, giving me time and space to let my mind go.

The thought of dreams brought to mind a night years ago when Amanda was a toddler and had what I thought was an extreme nightmare. I later learned it was a "night terror," a kind of panic attack that hits while you sleep and you can't wake up. It was terrifying for both of us.

My poor little girl was sitting up in her bed, eyes wide as saucers, her teeth gritted in terror, trying to scream, but her jaw was clenched too tightly to open. Only a guttural sound escaped her tiny throat. She looked past me as if I wasn't there, pointed at something behind me that I couldn't see, then finally her jaw released and she screamed bloody murder.

I was desperate to wake her. Calling her name and jiggling her weren't working. I recalled what I've seen on TV shows … when someone is hysterical, you slap their face and they snap out of it immediately. I didn't slap her hard, just enough to make noise as my fingers gently struck her cheek, like clapping my hands. I didn't want to hurt her, just startle her awake.

Mission accomplished. She stopped screaming immediately, looked me dead in the eye and said, in a voice more grown up than I'd ever heard her use, "I hate you." Then she lay back down and went to sleep, with no memory in the morning of anything ever happening.

For me, to see my darling baby girl in the clutches of a nightmare she couldn't describe—from which she could not wake no matter what I did— was even worse. After all, the nightmare ended for her once I figured out how to wake her. I, on the other hand, would be haunted by this scene to this very day. She didn't remember and I never forgot.

Then the question splattered across my mind: Is this how our guides see us, the way I saw poor little Amanda? The Universe smacks us with a 2x4 to wake us because nothing else is working. Then we glare at it and seethe, 'I hate you.'

Perhaps anger at my situation was inappropriate.

That's when it occurred to me to ask, "What are my other choices?"

Gwyn ap Nudd said, "You cannot continue as you have been, without interruption. The parasite has taken notice of you and has made you its plaything. If you cannot learn to overcome it without reminders or tricks with bracelets, *Inntinn-lobhadh* will win. You will surely be taken over by illness, madness, or worse … you will begin to affect the world around you in much the same way as your power-mad ancestor."

He shook his head with sympathy and continued, "Therefore, Lola Garnett, you must choose: either undo everything that has been done—and take the consequences however they may land—or enter the Cauldron of Rebirth."

"What?" I asked, fighting another burst of panic. "What is that?"

Seren spoke up, "Father, please allow me."

"Aye, child," the King said, gesturing with both hands for his daughter to continue.

"You see," she said to me in a gently humorous tone, "Father is not talking about an actual cauldron. You will not be cooked in a pot."

Grateful for the moment of levity, I smiled and nodded my understanding.

"But you will be reborn," she continued.

Lord Gwyn interrupted. "Aye, 'tis but a metaphor. Only one of these choices leads forward. Your current state—unchecked power with *Inntinn-lobhadh* lying in wait—creates chaos. I am grateful we intervened before permanent damage was done. I am told by Aethelwyne and her wee sister that your own home is under attack, with your marriage becoming unstable. This is just the beginning."

Seren frowned, all seriousness. "When someone has access to great power while under the influence of mind rot, *Inntinn-lobhadh* can easily take over, as it is forgotten again and again. This is what became of your ancestor and what will become of you, as you've already seen."

"Aye," said the King, "and Padraic has been waiting for centuries for a descendant of good heart to be born, so the curse … as it were … may finally be unbound and the lineage restored. You are not the only human with *ath-shapach*. You are simply the first of his lineage to cross the thinning veil in so striking a manner."

"So, Lola Garnett," Seren looked me straight in the eyes and asked, "What is your choice?"

SEVENTEEN

Seems like a no-brainer, right? Choose between a living miasma of dreary forgetfulness or evolving into a state of blissful, instant manifestation: who wouldn't choose the ability to create whatever they want? Isn't that the wish of pretty much everyone deep in the woo? Don't we all wish for that ol' Law of Attraction to actually work the way we've been promised?

Thing is, it *does* work the way it's been promised. What we get back is exactly what we feed into the field through our filter. It just takes a long while, so we don't always put two and two together.

What would happen if I chose instant manifestation and I suddenly churned out everything I thought of? This used to happen to a lesser degree in the early days, until I learned to be careful what I wish for, but it was just small things. Once, Melinda's garden was filled with rabbits after I wished it to be so, not expecting anything to really happen. It was almost cute.

My thoughts are nowhere near disciplined enough to keep expanding my abilities. I don't know if these faeries have any idea what they're asking of me.

Plus, they never said what would happen to *Inntinn-lobhadh*. Would I become so enlightened that it couldn't exist in my presence? Or would it become an exponentially greater foe?

Even if that weren't an issue, Lord Gwyn mentioned my marriage and the trouble I've been having with Chuck. I grow by leaps and bounds, and he remains content with the status quo. At least if I went backwards, he and I would be alright. If I take that quantum leap forward, there's no way he and I will click anymore. So, essentially, I'm being asked to choose whether to stay married or not.

Although staying as-is wasn't one of my choices, I pondered anyway what it would mean. I was already seeing signs of what would happen. With *Inntinn-lobhadh* relentlessly nipping at my heels—and my continued need for reminders to name it—I had to wonder what would happen when I went home, without a circle of friends nearby to say, *"Look at your left wrist."*

I could see how, given the abilities I already have, manifesting from panic, fear and untamed rage would eventually make me sick. Isn't there some metaphysical truth to the concept that our bodies reflect our inner thoughts and feelings? What would I become if all my negative thoughts were rapidly internalized and physicalized into infections, cysts and autoimmune issues?

So, yes, I saw the wisdom in not being offered that option.

Leaning toward the choice of rapid evolution—after all, maybe one of my instant manifestations would be for Chuck to catch up with me—I then considered what would have to take place for this to happen. Whether or not, as Seren had joked, I was to be literally stewed in a Cauldron of Rebirth was not the question. The question was, what *did* that mean?

I wished Maddie was there. I really needed a friend by my side who understood the human ramifications of what I was being asked to do.

Throughout my journey in Annwn, Twink and Pea had been able to hear my questions. Perhaps if I thought hard enough, Maddie could do the same. After all, her psychic abilities were growing, too. And she was sitting on the Tor, right next to my physical body, tuned in to why I was there. Stranger things have happened than friends communicating psychically—especially since the veil was so thin at the moment, with an active drum circle nearby and an eclipse/equinox affecting the cosmos.

As if on cue, the drumming rhythm shifted again as did the quality of light … or should I say dark? The eclipse was peaking and the pressure was building. I had no time to fiddle around trying to connect with Maddie for a commiserating confab with my bestie. The moment was upon me, and I recognized that I was just stalling.

The time to make the choice between going backward or forward was *now* and it was, indeed, a no-brainer. I heard the words spilling out of my mouth, "The Cauldron … take me to the Cauldron of Rebirth."

I felt the words, more than heard them: "*It is done.*"

This wasn't Seren or Gwyn ap Nudd speaking. These words were timeless and distant, accompanied by a feeling of finality, as if a door had closed behind me.

"Well done, Lola Garnett." This time it was Lord Gwyn speaking. "It is now that you and I must part ways and I leave you in the care of my beloved Seren." With this the King of the Fae faded from view, possibly into yet another layer of the bizarre reality in which I found myself.

Seren smiled, her eyes filled with compassion as she reached out her hand to take mine. "Well done, indeed," she said.

I took her hand and the scenery changed once again. We were no longer in the great room with the tree pillars and the non-existent chairs. Now we found ourselves in a clearing in a forest and before us was a modest stone structure … not quite a temple, more like a walled and domed rotunda with a few steps leading up to a single wooden door.

"We, too, must part ways now," said Seren, releasing my hand, "as you must enter alone. However, I will be there waiting for you on the other side."

My eyes, wild with confusion and fear, must have cried out to her because she continued, "Go through that door before us. Inside you will step into the pool and immerse yourself before stepping out on the other side. There you will see another door, and I will meet you when you exit."

"Is that all I have to do?" I asked, relieved.

"Well, that is all you will do physically," she said. "What happens otherwise remains to be seen." With a gentle wave of her hand, she ushered me up the steps. "Now go. All shall be well, and all shall be well, and all manner of thing shall be well."

I recognized that passage but didn't have the brainspace to recollect from where. I did recall, however, that it wasn't exactly a soothing sentiment. It essentially meant that even if something horrible happens, everything works out in the end. Not very reassuring, but there was no turning back now.

I opened the heavy wooden door, which creaked on its ancient hinges, then entered the stone structure and closed the door behind me. The inside was palely lit as if by moonlight, bringing to mind the eclipse that was happening in the real world.

I saw no source of light … no candles or windows. Perhaps a skylight but, again, I couldn't see anything above me. I wondered if this lighting reflected what Maddie and the drummers were experiencing but quickly reminded myself not to get distracted. I needed to focus.

Inside the dimly lit chamber, I smelled the hot mineral water before I saw it, and I heard it gurgling just up ahead so I was careful with my steps. I didn't want to fall into the deep end of a pool I couldn't rightly see.

"It's too dark," I muttered. "How am I supposed to see where I'm going?"

An etheric voice drifted on the air: "*Ask.*"

"Um … okay," I said. "Can it be a little brighter in here?"

Just like that, the lighting brightened … a little. Perhaps I should not have hedged my request so passive-aggressively. But at least now I could see … a little better.

Before me, built into the stone floor of the rotunda, was a swirling pool with steps leading in and out at either end. The only way to get to the other door, where Seren said she'd meet me, was through the pool.

As my eyes adjusted to the light, I noticed that the pool wasn't built into the floor at all. It was a natural, hot spring and the structure had been built around it. Only the steps in and out were hand-crafted.

And the door that Seren said was on the other side was still difficult to make out. I supposed that it wasn't important for now. I could worry about that later. For now, it was the Cauldron of Rebirth I was dealing with.

This pool before me … I wondered … was it fed by the same source as the White Spring that flowed through the forest chamber and out through the spigot in the human world of Glastonbury?

If I was right, then that was a whole new facet to this journey, wasn't it? The White Spring was connected to the Divine Masculine, and I was about to immerse myself in it. I wished again that I had paid more attention to Maddie's book, so I would better understand what I was about to do.

'*Oh well,*' I thought, '*I'm here now. If I was supposed to know more than I do, surely one of my helpers would have made that happen. Time to trust, Lola Garnett.*'

I mentally patted myself on the back for not spiraling and inching lower. Before stepping forward into the pool, I allowed myself one last distracting thought: Should I take off my clothes? My shoes? Does it matter? How would I get them to the other side of the pool without being preoccupied over keeping them out of the water as I walked across?

"Enough," I said aloud. "Just … do it."

I stepped forward into the water, down the first step … then the next … and the next, until the sloping bottom of the pool took over my descent. It felt gross and weird being fully dressed and submerged in water, my shoes now heavy and slogging, but I couldn't allow the discomfort to distract me.

The deeper I got, the higher the soothing hot water rose up my body, and the more my surroundings evaporated. Not only the walls surrounding me and the water in which I was immersed, but also my awareness that I was inside a stone rotunda or walking through a pool.

Instead, I was split into both an observer and participant in a scene long ago and far away, as if seeing through two sets of eyes.

We were in a brightly lit chamber with impressively thick walls of lime-washed stone, draped with lush, embroidered tapestries—both a demonstration of exquisite artistry on luxurious fabric and a barrier against cold drafts seeping through the cracks.

Sunshine poured through the arched windowpanes and birds chirped outside in the blooming trees. My observer-self was briefly swept away by the ecstasy of spring fever. Goddess, we felt so alive!

Wait. We? I, the observer, was the one overwhelmed.

"Who is in this room?" my observer-self asked.

"Surely yeh recognize yournsel?" the etheric voice replied. It was the voice that earlier told me to ask for more light within the rotunda.

It was then that I realized I hadn't seen anyone there. I only sensed their presences in the lovely and homey space.

After her prompt (it was decidedly a female voice), I saw two men. I recognized Padraic and intuitively knew the other was his son, the one we had been discussing. They were both my distant grandfathers.

"Which one am I?" I asked.

"Why, yeh're bothuns!" she said. "They're you, and yeh're them. Yeh're all One! You carry them within yeh. Now hesh and listen."

The men were involved in deep debate, seated in finely crafted wooden chairs, the style of which led me to assume this scene was taking place several centuries ago. I wasn't enough of a history buff to guess exactly when, but I'd estimate maybe the 1300s.

"Nae mair dithering!" the female voice demanded, and time sped up to make up for me wasting so much with my distracting thoughts. Focus, Lola!

As minutes zipped forward we skipped over the discussion itself, but I had a gestalt knowing of what the men were talking about. This was the moment when Padraic's son informed his father that he was joining the military, as Gwyn had mentioned.

What Gwyn hadn't told me was Padraic's reaction. War went against the code of *ath-shapach.*

His words rang out in the stone-walled room, despite the embroidered tapestries' natural ability to dampen echoes: "To accept the power of *ath-shapach* is to swear allegiance to a sacred code of ethics, the first: Do No Harm."

I had mistakenly thought of Padraic and his people as almost superhuman beings who could do no wrong—magical folk who simply "walked in beauty," leaving a wake that naturally reflected their inner goodness.

Now I saw … sensed … knew … that it wasn't so simple. Padraic was *disciplined* in the wise and moral use of this vast power. But his son grappled with a rebellious streak. His father's righteous lecturing only egged him on to prove himself.

"Father," the son's words reverberated within me, "I know my own mind. Has it not occurred to you that I can use *ath-shapach* to end the war and bring peace?"

"Aye, but when battle is an ingredient," his father warned, "there can be no immediate outcome that brings peace."

Once again, the fast-forward sensation kicked in, leaving me mildly dizzy for a few seconds. The female voice, whose presence was beginning to feel closer and denser, said, "These'uns be yehr kin. Remember this."

Now, as with my experience in meditation earlier that day, I was shown a panoramic view of a timeline, like a strip of film where I could zero in on a frame and enter the scene.

I chose a frame at random and was presented with a victory celebration. Padraic's son was being honored as the victorious commander of a seemingly impossible battle, in which his side was dreadfully outnumbered and yet triumphed. His men lifted him onto their shoulders, and his heart glowed with love for his fellows and all the lives that were saved by his skillful wielding of *ath-shapach.*

As if the filmstrip was folding in on itself, many similar scenes overlapped—one incredible win after another—each victory leading to more awe-filled glory until he was raised by his people upon a metaphorical pedestal.

For a time, he maintained humility. His well-intentioned reminders to his fellows that their worship was misplaced fell upon deaf and superstitious ears, until he began to believe them. They saw him as godlike and eventually so did he.

"We watched over him," the etheric voice broke in, pulling me from witnessing my ancestor's slow but steady fall from grace. "Allowing mistakes that caused no harm beyond what might have happened anyway. But …"

Her voice faded and I moved my focus to another frame in the film strip.

This time I saw, and felt, his longing to engage in combat, down there on the ground with his men. Mastery had become boring.

No longer content to lead from the rear using his ability to oversee the entirety of the battlefield—a puppet master pulling the strings to manipulate his desired outcome—his wish was to get down from his high horse and join his brave army in man-to-man weaponry.

It was bloody, gory work, this. But it filled a need within him to get his hands dirty, to plow down those who opposed his battalion, to dispatch them as painlessly and quickly as possible, moving on to the next foe. And once again, he was lifted upon the victorious shoulders of his men, exalted for his skill at hand-to-hand combat.

While my view of his actions from the distance—the blood and guts—was appalling, I respected his intention to show mercy to the opposition. He was mucking in with his men instead of standing out of harm's way. My admiration faded, however, as the next scene in the filmstrip showed me his progression.

Using *ath-shapach* he was unbeatable, and this knowingness festered within him like an infection. Soon he began to anticipate each upcoming battle with a bloodlust that gritted his teeth and hardened his manhood. There was nothing like wielding his axe and witnessing the look of horror on his enemy's face. It fed something deep inside him to watch the lights go out in his victim's eyes.

He held power over life and death, and no one could match him. He may not have seen it, but I recognized that mind-rotting infection. It was *Inntinn-lobhadh.*

His reputation as a ruthless and unbeatable warrior grew and soon no one would, or could, challenge him. Battles no longer came to his country, and the boredom once again took over. He began to look for prey close to home.

"Aye, lass," the voice interrupted, "do I need to show yeh more? Or can yeh imagine what comes next?"

Unbidden, images spilled through my mind … horrific scenes of cruelties to women, children and servants as this wretched ancestor of mine began to settle into an after-war routine of everyday abuses, magnified by his unbridled access to *ath-shapach* tainted by *Inntinn-lobhadh.*

"Yes, I can imagine," I cried, tears springing to my eyes and nausea brewing in my gut. "Please make it stop!"

"That yeh want it to stop is what I needed to know." The voice grew louder, more in-the-room, as she said. "Step forward, child, out of the pool."

And just like that, I was back inside the rotunda, moving forward through the now shoulder-deep waters of the Cauldron of Rebirth. My hair was dripping wet, so at some point I must have been completely immersed and somehow able to breathe.

Ahead of me were three steps up and out. The door I couldn't see from the other side of the pool was now there. At the top of the stairs stood the form of a radiant old woman draped in a flowing robe, offering her hand to help me out.

Holding onto the crone's hand, I climbed up the steps until I stood next to her on the far side of the stone structure, in front of the second wooden door. She handed me what looked like a large, fluffy towel. I didn't bother to wonder about the anomaly or the towel's thread count, as I might have earlier. Magic is as magic does.

I simply dried my face and hair and squeezed some of the excess water out of my clothes. I laughed aloud when I realized that, with so little effort, I was already completely dry.

"I knew yeh'd come through it," the old woman said. "I telt Padraic you were the one." She grinned triumphantly and, as she did so, grew younger before my very eyes, her glow softening. What had appeared before to be a draped robe was now a long, elegantly embroidered dress of off-white linen, with a small nosegay of flowers tucked into her waistband. She settled into a form that appeared to be in her vibrant sixties or seventies.

"You knew Padraic?" I asked.

"Knew him?" She laughed. "I married him. I'm yehr wee granny, lass. Yeh may have just come through the healing of the menfolk, but yeh'll notice it was done by the women, eh?"

I matched her grin and asked, "Now what?"

"Now yeh set here a spell and rest," she said, directing me to a stone bench at the edge of the pool, "and tell yehr Granny Myrta what yeh saw. That way I'll know if yeh're done here or no."

She sat beside me and patted my knee as I sighed with relief. "Give me a sec, would you?" I asked. "I need to gather my thoughts."

"Aye, lassie," she said, pulling my head down to her shoulder and giving me a warm hug. "You rest a while. We have time. All the time in the world."

EIGHTEEN

Granny Myrta patted my back as she rocked us both, there on the stone bench. The scent of the flowers tucked into her belt was faint and familiar, but I couldn't quite place it. I rested my head on her shoulder, sinking into the grandmotherly comfort she offered, but I couldn't wait to start with the questions.

"You said that I came through the healing of the menfolk," I said, "but that it was done by the women. What did you mean?"

With her cheek pressed into the top of my head, I felt her facial muscles shift as she smiled, "Aye, that's a good question. I misspoke, though. We're no' done yet."

She released her embrace and sat up straight, and I did the same. She faced me, peering into my eyes. "Now it be my turn to ask. What did yeh see?"

I gave her a rundown: I saw who I now knew to be her husband and son, and the subversion of her child's use of *ath-shapach*—how he was driven power-mad and became a danger to himself and others.

"I couldn't bear to watch the horrors he eventually drifted into," I said. "It felt as if his madness would infect my mind."

"Aye," she replied, shaking her head sadly, "the mind rot took him over. *Inntinn-lobhadh* became his constant companion … his lord and master. His father and I were distraught, witnessing our beautiful lad's outrageous misuse of his birthright inheritance."

Once again she looked me in the eye and said, "'Tis your inheritance, too, only it's been bound … shut off … for centuries. Yeh're the first of our kin to show signs of the madness having faded."

"Yes," I said, sitting up straighter, excited by this turn in the conversation, "that's what Lord Gwyn suggested. But that means it's upstream for one of my parents. Was this my mother's or my father's side of the family?"

"T'was yehr father, lass," she said. "My distant grandson. This strain has passed from father to son, lo these many years. P'rhaps it took a girlchild to finally break the pattern. Or p'rhaps it was simply time, as our race evolves."

I nodded, filing that bit of information away for later discussion. Instead, I said, "Tell me what happened to your son … my many-times great-grandfather. What was his name, anyway?"

Myrta smiled wistfully, a far-away look in her ancient eyes, and said, "My poor wee lad. We called him Gillebrid. Such a beautiful boy. It broke our hearts to watch his downfall, helpless to save him."

She wiped away a few tears and continued, "We had to stop him, but *how* was beyond the ken of any of us. It was Padraic's suggestion to consult with Gwyn ap Nudd, as we couldnae contain Gillebrid and *Inntinn-lobhadh* once they were joined, even with the full force of our community behind us. It took the magic of the Fae."

My ancient granny reached for my hands and held them clasped within her own. "We've waited so long for yeh, lass. So very long."

Raising my hands to her lips, she kissed them both before releasing them. "We couldnae override Fae magic and had to wait for someone of Gillebrid's lineage to earn back the birthright."

She crinkled her face with a broad smile and beamed, "That's you, lassie. But it's no' just our bloodline, it's our community. *Ath-shapach* belongs to a people."

I was about to interrupt with a question, but she continued, "We're no' as widespread as we once were—far too many of our bairns were overtaken by *Inntinn-lobhadh* once the parasite discovered how to worm its way in. The elders, taking their cues from Padraic and me, made the hard choice of dimming their lights over the generations. The only way to hold *Inntinn-*

lobhadh back was to bind *ath-shapach* entirely. We all made the sacrifice. And now, *ath-shapach* is all but dormant."

"Thank goodness," I said. "I can't imagine what the world would look like if bad actors were allowed to run loose with shapeshifting power."

"Ah, but yeh see, lass," Myrta said, "therein lies the rub. *Inntinn-lobhadh* has elevated a host of… bad actors… as yeh called them. Surely yeh've seen it at work in the world. They are of another order than our people—with power much like our own—but they act under a different set of ethics. In the meantime, many of good will have been disempowered and therefore unable to stand against them. Until now."

I gulped. "Do you mean me?"

"Aye, you and others like us," she explained. "Yeh're beginning to wake up, slowly … although no' so slowly in yehr case," she chuckled.

"But why me, if there are others like me … like us?" I asked, recalling Lord Gwyn's reminder that I'm not a 'chosen one.'

"Why, yeh're our own wee grandwee'un!" Myrta beamed. "Yehr great, great granda Padraic and I have been waiting and watching, praying and beseeching all these many centuries for one of our'n to finally come into the world without such a heavy load of brokenness on their back."

"Oh!" I replied, nonplussed.

"Yeh see," she continued, "it had to be one of our'n, for it was our bloodline that cracked, and it was Padraic and me who made the arrangement with Lord Gwyn. Yeh've struggled with *Inntinn-lobhadh*, sure, but yeh had the wherewithal to see it, recognize it and … more importantly … name it. That broke its hold, but the binding could only be undone by the final step, here."

Pondering all she had shared, I finally asked, "Who else is one of … our people? Anyone I know?"

"Oh, surely yeh've run into them here and there," Myrta said. "Have yeh no' met someone and felt, 'I know them from somewhere … they feel like kin,' even though yeh've ne'er met?"

Maddie immediately came to mind, as did Seth, but I already knew that Seth and I had shared past lives. So I said, "I do have two friends, but one of them is someone I've had many lives with, as family. The other one, I feel like I've known forever, but I don't get the feeling that she's family in the same way."

"They can both be one of our people, but one may be of yehr lineage," she replied, nodding, "as you and I are family. T'other may not be in yehr direct bloodline—the parent of a parent of a parent—but they may still be one of our people."

That made sense. Maddie and I clicked in a way that I've rarely experienced, but our friendship had a different quality than my relationship with Seth. Different in a way I couldn't quite name. She and Seth hit it off immediately, and she trusted him to take over her shop and even live in her apartment when she moved in with Paul. And, more than anyone I've ever met, Maddie literally embodied the word "shapeshifter."

Melinda, on the other hand, absolutely played a role in my current adventure—after all, without her I wouldn't be here now—but she did not feel like family. At all.

"What about someone who causes nothing but mayhem?" I asked. "The two I mentioned are dear to me, but I'm thinking of someone who uses her abilities selfishly and cruelly."

"Ah, lass," Myrta said, "someone like that can also be kin, playing a difficult role agreed upon before birth into the human realm. But they could also be one of the others I mentioned—one of the other kind."

My mind reeled as possibilities flooded through. What about powerful world leaders, those who genuinely worked for the good of their people?

What about others who did just the opposite? Who were they, and why did the harmful ones get their way so often? Did they outnumber us, or were they just really good at disempowering their constituents?

If enough of us with *ath-shapach* woke up, could we overpower them? Is that why those in power resist us awakening?

If we did awaken and try to overpower them, would we run the same risk as Gillebrid?

While lightbulbs popped in my head at a blinding pace, Granny Myrta continued speaking. I was finally pulled back into listening when I heard her say, "… and that's what we need to do to complete yehr journey here."

"Uh … what?" I sputtered. "I'm sorry, I didn't catch all of that. What were you saying?"

"It's a lot to take in, I know," she said, smiling, then ran her hand across my cheek. "Here, take in a deep breath," she added, handing me the small bouquet of colorful buds she had stashed in her waistband.

I held the flowers to my nose and breathed deep. I knew this scent, and it was driving me batty trying to name it. Meantime, I allowed it to work its magic, easing all anxiety and clearing my head, as Granny Myrta intended.

Handing them back to her, I asked, "What are those? I know that smell."

"That's *Anail na Sean*," she said. "I grow them in my window box, one of my many botanicals. 'Tis my own wee magic."

Finally, it hit me. "That's Clary Sage!" I cried.

"Call it what yeh like," she nodded. "Me, I prefer *Anail na Sean* … it means Ancestors' Breath."

"Wow," I said, entirely flummoxed by all the synchronicities. "We'll get back to that, but first, what were you saying about completing my journey? I feel like I've been here a long time, and the light is shifting … I can hear the drumming getting louder. Does that mean I'm slipping away from here?"

"Aye, could be, lass," Myrta said. "And that's what I was saying when yehr mind wandered. It's time for you to go, but first … as without, so within. The final step."

She paused while she reached into a deep pocket of her linen dress and retrieved a small glass bottle, so exquisitely carved that it sparkled even in the rather dim light of the rotunda.

The bottle was so beautiful that I hungered to own it—I literally salivated, I wanted it so badly. I could barely concentrate on her words, but I forced my attention back.

I had to ask. "You said 'as without, so within.' I keep hearing a few repeated phrases: 'as above, so below,' 'masculine, feminine,' 'we are one, the King awaits.' There's one more, without a second half. 'The ties that bind…'"

"Aye," she said, "up 'til now, there was no second part to that phrase. But now …" Myrta's face beamed.

"Now?"

"The ties that bind," she said, "have been released."

Granny Myrta pulled the cork from its neck and offered the bottle to me. "Just a few drops, mind, yeh'll need no more than that."

I brought it to my lips—blissfully grateful to even be allowed to hold the magnificent bottle—and took a sip. It tasted of iron, like water from the Red Spring. As the drops made their way down my throat, I 'saw' myself lighting up from the inside out. My spine became a pillar of brilliant white light and each of my chakras blazed in the spectrum of full color. The luminous donut I'd seen earlier glowed brightly, lit up in color as a looping, shimmering rainbow.

It took my breath away to witness the spectacular radiance of my own energy field. I'd seen artistic renderings of the toroidal field, but even the most perfect illustrations could never express the true beauty that light brings to color. The scent of Myrta's flowers, the Ancestors' Breath, wafted by and it steadied me, enabling me to breathe normally again.

"Aye, lassie, now yeh've got the way of it," she said, her voice bringing me into balance.

I handed the bottle back to her, easily releasing it into her hand, which surprised me considering how badly I coveted it just moments ago. It was still gorgeous cut crystal, but it was no longer my precious.

Now, though, Granny Myrta glowed the same way as I … a pure white pillar of light surrounded by a prismic torus, with a solidified human shape formed within it.

"Oh, lass, yeh've done it," she said, tears glittering in her lit-up eyes. "Padraic, come see," she called out.

Next to her, the shape of the man I'd seen earlier—my distant grandfather Padraic—materialized in similar form to hers, another spectacular display of light. The heartfelt power of his beaming smile was only slightly surpassed by the pure gratitude that radiated from every facet of his light body.

He was the embodiment of gratitude and, in that instant, I recognized *ath-shapach*—I had felt this brilliance before, but not in this lifetime. It rippled outward from him, filling the rotunda until my own field shifted and I, too, was gratitude. Everything around us shifted in response to him. He did not impose himself upon the space; he harmonized it.

'*But what about Gillebrid?*' I wondered and, as if my thoughts were spoken aloud, I saw—there between them—their son. As he materialized and realized where he was, who he was with, and what had happened, he fell to his knees and sobbed as if his heart were breaking.

His glow was nowhere near as strong as that of his parents or even me, for that matter. His mother, my Granny Myrta, knelt and folded him into her arms, crying with him, "Och, my poor wee lad."

Padraic joined his family on the stone floor of the rotunda, embracing them both. He patted his son's back, offering soothing words, "All shall be well, Gillebrid, and all shall be well …"

Myrta wiped her eyes and stood before me. "Yehr work here is done, dear child. Yeh'll likely have more to do on yehr own, but the hard part is behind yeh … behind us all, thanks be to you."

"Aye," said Padraic, turning his head to face me, still on his knees with his son, "yeh've done yehr family proud. And now, we've to get this'un to Lord Gwyn for permission to enter the Cauldron."

Gillebrid, my distant grandfather, finally became aware that I was even there. He reached out both hands to me, and I took them in mine. He said, his voice cracking, "I'm in nae condition to fully express …" he stammered a bit then continued "… give me time, lassie …"

"Of course," I said. "I'm grateful, too. You're not the only one who's been released."

"Seren awaits," Granny Myrta reminded me, touching me gently on the shoulder.

I released Gillebrid's hands and glanced at the wooden door on this side of the rotunda, this side of the Cauldron of Rebirth. Before turning to go, I said, "Will I ever see any of you again?"

"Aye," Granny said, and the men both nodded. "Whenever yeh smell the Ancestors' Breath, yeh'll know we're nearby. And should yeh need us …"

"Aye," Padraic said, "yeh've got *ath-shapach*. Use it. We'll hear yeh."

Reassured that this wasn't the end—in fact, it was just the beginning—I opened the wooden door and stepped outside, where I was greeted by Seren and the King of the Fae, Gwyn ap Nudd.

"Lola Garnett," he said, "welcome, and well done."

I bowed my head, pressed my hands together, and said, "Thank you, Lord Gwyn, for all you've done for my family. We're not out of the woods yet, though. I believe you're needed inside."

Without a word, he strode up the steps and into the rotunda, his part in this phase of my journey complete. Seren reached out her hand and said, "Shall we? Your friends await, and I believe your physical form needs you to rejoin it."

And just like that, I opened my eyes to find myself in my body, lying atop the grassy Tor on the sweatshirt and afghan, shivering with the cold. Maddie had covered me with her jacket, but I was chilled through anyway.

Looking down at me, eyes filled with concern, were Maddie and the crystal vendor, the red-haired young woman who yearned to visit America. Standing behind them, still in their full-size, Pea and Twink also looked down at my reclined body, and Myx and Maj fluttered over Maddie's head.

"I think she's okay," said the woman.

I sat up, pulled my sweatshirt on and rubbed my arms to warm them. "Brrr," I said, "it got chilly, didn't it?"

"Not a moment too soon," Maddie cried. "I was about to jiggle you awake, you were gone so long. I knew you must be freezing, with your back on the ground like that!"

"I'll be fine," I told her. "But I am looking forward to a nice, warm cup of tea. Let's go home."

"Yeh're going nowhere yet," the young woman said. "I have some tea right here." She opened a thermos, poured steaming tea into the cup from the lid and handed it to me.

"Oh, you're a lifesaver," I moaned, turning on the drama. "Thank you." I sipped the tea, surprised to notice that it was washing away the taste of iron at the back of my throat.

As I settled back into my body, I finally observed the quality of light in the late afternoon sky. It was slightly off—borderline spooky. "How far along is the eclipse?" I asked.

"We're on the other side of it," Maddie said. "That's what had me worried. You were out for quite a while."

"Hmm," I nodded, taking another sip of hot tea. "It felt like I was down there forever. So much happened! But as Twink has reminded me so often, time doesn't move the same across the veil."

At the mention of her name, Twink stepped forward. No one but me could see her ... I could tell by the lack of reaction from the two humans with me.

"Aye, and so it cannot," she said. "Otherwise yeh could never have done so much powerful work. Well done, friend."

My jaw dropped. Twink had *never* shown me that kind of respect. Something had shifted here, as well. Before I had a chance to respond, she faded from view.

"Lola, what is it?" Maddie asked.

"Huh?"

"Your jaw was hanging open," she explained, "like you were seeing something bizarre."

I chuckled and said, "Yep, it was bizarre alright. I'll tell you later."

"Help me get up, would you?" I said, reaching my arms out to Maddie and the woman. "I'm a little stiff from lying on the cold ground for so long."

"Are you quite well?" the woman asked, hoisting me up with Maddie.

"I'm better than well," I said, my heart swelling with appreciation for the concern shown by a newly found soul-friend. "All shall be well, and all shall be well ..."

"... and all manner of thing shall be well," the woman finished the line with me. "Aye, Julian of Norwich. I love her work."

"That's who it is!" I cried. "I couldn't remember." I wobbled a bit, so she took my arm.

"We're in no hurry," she said. "You wait until you're steady. Paolo won't mind waiting." She turned to wave assurance to her man, who was watching from the other side of the Tor, that she'd be a bit longer.

I tuned into my body. Was I okay to make that long trek back to the rental? Now that I was paying attention, I sensed that a few parts of my consciousness had not yet returned, so I took a moment to allow everything to fall into place.

I knew I was complete when I felt ... whole. Literally whole, like never before—except maybe inside the rotunda with my ancestors.

This reminded me. I stooped down and grabbed my bottle of Clary Sage oil. I opened it and took a sniff ... Ancestors' Breath ... and instantly sensed my field's donut shimmering brighter. With a childlike giggle, I thought, '*Cover that donut with rainbow sprinkles,*' and it was so.

"I'm good," I grinned. "Let's go."

"Wait," the woman said, reaching into the back pocket of her jeans. She handed me a business card and said, "Let's stay in touch, shall we?"

I read her name there on the card, above her email address and phone number, and slipped it into my own back pocket.

"Angel," I said, reading her name aloud, "I would love that. I'll text you."

She gave me a big, warm hug, then ran across the Tor to rejoin her compatriots, waving goodbye. I waved back and stooped again to gather my things into my backpack, while Maddie rolled up the afghan to stuff it into her bag.

One last time, I looked across the top of the Tor to the drummers and beamed blessings toward my new friends. The atmosphere around me had changed. It shifted to match the beauty of all they had created while I journeyed.

All was well as we set off down the hill, back the way we came.

NINETEEN

"Angel was so nice, wasn't she?" I asked Maddie as we followed the path down the back side of the hill. "Everyone was so nice!"

"Yes, they were," Maddie said, "but that's not what we need to talk about, is it? The suspense is killing me. *What happened up there?*"

"Can you feel it?" I asked. "Or is it just me?" I stopped for a few moments, soaking it in.

"It feels like everything's different now. That was a profound vibe up there, with the drumming and the eclipse … everyone was tuned in to … well, Avalon!"

A bench just ahead on the trail caught my eye, and I said, "Let's sit so we can focus. It's hard to concentrate when I'm trying not to tumble off the side of the Tor."

Once we sat, I continued. "Honestly, Maddie, I don't know where to begin, aside from asking if you can feel the difference. I need to know whether it's just me."

She pondered for a moment, then said, "Yes, I can feel it. I think anyone with psychic sensitivity would. But how do I know it's the same as what you're feeling?"

"Good point. Let me start over," I said. "I had a profound experience under that hill and, by the way, it wasn't a cave or a hole dug in the dirt. I was surprised by that, but it was similar to a shamanic journey like we learned in class from Glenna. She would probably call it the Lower World."

Maddie nodded, following along, so I kept going. "But this was more palpable, like I could taste and smell things as if they were really there. There's a difference in density between the land of the Fae and the shamanic worlds. Does that make sense?"

"I think so." She nodded again. "But it still doesn't answer my question. I want to know what happened."

"Okay," I said, "I'll tell you, but I'm afraid it'll only be words. I don't know if I can convey what happened without first making sure you *really get* the … dimensionality … of the whole experience, but I'll try."

"Lola," she said, looking me square in the eyes, "this ain't my first rodeo. I get it."

I chuckled and said, "No offense, but I'm not sure *I* even get it."

"I promise I'll interrupt if I need to," she said. "Now spill it."

So, seated there on the little bench, I told her what happened. I filled her in, her eyes growing wide in wonderment at all the appropriate times. I even offered her a sniff from my bottle of clary sage oil to bring it home and inhaled a deep whiff myself while we were at it.

"You know what, though?" I said, "You're probably the only person I can tell this to. Well, maybe Seth. There's no way I can expect Chuck or Amanda to understand. Okay, maybe Raven … and Glenna … but not my own family."

"Does that matter?" she asked. "I don't suppose it's much different from being a Freemason or a member of some other mysterious order. You don't discuss what happens in the meetings with civilians, so to speak."

That sank in. "I never thought of it that way," I said. "Thank you. That helps."

She beamed, pleased with herself, and egged me on. "So, what else? Tell me more. I feel like there's more."

"There is more, but it's like I said earlier. I've used all the words I can. There is no way to describe what that embodiment felt like—the shift itself, how *real* it was."

"Was it real?" she asked. "Do you think these are your actual ancestors, or is this metaphorical? I mean, is there really a lineage of people with the power of … what did you call it?"

"*Ath-shapach.*"

"Ah-shoppick," she said.

"Close enough." I nodded. "I have no way of knowing if a lineage like this really exists—at least not without a lot of research. This supposedly happened hundreds of years ago on my father's side of the family. I would have to trace his genealogy to see if any names from that long ago are even there."

"Oooh! That would be quite a find!" she replied, her eyebrows raised and her fingers tapping my forearm. "That's the first thing we've got to do once we get back to Ohio!"

"Right, but to answer your question about whether this is all real or metaphorical," I said, "like you said earlier, I don't know if it matters. The fact is, I'm changed."

As I spoke, the air before me rippled and I gripped the bench to steady myself during the brief spell of wooziness.

It passed quickly, and I paused for a moment to tune into my field, like a dog sniffing the clean, clear air. "I don't feel even a hint of *Inntinn-lobhadh* anymore. At least right now, I don't. And now that it's gone, I think I can say it's always been there. Ever since I was a kid, I've felt something like that messing with me, suppressing any joy, making me doubt myself."

This train of thought brought up a memory buried long ago. I told Maddie, "When I was maybe four years old, there was a song that played on the radio all the time. It was my favorite song. It was so beautiful that it hurt. Do you know what I mean?"

"I sure do," she said, nodding.

I continued. "I don't know why this song was especially moving... I don't know if that even matters. What does matter is that I used to bawl my eyes out whenever it played, and I couldn't explain why. I was too young to put it into words. It frustrated my parents so much that at first they were compassionate, but eventually they grew impatient, then angry. I learned to cry unseen in the closet."

I thought for a moment to gather my thoughts and went on, "Something about the song resonated so strongly that it woke something in me ... the sound of pure beauty? I don't know, but it allowed me to sense something gorgeously in tune. I wish I had the words for it. I don't know enough about music to describe what I felt, but it was a perfect expression of harmonics."

I watched Maddie's face, and she seemed to be following me. I went on, still struggling to describe the ineffable. "Perhaps it made me cry because…" I mimicked clutching at something. "…I couldn't have it. It wasn't mine. It was like *Inntinn-lobhadh* was taunting me, saying, 'look what you can't have!'"

Tears filled Maddie's eyes and she nodded. "I know exactly what you're talking about. I've always felt so … wrong … so awful. It would be bliss to be rid of that!"

"Oh, I'm sorry," I said, pulling her into a warm hug. "I didn't mean to make you cry. I meant to tell a happy story, that I don't feel that way anymore, but I've made you feel lousy."

She gave a little laugh and pulled a tissue from her pocket to wipe away the tears before they could run her expensive mascara. "It's okay, you didn't make me feel lousy. I already did. I was just saying it out loud."

I wanted more than anything to use what I'd learned today to help my friend. What would Granny Myrta do? Then it hit me, a memory like a lightning bolt. "Oh!" I said, "I forgot to tell you this part. It may be that you and Seth are both *ath-shapach*, too! Granny Myrta suggested as much."

Maddie's eyes grew wide, and she grinned but didn't say anything yet as a group of people descended the hill, passing us on the trail. The drumming circle and ceremony must have ended. Everyone was exuding such peace and joy that they glowed in their own way.

"Bright blessings," a few of them said as they went by.

"Bright blessings," Maddie and I both replied. Maddie was practically bursting with anticipation.

Once they finally passed us, the words surged out of her. "Say more now!"

I laughed, enjoying her enthusiasm, then noticed Myx and Maj fluttering over her head. "You seem to have a couple of little buddies," I said, pointing them out. "Myx and Maj are here."

"Oh, yes," she said, "I have a story as well. You first."

"There's not much more to tell," I said. "It's like recognizing someone you've never met because you've shared past lives with them. Myrta said … well, suggested … that you and Seth might both be from this community of people. It's not only me. I just happened to be from the lineage that was bound, so I had to brave the claws that catch."

"But how can I know for sure?" she interrupted.

"You know what?" I replied, gesturing up at the evening sky as night was beginning to fall. "It's getting darker and colder. Let's get down the hill and back home while we still have some daylight. We can do a reading after dinner, and you can tell me about these two." I pointed again at the twin faeries floating above her.

"Oh, yes," she cried, all drama, "I am starving. And then, we had better get packing. We leave for London tomorrow."

Her words hit me like a punch to the gut. The thought of not just going back home to Ohio but leaving this place—this magical, magnificent place—broke my heart. And that was not *Inntinn-lobhadh*. It was premature homesickness for a place my soul had grown to love.

I was already home.

TWENTY

Here it was, the first day of autumn, and I had spring fever. At least, that's what it felt like. My chest was bursting with joy, the air smelled ripe with promise, and I practically floated instead of walking down the hill. We got back to the cottage just in time, though, because we were about to lose all the daylight and it was getting *cold*, especially just wearing sweatshirts.

We hurried inside, rubbing our hands together for warmth. "I'll start a fire," Maddie said. "You put the kettle on."

"Will do," I said, scurrying into the kitchen to make some tea. I also turned on the oven to preheat. Tonight, we were sharing a steak pie for two, with a gorgeous flaky crust, along with mashed potatoes and gravy. Have I mentioned how excellent the frozen food selection is in England?

"Do you want to do a reading before or after we eat?" Maddie called from the other room.

I thought for a moment then stepped closer, leaning against the door jamb between the two rooms. No need to shout. "I think we should do it before. I have a couple of canned Pimm's I want to finish off before we go home, and I avoid alcohol when doing readings."

"Right," she said. "Forgot about that." With a roaring blaze in the gas-powered fireplace, Maddie clapped her hands together. "Voila. I'm going to put on my jammies and get comfy. Be right back."

"Grab your oracle cards—the ones you bought in Avebury," I said.

"Ooooh! Good idea!" she said and hurried off to her room.

While the kettle boiled, I busied myself unwrapping and preparing our frozen dinner items for the oven, reminiscing about who I was when I set off that morning. Just a few hours ago, I was plain ol' Lola Garnett from Chagrin Falls, Ohio.

Now I was Lola Garnett: Eclipse Rider.

Lola Garnett: Equinox Wrangler.

Lola Garnett: Shapeshifter!

That last one had a ring to it. I'd have to get a T-shirt made.

I chuckled at my own silliness, but the more I thought about it, the more I realized these titles actually fit. I actually did all that. Me. Lola Garnett from Chagrin Falls, Ohio, actually spent the afternoon receiving a generational healing from the friggin' King of the Fae! Oh my God!

Even with all this wonderment, though, everyday life went on. What does a monk do after enlightenment? Chop wood, carry water. What does Lola Garnett, Shapeshifter, do after rubbing elbows with Fae royalty? Brew tea, cook TV dinners.

The kettle was boiling, so I poured hot water over a couple of tea bags in the souvenir cups we had bought at the grocery store.

Maddie returned from her room, cozy and warm in her flannel jammies and fluffy slippers. She plopped herself down on the couch, unpackaged her oracle cards, and flipped through them. "These are so beautiful," she said. "Can't wait to see what you read from them."

The oven was preheated, so I popped our food in and set the timer. We'd have plenty of time for a reading.

By now, I was plenty familiar with how Maddie liked her tea, so I fixed us both a cuppa and brought them over to the coffee table and wondered why they don't call it a tea table here.

More silliness.

I sat in the comfy wingback chair across from Maddie. She handed me the cards once she was done shuffling.

"Okay," I said, settling in. "What are we asking about?"

She rolled her eyes upward, trying to recall what we had discussed on the hill. "I don't remember exactly. We talked about a lot today." She tapped her perfectly manicured index fingernail against her front teeth as she thought.

"Oh! That's right—you said Granny Myrta said I might be ah-shoppick, just like you!"

I chuckled. "It's *ah-SHAH-pukh*. Say the final 'ch' like you're hocking up a loogey."

"You are so gross," she said, laughing. "No pretending you didn't grow up in the Midwest."

"What can I say?" I laughed, too. "Buckeye born and bred. Anyway, you're right. You asked how to tell if you're *ath-shapach*, too. Maybe even Seth, for that matter, but we can get to him later."

I shuffled the deck with this question in mind, the cards slippery with newness. One of them popped out of my hands and landed on my lap, so I set it on the table in front of me. "There's your first card," I said, and continued to shuffle.

Once I felt complete, I stopped and flipped three cards indicating past, present and future, then set the deck down on the table. First, I examined the one that had leapt from my hands as the significator card … the one that represented Maddie in this spread.

"Holy accuracy, Batman!" I cried. "This first one … you saw it jump out, right? This first one literally says, '*Remembering your lineage awakens the abilities woven into your blood*.' I shit you not. Look." I handed her the card and watched her jaw drop as she read it.

"Girl," I said, "you don't even need me to do a reading. There's your answer right there."

Shaking her head to clear it, she pointed at the other three cards on the table. "You may be right, but what do the rest of them say?"

I picked up the first one. "This card represents your past. It says, '*These abilities are not new. They are yours. Trust what rises through you*.' Wow, Maddie, I don't know if it's the cards doing this or if we're both so deep in the zone that they're coming up bang on. I've never done a spread like this where I don't have to interpret them *at all*."

"Well, hold on," she said. "You said this card is about my past. But does that mean my past in this lifetime, or a lifetime with ah-shoppick … I mean, ah-SHAH-puchhhh?"

I chuckled at her absurd exaggeration and said, "Give me a sec to tune in."

I closed my eyes, held the card to my chest, and opened my psychic channel. The first thing I saw was Maddie as a tween—when she was still called Matthew—playing in his bedroom with a Ouija board. He was startled by the sound of his bedroom door opening. No one was supposed to be home. It was his father, who whipped off his belt and began leathering him, screaming about inviting evil into the house with "the Devil's oracle."

That was all I could see. Maddie had tight reins on allowing anyone psychic access, even me. But it was all I needed to know. I dove back in, asking about the second part of her question.

There she was—a woman in this scenario—conferring with Granny Myrta. My surprise at seeing that they knew one another nearly pulled me out of the vision, but I held on.

The two women were discussing the dilemma Myrta had told me about … whether their people would have to sacrifice their way of life to save future generations from the abuse of power by just a handful of youngsters. It wasn't just Gillebrid. Others had begun testing the waters, pushing the envelope, seeing how far they could take *ath-shapach*—some even succumbing to *Inntinn-lobhadh*.

I wasn't hearing words, just sensing the scene. A decision had to be made, and these two were part of that process. Sisters.

Maddie was Myrta's sister.

"Wow!" I said. "You're not going to believe this. You and Granny Myrta were sisters. My zillion-times-great auntie! So, yeah, I would say you had a life with *ath-shapach*."

"Wha? Shut up!" she laughed, then asked hopefully. "Are you serious?"

"I'm telling you what I saw," I said. Then I remembered. "I saw something else that answered the other part of your question, whether it was this lifetime or another. I think it was both. I saw you playing with a Ouija board as a child, during this lifetime. Does that ring a bell?"

A shadow crossed her face and she scowled. "It certainly does. I borrowed one from a friend. I was starting to have psychic flashes, I guess you would call them, but I didn't know how to control them. Kind of like you after Melinda, but nowhere near as extreme. I was just experimenting. I only tried that one time, I can tell you that!"

I didn't push it. This was a painful memory, and I had my answer.

"Do you want to talk about it, or should we move on to the next card?" I asked.

"Let's move on."

I picked up the "present" card and burst out laughing. "Oh, come on. Did you stack the deck?"

I turned the card toward her. It said, *Equinox: Day and night meet as equals. Choose the version of yourself that walks in greater alignment.*

Maddie furrowed her brow and said, "I most certainly did not stack the deck. Besides, you shuffled after me. Lola, this is getting spooky."

"You know, I would have thought so, too," I said, "if I hadn't just experienced the day we've had. Come to think of it—after the week we've lived—is *this* really the unbelievable part?"

She sputtered, unable to make any other sounds, and finally threw her hands in the air.

"Right?" I said. "I don't think we even need to examine that card's meaning, do we? Shall we see what the future card is?"

"Go for it," Maddie said.

The final card took my breath away—quite literally. On it was a single word: *Breathe.*

Tears sprang to my eyes, and I was immediately taken back to yesterday—our first trip up the Tor—when that singing man filled St. Michael's Tower with the echoes of Pink Floyd's song *Breathe.*

"Maddie," I said, "we're both *ath-shapach.* I don't think it gets any more certain than this."

She was silent for a long moment, then finally blew out a long exhale. "Wow," she said. "Now what do I do with this? What does that even mean?"

"Hey," I said, sitting up straight in my chair. "Remember I told you that Granny Myrta uses botanicals for her magic?"

"Yes ..." Maddie said, waiting to see where I was going. Then it hit her. Hard. "Oh. My. God."

"Yes! You get it, too?"

"Yes!" Maddie cried. "I do the same! When we first met..."

"You gave me a bottle of magical rose oil."

"I did ... I still work with oils, but not to sell them," she said. "I don't need to anymore. But that's not the point."

I nodded, urging her on.

"It's the same thing," she said, almost in awe. "What she does is what I've always done. It's the same thing.'

We stared at one another, unsure what to say. In that moment, it felt like the biggest synchronicity of the entire trip.

Finally, she repeated her earlier question. "What am I supposed to do with all this?"

As she spoke, the twin chameleon faeries, Myx and Maj, sparkled into view over the coffee table, where the oracle cards still lay. One of them said, "We told yeh, up on t'hill, we'd help yeh with yehr next steps."

Maddie, who apparently had no trouble seeing these two now, replied, "Yes, but I didn't know this is what you meant!"

"That's right!" I interrupted. "You mentioned that you have a story about what happened to you up there on the Tor. I suggest that now is the time to spill some tea." I took an exaggerated sip from my cuppa, slurping loudly for emphasis.

"I did say that, didn't I?" Maddie grinned. "Tea spillage begins now." She lifted her teacup to her lips for an equally loud sip and then began, "Well, you were out for a long time. I started out just sitting there by your side, reading my book, but after what felt like too much time had passed, I began to get worried."

The twins then materialized at their full size, standing next to the coffee table—younger, smaller, and bonier than Pea and Twink, their features sharper but harder to see. As with so many things we'd experienced the past week, their vague invisibility was difficult to put into words.

They rather blended into their surroundings … not that their coloring changed so much as their visibility sort of faded. If you didn't know they were there, your eyes might pass right over them, like the nonexistent sky under the hill and the invisible chair beneath my tuchus.

Small enough to both fit in the empty wingback chair next to me, facing Maddie, they squeezed in side by side, their feet swinging several inches off the floor.

"Finally," Maddie continued, "after reading the same paragraph for the fourth time, I put the book down and started making small talk with these two."

"Much to the chagrin of Miss Thel," one of them grinned, using their familiar nickname for Twink.

"Aye," said the other, "but she were mostly putting it on. If she were truly bothered, she'd have shut us down, yeah?"

Maddie watched them banter, delighted by their presence, before finally interrupting. "I didn't notice any disapproval. I was just so grateful for some distracting conversation. We talked about the synchronicities of us being there during the eclipse and the equinox, and the drum circle just happening to show up at the same time as us—yada yada—when one of them said …"

"It were me," one faery said.

"I'm sorry," I said. "I still can't tell you apart. Which one is who?"

"I'm Myx," said the one who had just spoken. "I'm the older sister."

Maj nudged her in the side with a sharp elbow. "Aye, by mere seconds! It hardly counts."

"Every second counts," Myx replied.

Maddie interrupted, laughing, "… when *Myx* mentioned that this adventure wasn't all about you. I mean, I knew I had something to gain from being here at this sacred spot during this auspicious time. How could anyone not be affected by all this cosmic flow? But I didn't realize that our adventures were connected."

"Oh?" I asked, eyebrows raised. "Do tell." I settled back in my chair, getting comfy.

"Well," Maddie continued, "we were talking about the ley lines and the intersection of the divine masculine and feminine and all that, and Myx pointed out that I'm a genuine embodiment of all of it, more than anyone else on that hill. I was the only one up there literally living with a foot in both worlds."

This had occurred to me as well, but now wasn't the time to point it out.

"In other words," she said, "we both have a reason to be here. This spur of the moment trip wasn't about me going to an estate sale and bringing you along as a travel buddy. We were pulled here, at this specific time, for a reason. At the risk of sounding full of myself, we're both doing important work."

I grinned. "I'm so glad to hear you say that. Every time I let myself think that, I shut it down as egoic, the so validation is appreciated. Tell me more."

She nodded, also smiling. "You're the only one who truly knows why you're here. Same for me. And my work begins with what I was saying earlier—about how I've always felt ... wrong."

Pausing to gather the right words, she finally continued, "I still do feel ... wrong ... sometimes, although not as much as I used to, thank God. As I get older, and now that I'm settled with Paul—who doesn't just accept me but genuinely *loves* me, in this between-two-worlds body that offends and angers so many—it's getting easier. But there's still something I can't put my finger on that makes me feel bad."

Maddie shrugged and continued, "I've done enough therapy and soul-searching to know the difference between early programming, society's expectations, and my own inner bugaboos. This is a bugaboo."

"I've always admired your inner strength," I said, "especially knowing how much hostility is out there."

"Yes, there is that," she said. "But it's not just the haters. I don't want to be a symbol. I'm just Maddie, but I'm torn between living a happy, private life and being an outspoken fighter for the cause. I cannot wait for the day when this isn't even an issue anymore. I'm not a fighter. And that makes me feel awful."

Nodding with sympathy, I placed one hand on my chest and said, "I feel you. Do you think some of that awful feeling might be *Inntinn-lobhadh*? The part that says you're not doing enough 'for the cause?' It's not just me it targets, it's all of humanity. Heck, it's probably *Inntinn-lobhadh* that makes the haters hate."

"That's very likely," she said. "I've been giving that mind rot a lot of thought this weekend, applying it to my own life. I may need to get one of those bracelets for my left wrist." She chuckled, pointing at my arm, and continued, "It really does explain a lot."

"Want mine?" I asked, slipping off the labradorite bracelet and tossing it to her. "I don't think I need both of them anymore." I moved the string of quartz beads from my right wrist to my left. "There. This'll do."

"Goody!" Maddie said, snatching the bracelet from the air and slipping it onto her wrist. "Thank you." She rolled the beads between her fingers for a minute or so, gazing into the flames dancing in the fireplace.

"Oh!" I gasped, jumping up from my chair. "I'll be right back." I hurried to my bedroom and grabbed my bottles of spring water—both Red and White—and returned to the living room. "Hold your wrist out."

Maddie extended her left arm and I poured a few drops from each bottle over the bracelet, mindful of the carpet below. I didn't need much. Just enough to make it hers.

She beamed as I did so and, as I screwed the caps back onto the bottles, she said, "Thank you for the cleansing. I can *feel* the difference. Isn't magic fun?"

"Aye, it is," Maj said, her voice pulling my attention back to them and the conversation we'd been having just a few minutes ago.

"Yes," said Maddie, "and these two"—she gestured at the twin faeries— "have promised to help me!"

"Really?" I asked, seating myself again. "How so?"

"We hadn't really discussed the hows," Maddie said, turning toward the sisters. "But now that I know I'm part of the bigger picture—the *ath-shapach*—I'm relieved to have some assistance, just like you have Twink and Pea."

Myx and Maj both broke into giggles. "Heehee … Twink! Heehee …"

Just then, the oven timer went off, and I leapt from my seat. "Oh, I have to put some foil around the edges of the pie so the crust won't brown too much," I said, and hurried into the kitchen.

After dealing with the cooking, I called into the other room, "Do you think we're done with readings? That Pimm's has my name on it."

Maddie laughed. "I think we've done enough for one evening. Bring me a glass of wine, would you, doll?"

With a glass in each hand, I returned to the cozy fireside and handed the wine to Maddie. I sat, and we reached across the table to clink glasses.

"Here's to a most unusual adventure," she said.

"Here's to a most unusual friendship—well, friendships," I said, tilting my glass toward Myx and Maj, then lifting it slightly to include all the other friends and faeries we'd encountered over the past several days.

I took a sip and sighed. It was going to be hard going back to Ohio.

TWENTY-ONE

"Is it morning already?" I asked aloud to no one when I opened my eyes to see sunlight streaming through my bedroom window. Waiting for that old, familiar 'ugh' feeling to settle in, it finally dawned on me—yes, dawned; that word made sense in a whole new way—that it wasn't going to happen. I hadn't awakened with the same-as-it-ever-was dread I was so used to.

I giggled with anticipation. If this was what life was going to feel like now, I was all for it.

I hopped out of bed, my feet hitting the cold floor, yearning for a hot cup of tea. My metamorphosis into an official Brit was complete. No longer content with a cup of morning Joe, I understood now the joys of a nice cuppa. I hoped Maddie had risen before me so the kettle would already be on the boil.

My luggage sat just over there, mostly packed, with a few last-minute things piled nearby. My clothes for the day were neatly folded, waiting for my decision: should I do a quick rinse this morning, or wait for a before-bed shower in the hotel in London?

I didn't want to wash off the Glastonbury buzz, so I got dressed and went to the kitchen, where I was delighted to find the kettle already hot and ready for a brew. Maddie must have beat me to it.

As I waited for the teabag to steep, I dug out Angel's card to text her my email address while I still had a British phone number. Before I could do that, though, a notification popped up on my phone—a message from Chuck: *Love you, miss you, can't wait to see you.*

There it was. That familiar dread I had not missed when I first woke up. And it wasn't about Chuck, per se, it was everyday life back home. I didn't want to leave England.

I wasn't unhappy back in Ohio. Not really. I had everything a person could want: a nice home, a happy-ish family, a job I loved … all the things. But that undercurrent I hadn't even noticed until it was gone? It was back.

Was it *Inntinn-lobhadh*? I looked at my left wrist, where I now wore the quartz beaded bracelet, and nothing shifted. Not this time.

Maybe it was about Chuck, after all.

Before I left for England, I'd been doubting the quality of our marriage but, over the course of the past week, that doubt had faded a bit. Perhaps I'd just needed a little distance between us for a while.

Was it just the typical traveler's woe of leaving vacation behind? I couldn't tell. I wished Maddie's cards were there on the table, easy access.

As if on cue, Maddie came in, her hair wrapped in a towel, fresh from the shower. "Oh good," she said, feeling the kettle, "you've already turned it on." She poured steaming water over a teabag in a cup, humming a tuneless melody.

"I didn't turn the kettle on," I said. "I thought you did."

"Nope, wasn't me," she said. "I hopped straight into the shower when I got up. I know we have to hit the road soon, but I wanted a fresh start before we head back to the big city. I won't take long to get ready, I promise."

"I'm just the opposite," I said. "I didn't want to wash the grass out of my hair, so to speak."

"Gotcha," she grinned. "I'll be back in a sec. Just want to towel off my own hair."

It was only after she left the room that it sank in. Maddie had not turned the kettle on. It was already hot when I became the first person in the kitchen that morning.

"Huh," I said, adding some milk and sugar to my cup. I sat at the table, texted Angel, and took my first life-affirming sip of the day. "My God, that's good," I said to no one.

I sat and gazed out the kitchen window, the view of the Tor a spectacular reminder of all that had occurred. I felt changed. Content. Blessed.

And I didn't want to go home.

Maddie returned to doctor her tea, her damp hair now combed straight and pulled back behind her shoulders. "Here," she said, "something told me you might need these." She set the deck of oracle cards on the table.

"Will wonders never cease?" I laughed. "I was just wishing they were handy."

"There are no coincidences, right?" She sat to join me at the kitchen table, also facing the Tor. She blew into her cup to cool her tea. "Isn't that a gorgeous view?"

"It is," I agreed. "I've been sitting here burning it into my memory."

"I've got a better idea," she said, picking up her phone and taking a picture of the view, windowsills and all. "There. Now I don't have to rely on my memory."

"Good idea," I did the same, then made the photo my phone's wallpaper.

As I fiddled with my phone's settings, Maddie's voice broke through my concentration, her dismay mixed with aggravation. "Oh no! Our flight's been cancelled!"

"What? Cancelled?" I replied. "How are we going to get home?" I didn't say it aloud, but part of me was relieved. I wouldn't mind an extra day or two. Or twelve.

"Let me work on this," she said. "There's got to be another flight tomorrow, and I'm sure the airline is already on it. They can't leave international travelers stranded."

All business now, Maddie focused on fixing the problem. Meanwhile, I picked up the deck of cards and gave them a shuffle, asking, *What is this dread about? Why do I feel so reluctant to go home?*

I only pulled one card this time. I didn't need a whole reading, just an answer to that one question. The card said, *Habit: Release the past you keep rehearsing. The future does not require yesterday's script.*

"Dude."

Maddie wasn't listening. She was tied up on the phone with the airline, so I sat there sipping my tea, gazing out at the Tor, pondering the accuracy and depth of the card's response. I needed one of these oracle decks.

Once Maddie hung up, before she could even tell me what happened, I asked, "How far out of the way would it be to drive through Avebury so I can get a deck of my own? If it's too far, I can order one online when we get home, but the cost of international shipping …"

"I don't know," she replied. "I can check. But first, you're not going to believe this …"

She paused, building the suspense. Waiting until I was clearly champing at the bit, she finally said, "I just booked another flight. It's a little earlier than the original, but get this …"

Again, she waited until I finally hollered, "Tell me!"

She grinned and beamed so broadly I thought she would burst. "They comped us first class seats."

"Oh my God, you are KIDDING ME!" I shouted.

"NO!" she shouted back.

We both leapt from our seats and did our own versions of a happy dance, giggling like children, hooting and hollering. Once we finally collapsed from the exhaustion of celebration, we landed back in our chairs at the kitchen table.

Maddie grinned. "You know what? I don't care if it is out of our way to stop in Avebury. I saw a crystal at that shop that I didn't buy, and you want those cards. Let's do it."

"Alrighty," I replied, "but we'd better get moving. We have to check out soon. Are you done packing?"

"Just about," she said, "but I still need to dry my hair and put on my face. How about you?"

"Pretty much," I said. "I'll do a last check around the place and turn on the dishwasher. You finished there?" I pointed at her teacup, which she lifted and drained before handing it to me.

"I'll be quick," she said, and darted back to her room.

It didn't take long to get the cottage spic and span, so I grabbed my luggage and stacked it by the front door, waiting for Maddie to join me. She was still humming away in her room, which meant that she was nowhere near ready, so I wandered outside for one last communion with that gorgeous hill out there.

I stood for a while in the grassy yard, gazing up at St. Michael's Tower, recalling how the sight of one of these towers would have sent me spiraling with fear, just a few days ago. I glanced down at my left wrist, now adorned with crystals associated with the bright light of the Divine Feminine, and thought about what a new person I was becoming.

I called out to Twink, my voice dreamy with retrospect, "Hey, are you there?"

In a flash, she stood next to me, full-sized, the top of her head just about at my shoulder. "Aye, I'm here." She sounded as wistful as I did.

"We've come a long way, you and I," I said.

"Aye, we have," she sighed.

I finally noticed her tone. "Is something wrong?" I asked.

"Not 'wrong,'" Twink replied. "Just … difficult."

I waited.

"This is where we part ways," she said. "My work is done."

"What? Wait!" I cried. "No!"

She moved to stand in front of me, looking up at my face. "Aye, Auntie Jennett needs me elsewhere. I've taken yeh where yeh need to be, and now yeh're off and running."

"But …" I stammered, "… I may not *need* you, but I *want* you to stay."

"Oh, I'll still come around to check on yeh from time to time," she said, reaching her tiny hand out to touch my arm. "But not at yehr beck and call."

"What about Precious Pea?" I asked. "Myx and Maj have kindled a friendship with Maddie. Will I be alone now?"

"Pea will come around, too," Twink said, "but I don't know if yeh're hearing me. Yeh don't *need* any of us."

This hurt. This really hurt.

The pain in my heart threatened to overwhelm me, but I caught myself. I had just discovered *ath-shapach,* with Twink's help. And Pea's help. And Myx and Maj, and Seren and Celesta … and Gwyn ap Nudd. I wasn't alone. They all lived in my heart.

I bit my lip to keep from crying—not just from longing for what I was leaving behind, but from overflowing love for those who had stood by my side this past week. Maddie … and Padraic and Gillebrid … and, most of all, Granny Myrta.

"I'll always be with yeh, lassie," a familiar voice said. As Twink faded away in a sparkling mist, she was replaced by the form of my distant great-grandmother, whose eyes twinkled at me. "I live in yehr bones, in yehr blood. I'm only a heartbeat away."

Behind me, I heard the cottage door open and the scrape of luggage wheels on the cement walkway. Maddie said, "What a beautiful day! Let's drive with the top down."

With that, Granny Myrta vanished, and I was alone.

Well, not really. I would never be alone again.

TWENTY-TWO

Maddie popped the trunk open there in front of my house, and the sound of the latch releasing felt so final. I was home.

The trip back to the States was almost as interesting as our visit to England. I couldn't imagine what it would be like to walk through my front door and settle back into everyday life in Midwestern America, back with my family instead of spending every waking, magical moment with Maddie.

Chuck was right when he had suggested that things always got a little crazy when she and I were together. They did, but his implication had been that bad things occurred and I had corrected him, identifying Melinda as the source of the "bad" in those incidents.

I wouldn't argue now, though, that the Lola/Maddie combo attracted … curious … events.

On the trip home, those events began to get interesting when we went through security at Heathrow Airport. We had both carefully packed our bottled Glastonbury water in our checked luggage to comply with the restrictions on carry-on liquids in containers larger than a few ounces. Maddie had even had the foresight to buy packing tape so we could seal them tightly against leakage.

Neither of us had considered, before packing for the flight, how heavy so much water would make our bags, so we had to juggle some things and overfill our carry-ons with heavier items we didn't necessarily need with us in the cabin. However, neither of us anticipated our carry-ons being pulled aside for inspection after going through the X-ray machine.

"What's that?" the security agent asked me, pointing to the screen displaying the contents of my backpack. A dark, round, opaque object stood out in stark contrast to everything else, which appeared somewhat translucent. It looked like one of those cartoon bombs, without the wick. No wonder the agent eyed me suspiciously.

Momentarily flummoxed, I searched my memory, unable to recall what I had placed in the bag just hours ago until it finally came to me. "Oh! It's a labradorite sphere."

The agent stared at me, unblinking, waiting for me to elaborate.

"It's a rock," I said.

"You have a rock in your bag?" She handed the backpack to me. "Show me."

"It's really pretty," I explained. "You'll see." I dug through the backpack, feeling for the sphere, and finally pulled it out, wrapped in a T-shirt to protect it from damage. I unwrapped it and held it out for her to examine. "See?" I asked. "Isn't that gorgeous?" I turned it about in the light, showing her the heart-shaped flash.

"Oh, that is pretty!" she said, softening a bit. "What's it for?"

"It's just a decoration," I said. "There's a matching display stand somewhere in the bag that goes along with it, so it doesn't roll around. Is it okay if I put it back?"

"Sure," she said. "Go ahead." She waved me on, so I rewrapped it in the shirt, stuffed it into my backpack and moved out of the way for the next person in line—Maddie.

"Don't tell me," the agent said to Maddie. "You have a rock, too? Only that doesn't look like a rock."

On the screen, the X-ray of Maddie's carry-on showed a long, opaque, unmistakably phallic shape. Maddie burst into laughter and said, "I know what it looks like, but I promise you, it's also a rock."

"Show me," said the agent, her raised eyebrow conveying more than she dared to say aloud.

Just as I had, Maddie dug into her bag and retrieved an impressive quartz crystal wand, about seven inches long and nearly two inches wide. It was the one she saw during our first trip to the shop in Avebury—the one she bought on our return trip to London.

The agent rolled her eyes. "Go ahead." She moved on to the next person in line.

Maddie, in a fit of giggles, replaced the quartz and zipped her bag. "You'd think she'd never heard of crystals before."

"I don't think she has," I said. "Can you imagine? Between the two of us—me with a cartoon bomb and you with a …"

"Honey, those sharp edges should have tipped her off that it's not what she thought it was." Maddie vamped a bit, then added, "Although, you know what they say … anything'll do if you're brave enough."

I cracked up laughing and, once I was able to speak again, said, "I was going to say it could have been mistaken for a cartoon stick of dynamite …"

"Either way," Maddie said, "explosions galore!"

The rest of the trip was magnificent, with our rescheduled flight two hours earlier than the one that had been cancelled. And now I understood why Maddie had so strenuously objected to flying in the main cabin on the way to England.

First class was the way to go, and I wondered how I would ever go back to flying coach. I made a point of luxuriating, soaking up every amenity and the royal treatment we received from the flight attendants, as if I would never be able to do this again.

Then I remembered *ath-shapach*. If I *never* wanted to do this again, all I had to do was keep thinking those limiting thoughts. Otherwise, if I played my metaphysical cards right, I could do this whenever I flew again.

Even our arrival in Cleveland was smooth. Going through customs was a breeze. They didn't even ask about the rocks or the Glastonbury water. We just showed our passports and sailed through. Traffic going back to Chagrin Falls was non-existent.

Back in our hometown, I was flooded with nostalgic warmth as we drove through the uptown area—the Popcorn Shop, the waterfall and Raven's shop … all the things that I love about this place. I didn't feel any of the dread I had so anticipated and worried about before leaving Glastonbury.

That is, until we pulled up in front of my house and I heard the trunk latch pop open, the sound that meant this was it. I was home.

I turned to Maddie with big, puppy dog eyes. "I'm going to miss you! We had so much fun. Let's turn around and go back, while we're still packed—before anyone even knows we're home."

"I wish," she pouted, making sad eyes back at me.

"Thank you for inviting me," I said, leaning over the console to give her a big hug. "Thank you for listening to the Universe when it nudged you."

"Thank you for coming with me and letting the Universe override all that panic." She hugged me back.

We released the hug after a long moment, and Maddie laughed. "Look at us, acting like this is the end. It's just the beginning, isn't it?"

"You bet, Auntie Madeline," I said, getting out of the car to fetch my bags from the trunk. I waved as she drove away, then trudged up the walkway, up the steps to the squeaky screen door on the porch that Chuck had built to protect us from Melinda.

Ah, memories.

No one was home but my cat, Missy, who sat on a windowsill glaring at me for daring to leave her. "Kitty kitty," I said, dropping my backpack and giving her a scritch behind the ears. She allowed me to do this for only a few seconds before giving me a look of disdain and hopping down, heading straight for her not-empty bowl. At least Chuck or Amanda had kept her fed.

The house smelled musty, as if the windows had not been opened the entire time I was gone. A thin layer of dust covered everything, and the rug needed vacuuming.

I shook my head with mild disgust, as I made my way around the first floor to open some windows, but caught myself before I spiraled into true anger. *'Ath-shapach, remember?'*

Fresh air flowed through the house, and I wondered if the weather had been rotten while I was away. Maybe it hadn't been aired out because it had been cold and rainy. Then I recalled that both Chuck and Amanda weren't home during the day, like I would have been. It probably wouldn't have even crossed their minds to let in some fresh air.

Problem solved. A cup of tea would hit the spot. Tossing my suitcase onto the couch, I unlatched it and retrieved a package of teabags I'd purchased at the grocery store in Glastonbury. I knew I wouldn't have English Breakfast tea at home so I brought some with me, packed in my checked bag to help balance the weight.

My stevia packets were in the backpack and, as I felt around inside for them, my hand bumped into the rock that caused such a ruckus at security. Grinning at the memory, I retrieved that as well. I turned it in the light, gazing into the flash.

I couldn't help reminiscing, thinking back to the street where I'd bought the stone from Angel and Paolo, just down the road from the White Spring, on the other side of the wall from the Red Spring. I held it to my chest, closed my eyes, and breathed. Just … breathed … as the Pink Floyd tune played on my internal radio station.

After a minute or so of reconnecting to those magical experiences, I set the labradorite sphere on its stand on the coffee table—which I would henceforth call the "tea table"—making a point of turning the lopsided-heart flash toward the light: my first step in bringing that experience home with me. My second step was to recall Angel's wish to visit America, and my promise to allow the stone to be an anchor for her dream to come true.

Tea would be the third step. Ignoring the pile of dishes in the sink and the countertop which had not been wiped down recently, I dug the old stovetop kettle out of the pantry and rinsed it out. I couldn't even remember the last time I used it.

After filling it and putting it on a burner to boil, I finally noticed the straw that broke the camel's back—there on the kitchen table.

Up until then, I had been able to calmly witness all the signs that both Chuck and Amanda had left their messes in place, waiting for me to come home and clean up after them. I had only mildly reacted … I had successfully kept *ath-shapach* in mind.

After all, I was a new person, and they were still living their old ways. They had not been through the Cauldron of Rebirth, so it was unfair of me to expect them to behave as if they had. It would be up to me to lead by example.

I laughed at my mental course correction and rolled my eyes at myself. How high and mighty am I? I sounded exactly like one of those poseurs I had been making fun of all along. *Oooo, I'm so enlightened and you're … not.*

But this … mess … on the table …

One of the primary rules in this house was: if you're going to work on a craft or project and leave it only partially done, do it in the garage or the basement. Do NOT leave your shit strewn across the kitchen table.

There it was, though, some sort of wooden box, half assembled, surrounded by little cans of stain, sandpaper, and paint brushes. At least whoever left the mess had spread newspaper under everything to protect the table, but that was beside the point.

The kettle began whistling, mirroring the shrieks inside my head as we both boiled—the kettle with heat, me with rage. I paused, struck by the analogy, marveling that this was something I wouldn't have done two weeks … er … ten days ago.

The kettle transformed cold water into something useful, the shriek signifying that it was ready to do its work.

The mess in the house—waiting for me to take care of it instead of two grown people taking responsibility for their own clutter—was a boiling point, offering me an opportunity to respond differently … not as a victim, but as one imbued with *ath-shapach*.

I poured the hot water over the teabag and pondered the question: How can I overlay this analogy onto what was boiling up inside of me? What could I pour that over to transform?

Before I could come up with a suitable parallel, I heard the familiar, unmistakable sound of Chuck's truck pulling up outside. Unless I wanted our first moments together to explode into a fight, I needed to dial it down. Not only that, now that *ath-shapach* was showing itself to enact relatively instant karma, this was not the time to experiment with rage.

There was the sound of his key in the lock. I hadn't locked the door behind me, so he jiggled his key a couple times, probably noticing it was already unlocked, probably wondering why. I took a few more deep breaths, settling my anger, willing myself to allow him a little grace.

Chuck swung the door open and stood there for a moment, staring at me in astonishment. "You're home! I didn't expect you for another two hours." He checked his watch, tapping it to make sure it was running.

"Oh, right," I said, remembering. "Our flight was changed. We got in a little earlier."

"That's great!" he said, stepping toward me and reaching out for a hug. "Welcome home. We missed you."

"Thank you," I said, returning the hug but unable to return the sentiment.

He kissed me on the cheek, then released me and dashed toward the kitchen table. As he hurried to clean up the mess, he said, "Sorry about all this. I tried to beat you home to get it cleared away before you got here. You must have been so pissed …"

"Well," I admitted, my arms folded over my chest, "I certainly wasn't happy to see it there." I didn't mention the mess in the kitchen or the dust on the furniture. Or the unvacuumed floors.

"Amanda was supposed to make sure the kitchen was clean before she left for school," he muttered. Then he turned to me, his hands full of his craft supplies. "I see what you mean now. She really does need a kick up the backside once in a while."

I chuckled and unfolded my arms. "I'm glad something good came of my time away."

"We both appreciate you a lot more," he said with a laugh as he set his supplies inside the partially assembled box.

"What is that?" I asked, curiosity finally getting the better of me.

"It's an old letter box," Chuck said. "I got it for my desk. Paul took me to a high-end flea market, if you can imagine such a thing. Talk about an oxymoron, right? Anyway, it wasn't quite an antiques fair, but all sorts of upscale vendors gather at this venue twice a year, and he wanted to see if he could find anything for Maddie's shop."

"How sweet," I said, helping him by clearing away the protective newspapers from the table after he lifted his supplies.

"Leave that, hon," he said. "I made the mess; I'll clean it up."

With those words, the last of my aggravation melted away. Wow. Had he changed or had I? Or was it both of us?

"Okey dokey," I said. "I'm just going to take my stuff upstairs and unpack. It's been a long, long day, and I'm a little jet-lagged."

"Of course," he said, leaning in to give me another quick kiss. "I'll get to those dishes next. I really didn't expect you home so early."

I kissed him back, meaning it this time. "Thanks."

Gathering my bags, I headed up the stairs and, just as I reached the top, Chuck called out, "Hey, by the way, I got you something at the flea market, too. No idea if you'll like it or not, but it practically jumped into my hand, so I brought it home. It's in your office."

"Okay, thank you," I called back.

I dropped my bags on the bedroom floor and reached into my backpack for my new oracle card deck, which I hadn't even opened yet. Sitting on the bed, I opened the box and shuffled the shiny new cards. Not surprisingly, one of them popped out and landed on my lap.

Step back. Let your heart and mind stretch wider than ever before. You are becoming more than you were.

"Holy cow," I said aloud to no one. "Sure am glad I stopped in Avebury. Eh, Granny Myrta?"

I didn't see or hear her, but her presence was palpable, her heart filled with love. I tuned in to that love and felt, for the first time since landing in the States, the full power of *ath-shapach*, just as I had in Glastonbury. Before I let the feeling fade, I checked in with my glowing donut. I could see it in my mind's eye, lit up in the full spectrum of color. I practically floated off the bed.

Maybe everything would be okay, here at home, after all. It was entirely up to me. If I gave my power away, *ath-shapach* would reflect that very thing right back—Powerless Lola.

For a moment I despaired that Twink was no longer by my side to remind me not to slip into old habits, even if she was usually snotty about it. But then I remembered—on my own, mind you—to look at my left wrist. I didn't even need a bracelet. Just the mental touch-the-grass moment was all it took.

I could hear Chuck putzing around in the kitchen, running the water, dishes clattering as he stacked them in the dishwasher. Then I remembered that something was waiting for me in my office. I put the cards back in the box and took them with me, tucking them into my desk drawer with all my other decks. I had quite a collection by now.

I didn't have to look hard for Chuck's gift. It was right there, leaning against my desk—a carved wooden staff with a large labradorite sphere embedded at the top. Its size and carved design wasn't exactly the same as the one in Annwn, but it was pretty darn close.

Most importantly, though, the stone bore the same lopsided, heart-shaped flash.

Chuck had said it practically jumped into his hand. That made me smile. That's what happened to me when I reached for my ancestor's staff under the hill with Lord Gwyn.

So much had happened in these past ten days … heck, over the past couple years. Ever since Melinda had disrupted our lives with her enraged spell casting, I'd doubted my sanity more than once. This kind of thing doesn't happen to ordinary people! These are the kinds of stories you binge-watch on streaming services.

Over these past couple years, as I struggled to accept that it *was* all real and there could be no turning back, I had assumed that I was the only one having such extreme psychic experiences. I had judged a lot of people as New Age wannabes—phonies and poseurs.

It wasn't until this trip abroad that I witnessed so many others with legitimate experiences of their own. Maybe their psychic encounters were just as real as mine. Maybe I'd been projecting my own imposter syndrome onto them.

I grinned, overcome by a sudden sense of belonging unlike anything I'd ever felt before. Until now, I hadn't realized how alone I had been. All it took was meeting others on the same path and reconnecting with my own DNA, my ancient birthright. The knowledge that there were others waking up like me filled me with such brightness that I couldn't help but giggle in anticipation of our collective future.

I reached for the staff, and it settled easily into my outstretched hand. It didn't matter who had owned it before. When I held it for the first time, I knew.

This staff was mine.

THE END

AUThOR'S NOTES

Hi, it's Lisa. I just wanted to add a few notes here, because I love when this kind of thing is included in a book I've just finished reading.

Some of what's in this book is based on real events and some is, of course, fiction. It might be fun to let you know what was real or slightly fictionalized from our trip spanning the eclipse/equinox weekend of Autumn 2025 in the U.K, during which we were in Glastonbury.

Starting in Avebury, Jeff and I were let into the fenced-in field by a man dressed in wizardly garb and his magical lady. We remarked upon this, as did Maddie and Lola.

Also in Avebury, I visited the gorgeous little metaphysical shop described herein and purchased a quartz sphere, an oracle card deck designed by the owner, and a bottle of clary sage oil.

Speaking of those oracle cards, I used my deck whenever Lola did to create a spontaneous reading for the book. I didn't know how they would come out—I was prepared to write the rest of the chapter based on whatever appeared.

I was just as blown away by the cards I pulled as Lola and Maddie were. They were right on the money. I reworded the text but kept the meaning of the cards so I didn't step on any copyright toes. It's a lovely deck and you can order it online.

Oh, by the way, the well table at the Red Lion pub really is haunted by a ghost named Florrie who hates men with beards.

In Glastonbury, we saw the same wizard and his woman at the Chalice Garden.

Before spotting them in the gardens, when we came down from the Tor, Jeff and I did see a row of vendors, and I bought a beaded bracelet, but not from the couple from York (more about them in a minute). The vendor was a man who told me that he had also been in Avebury the same day as I.

Fun story about that real-life bracelet ...

Last time I was in Helper, Utah (doing a book signing for *Castle Gate*) I purchased a bracelet made of tiny rose quartz beads at what is quite possibly the best rock shop I've ever found. At the same time, I also bought a large rose quartz sphere in honor of my great-grandmother Helen (one of the main characters in *Castle Gate*). That sphere sits on my coffee table ... er, tea table ... so I see it every day, and I never took that bracelet off (except for practical reasons, to protect it).

As Jeff and I were leaving the house on our way to the U.K. from the U.S.—the trip that inspired this book—that bracelet caught on my suitcase handle and snapped, sending beads flying all over the garage floor. I didn't have time to mourn the loss. We had to go.

So, when I saw that vendor at the bottom of the hill, who had just been in Avebury the same day as the wizard and I, selling rose quartz beaded bracelets, well ... the story finishes itself.

Okay, maybe it doesn't. Aside from not having time to mourn my broken Granny Helen bracelet, I felt in my bones there was a reason it snapped just as I was heading out the door to visit the ancestral homeland. When I found another rose quartz bracelet, this time with beads the size of garden peas, after I had journeyed up the Tor on eclipse/equinox weekend, tuned into the ley lines and heard an incredible voice singing Breathe (yes, that happened, too) I knew this bracelet was why the old one broke. The beads had grown, and so had I.

Regarding the vendor couple (Angel and Paolo ... not their real names), I didn't meet them in Glastonbury. I met them at Shambles Market in York later in our trip, but they made such an impression that I had to include them here. I did buy a labradorite sphere from them. I had been looking for that exact stone for a couple of years, in numerous crystal and rock shops. In fact, when I was in Helper and bought the rose quartz sphere, I was originally looking for the labradorite I kept seeing in my mind.

They were also selling labradorite "UFOs," and I wanted one so badly, but I had already spent my souvenir money. I couldn't stop thinking about it, so once I got back home, I tracked them down online and ordered it via email. Both of these stones, along with the quartz sphere, sat on my desk in front of me as I typed this story.

(*Note: this was a huge lesson to me ... when you see something overseas that you'll definitely want later, just buy it. The cost of shipping—and unexpected friggin' tariffs—more than erased the money I "saved" by not buying the UFO when I first hungered for it. As Twink said, "Do yeh think we brought yeh in here just to buy trinkets? Cut yehr costs elsewhere."*)

A lot of other moments in this book were drawn from real life, but I think you get the picture. Magic is as magic does.

If you want to know more about how to work with your own glowing donut, check out Tina Zion's video on YouTube about the Toroidal Field. Tina offers a beautiful practice that takes just a few minutes. Tina is a renowned medical intuitive, and her books are among my favorites.

Inntinn-lobhadh is based on my understanding of Wetiko, a topic my friend Paul Levy has written about extensively. Please check out his books on the subject. They will change your life. I've had the pleasure of interviewing Paul on numerous occasions, and every conversation has lit up my mind. You can find many of them on my NOW Podcast.

I especially enjoyed our discussions about how Wetiko has shown up by different names in myths, belief systems and fictional portrayals over millennia. Personally, I find it easiest to grasp through a modern parallel: the Silence in Doctor Who—terrifying beings you forget as soon as you look away.

This book is my attempt to take a whack at portraying that same phenomenon, which some traditions describe as so central to the human condition that it's been called "the topic of topics"—the subject beneath all others, worth seeing clearly if we want to understand anything at all.

Ath-shapach is based on my own understanding of how this whole being-in-a-human-suit works. If I can *remember* to do it—and keep from inching lower—then life hums along. The hard part is *remembering*. That's why I wear a labradorite bracelet on my left wrist.

My very first book, *Shape Shifting – the body/mind/spirit weight solution*, was based on my much younger understanding of this process. (In other words, that book was not my best writing … it was my first effort so, if you read it, please be kind.)

In the many years since Shape Shifting was first published (around the turn of the century) it hasn't been read far and wide, so I had begun to assume that I was wrong in my understanding of how life works. But then I started working with The Shift Network and had the golden opportunity to work with some of the most brilliant teachers of metaphysics in the world. It was there I realized that Sandra Ingerman's shamanic practice of Transmutation is in the same lane as my Shape Shifting, and HeartMath's coherence practices were as well.

In other words, I "got it" but there was something I was broadcasting that kept catching the attention of my inner doubts and fears. Now I see that Wetiko was keeping me from accessing my own *ath-shapach*. It's been hinted to me over the years, but my most recent trip to Glastonbury, during the autumn eclipse/equinox weekend, etc., helped me to clear the clouds.

Soon after I got home from England, my writing muse demanded that I set aside the other book I was more than halfway through and write this one. Now. I finished it during the following spring eclipse/equinox season.

One more thing …

I really did spend much of the trip shrieking at Jeff as he drove:

**"Take this exit! No, this one! You just missed it.
Gaaaah … I hate roundabouts!"**

Did you enjoy *The Shapeshifter's Cauldron*?
Your review makes a difference.

Visit

lisabonnice.com

The author, at the Glastonbury Tor in 2019 —
her first visit, when her hair was still long and dark.